MY

MY ENEMY
Part III

MY FRIEND IS MY ENEMY
Part III

MICHAEL J. COUCH

Although this novel is set in an historical context, the characters are entirely fictitious and any likeness in name or personality, to persons alive or deceased, is co-incidental.

MY FRIEND IS MY ENEMY
Part III

Copyright © Michael J. Couch

First published in Great Britain 1992 by Michael J. Couch
68 Chesil Street, Winchester, Hampshire SO23 8HX

Typeset in 10/11 pt Baskerville

ISBN 0 9517531 2 6

Made and printed in Great Britain by
The Guernsey Press Co. Ltd., Guernsey, Channel Islands.

Further copies may be purchased by sending cheques/postal order made out to M.J. Couch, 68, Chesil Street, Winchester, Hants. SO23 8HX.
Part I £4.99 plus 60p postage and packing.
Part II £5.50 plus 60p postage and packing.
Part III £4.75 plus 60p postage and packing.

This novel is dedicated to

DAVID

I wish to thank the following people who have been of assistance with research and advice.

Deputy Raymond Falla, O.B.E. — Occupation Essential Supplies and Commodities Committee.

Deputy Bill Green

Mr. R. Heaume — Occupation Museum

Mr. A. Benjafield and the Workers' Education Association

Mr. and Mrs. E. C. Robins

Mrs. D. Lawrence

Mr. A. Buckingham

Mr. J. A. McCormack

Mr. D. C. Maguire

Guille-Allès Library

Chapter One

At peace now, he lies there as though asleep, oblivious to the cares of this world. Who is this man, so bandaged and patched that the casual onlooker could not tell if he were old or young? Perhaps that is it. He is both old and young at the same time.

At times unconscious, at best semi-conscious, he is attached to tubes, kept alive by modern science. He is the victim of one human but fatal error, that lapse into inattentiveness when he had permitted his car to be in control of itself, as his thoughts had taken him back almost half a century in search of the friend who had never really left him.

From the moment of violating the red traffic lights (his vehicle, until then an extension of his very limbs), from the moment of that awful crash where flesh and bone, metal and glass, daydreams and intrusive agonising pain had all become intertwined, people had fought to save this man, to bring his very soul back from those decades long ago, so that he might be prepared for his coming demise.

* * *

This youth stands here, he is in a crowded room, yet he is alone. This place is foreign to him. It is not just that he is surrounded by Germans with all their trappings of glory and permanence, an order which will last for a thousand years. No, John Collins, fifteen year old Guernseyman, is well used to these Teutons, for he has lived for the past fourteen months in the only part of Great Britain to be occupied by them. John knows them well, for once he was conscripted to work for them. He even admired and adulated them in the past. John Collins also numbers one of their sons as his greatest friend.

1

So, why does the youth feel so ill at ease? This young person is little more than a child, yet in the past few weeks has been forced to rapid maturity, to enter this real adult world. He is well used to fear by now, for during interrogation he has experienced pain imposed by others, so it cannot be that. Recently he has lived with a sense of guilt and foreboding. He has lost his only friend, his enemy friend, and perhaps has been the cause of that same German's awful fate, but John is familiar with these feelings. He knows too that his own father, his father's friend Uncle Bert, the fisherman Keith de la Haye and his own parish priest Father Peters, are all in dire trouble, and all because of his selfish fraternization with his enemy friend. But although he has not yet learned to forgive himself, he has accepted this all as having to be.

No, John Collins, subversive spy, underminer of the Reich, corrupter of one of the master race, traitor and quisling, is aware that it has all begun, the end has started. He stands here now in this ornate room, bedecked with its large swastika flag. John stands in front of a large table, while various officers of the Wehrmacht take their seats behind, some with papers, others conversing, some just still and stolid. He is not unused to courts of late, this seasoned criminal, and cells are not unknown to him, be they those of the Gestapo, the civilian police station or the cold damp prison next door to his very home in Guernsey. This is all different, however, for today he is as alone and exiled as if he had already been sent to that Nazi empire of continental Europe. For already John has been plucked from his homeland, his island of Guernsey, which has always been his world. Today, fifteen year old John Collins faces court martial in the Nazi court in neighbouring Jersey.

Like most of his fellow islanders, John has never been to Jersey before. This might seem strange when only sixteen miles of water separate the two islands, but for most inhabitants of both islands, before the Occupation it had been more usual to travel the almost one hundred miles to England than to visit the other community. The Germans, however, do not seem concerned at the ancient rivalries— some might say almost feuds—as, for expediency they combine both states as though they were one. Similarly for

2

efficiency, without due regard for history, they put these proudly independent islands under the overall administration of nearby France.

There seems to be no-one willing to tell John what he must do. He just stands there, awkward and insignificant, yet he knows he is the reason for their all being assembled. He looks round cautiously as though such an action might be construed as disrespectful, as if he were in church. This court certainly is strange; no robed officials, no public witness, no reporters, just uniformed men. Apart from the line of officers behind the table, there are various lesser mortals scurrying and looking busy. There is even a Jersey policeman, armbanded for duty, and sentries standing at the door, bayonetted rifles at the ready, while civilian prison guards wait to receive their guest, for few accused ever leave this room as free persons.

In Guernsey, John's advocate had prepared the youth for what to expect, knowing he would not be permitted to represent and defend his client. This was a military court, and any representation would be provided by Germans for Germans. John had been told too that the proceedings would be conducted in the master tongue, and most likely the youth would not be afforded an interpreter. John would not be permitted to call witnesses to assist his case, and, as his German defence was unlikely to wish to cross examine his accusers, only statements would be produced, German statements which would be accepted without question by the panel of officers. The proceedings would be brief, for why should the Reich waste its time on one who was so obviously guilty before they even began?

John was to be denied any glory, for there would be no newspaper reporters at the ready. No, not even the German-edited local newspapers would carry reports of his stand against Nazism. If John was lucky, all that would be stated would be his crime and an announcement of his punishment, as an example to any other would-be miscreants.

Well, at least Dad, Keith and Uncle Bert were the lucky ones, for they, like John, had appeared in Guernsey's Police Court, but are fortunate that their trial is to be in the Royal Court. The Royal Court, with its ancient ceremonies of justice, will do the Germans' work for them, but at least their

3

cases will appear in the papers, for their crime has been deemed to be against the civil law only. The Germans do not wish it to be known that because of their lax security these criminals have also stolen from them. No, if the Royal Court does its job sufficiently thoroughly, the Germans will not feel obliged to appear involved.

For John, however, his crimes cannot be overlooked, just as for Father Peters with his seditious sermon against the Führer himself. John sees that same man now, sitting behind him, for they are going to try the priest this morning as well, both subversives on the same day.

As Father Peters acknowledges his young parishioner, at that very moment the assembly seems to focus, and John's ordeal begins. With the entry of someone who must be more senior, all the other officers rise and the room becomes still.

'Mum, where is Mum?' John so wants his mum. He is not yet ready to be a man, he wants to be a little boy once more, he needs his mum to take control and take it all away from him. She must be here too, she must be somewhere in this place.

Frances, John's mother, had been given a permit to travel to Jersey. As a minor, John had been allowed the presence of one parent. Brave woman Frances Collins had travelled across on a German boat.

They all sit. John is the only one left standing. All eyes are upon him. The senior officer confers with those on either side of him, and, barely looking up from the sheaf of papers before him, addresses the youth with staccato German. The youth does not comprehend. The voice rattles out its same words once more, only to be contrasted by a deep embarrassed silence as the assembly wills John to respond.

It is all right, Mum is here, John hears her slight nervous gasp, almost a cough, as it fills the hiatus. He feels he can almost cry with relief. What does it matter now, anyway? He does not want to be here, it is their wish, not his. They will do what they have to whether he understands what is happening or not. John knows he does not have to feel this sense of nightmare at not being able to understand their words, for it is all outside his control.

4

Well, Mum is here now, and so is Father Peters. John is no longer alone, he has nothing to lose. Why not use just a little bravado, why not show them he still believes he has rights, even if they think otherwise?

"What did they say to you?"

"Who?"

"That soldier and the SS?"

"Oh them," said Franz, as though no one had been further from his thoughts. "They just say I should get my friend home quickly before curfew."

"Is that all?" asked John. "Didn't they get funny or anything?"

"Get funny? What is this, 'get funny'?"

"You know, didn't they ask about me?"

"Oh yes, they ask who you are."

"What did you say?"

"Why you ask all these questions, John?" asked Franz angrily. "You are worse than my uncle!"

"Sorry about that!" retorted John, in a hurt tone. "But I would like to know what they said, especially as they spoke about me!" Then adding as an afterthought, "and you."

Anticipating the awkward silence, which would follow, John added:

"If they spoke about me I've a right to know."

"Right to know?" emitted Franz. "Rights? You are English. You have no rights!"

"Excuse me," said John, addressing the most senior officer, "but I do not speak German." He was trying to sound assertive, but the brave words which left him were diluted in the heavy silence of the room, and became rather weak and pathetic, as they reached the masters.

The senior man did not reply to this plea but, turning to one of his fellows, signified that he should see to the criminal.

A young officer, probably the most junior in rank, rose and walked to John.

"Collins," he lisped, "I am here for you with speaking. You must speaking with me."

His mastery of English was not perfect, but John quickly gathered this man had been assigned to be his only link to understanding anything which was happening.

Confident now that the criminal had his rights, that he had been granted an impartial officer of the Wehrmacht to keep him aware of the justice which was being wreaked upon him, the senior officer repeated himself once more.

John looked to the German next to him, the nearest hope to having an advocate of defence.

"Is nothing," hissed the Teuton. "He ask you are knowing these crimes."

Without consulting the criminal, the German affirmed his client was aware of the catalogue of wrong doing.

It was true, despite the German tongue being used to enlighten his judges, John was well aware of the charges against him. He had heard them so often during interrogation by the Gestapo and his own police, he had discussed them with his own Advocate in Guernsey, now prevented under martial law from defending his client. John knew them by heart:

'Subversive talk and actions against the Reich.

Attempts at spying to aid and assist the enemies of the Reich.

Corruption of a German national in an attempt to deflect him from his duty and loyalty to the Reich.'

How bleak it all sounded, how conclusive and oh, so utterly misrepresented. How could such innocent actions, at best following the propaganda exhortations to regard the Germans as friends and saviours, at worst just naive mistakes, have been so misconstrued by the authorities? Why now was John facing such distorted charges and a court martial, the outcome of which was sure to result in imprisonment if he was lucky, or even . . .? But no, such conjectures could not be entertained. Not yet.

Chapter Two

John Collins, shaped and seasoned by life, calm and peaceful in his latter years, as though by contrast with his former turbulent and youthful self, now prepares to die. Not that he is too aware of his state, for shock and disability for the most part shield him from such mundane musings.

Here is a man with no future, yet in the present, kept alive. John Collins will not be permitted to slip away yet, while the machines and dials, tubes and bottles, nurses and doctors effect their function. No, John cannot be allowed to pass too quickly, for there are those not yet ready to mourn, who need to prepare themselves, who need to say goodbye. Besides, the man still has too many memories, a surfeit of thoughts and recalls, to go yet. The old man has to stay vital, to live out the time when he was young.

* * *

It seemed so long ago now that John Collins, just a boy really, who had not evacuated to England with his school the year before, had been so lonely. It must have been all of three weeks previously, when his loneliness had led him into a friendship which was now wrecking the lives of his whole family, friends and associates of his family and even the very enemy friend with whom John had started his crime against the state of war.

It had all started when John had been conscripted to work for the masters. It was on his first day that he had met pathetic, frightened Franz, a youth of his own age, brought to Guernsey too young, in order to be under the protective eye of his Gestapo uncle–well, it suited Islanders to afford the like of his uncle such grand status, be they the Secret Police or just plain Feldpolizei. It was little wonder that Franz was so disoriented and so needed a friend; he also was ready to suppress the knowledge that they were really enemies, for he too had received only misery from this war.

Franz had not known where he had been running or why he had been doing so. Perhaps it had been something to do with his friend, Corporal Schmidt, who had been sitting next to him in the open launch bringing them the three miles from Herm. Maybe it had been to do with the bomb that had exploded on the breakwater above them, the bomb which had blown a shower of dust and granite blocks into the air, the bomb which had turned his friend into a faceless man. Had he run so blindly because of Corporal Schmidt's screams which had changed from burning, piercing sirens into gasping, choking gurgles as he had drowned in his own blood?

He remembered the horror of that moment. The gaping hole where the face had been. The gushing blood, the blonde hair turned pink and the pieces of flesh hanging by strips of skin like some grotesque and hellish decoration. The screams, those haunting screams which seemed to have gone on and on. Those screams which seemed to have followed him as he had jumped ashore at the jetty, as he had run on and on and on.

Franz had run away, like a coward. He knew the Führer had no room for weaklings, and, failure that he was, he had enlisted his new friend's help to get a message to his uncle in order to save him.

It was this action which had involved John's parish priest and the tapped telephone call which had drawn the Germans' attention to his father's illegal activities.

"Subversion! What do you mean subversion?"

"Come on, you don't need to put on an act with me," was Bert's reply. "This isn't a blasted interrogation you know!"

"I know, I know, but what the hell do you mean by subversion? Trading yes, but mixed up in that other, no. That's a mugs game."

8

"Well all I know," explained P.C. Bert, "is that we've been asked to check our records and make investigations about you and any connections you might have with Father Peters . . ."

"Father Peters! Father Peters! I haven't had any dealings with him. He's so straight I doubt he'd buy a tomato without surrendering a ration coupon!" shouted Larry.

What good times the two enemies had shared, what a lot of things they had done together in their innocence, as, childlike, they had got to know each other, as though they had been friends all their lives.

John had so enjoyed educating his serious German friend. In fact, they had both taken pleasure as they had good-naturedly put the other right, forgetting all the time that one was supposed to be the victor, the other the vanquished and humble foe.

"Do you hear those guns, John? They're German guns firing at enemy ships, yes?"

"Maybe," replied John with a shrug. "Maybe they're British guns firing at German ships? Who knows?"

"No I think they are German guns," insisted Franz, "for they are very powerful sounding and Germany now has control of the Channel and the oceans."

"Oh yes, sure," sneered John sarcastically. "And where did you get that idea from?"

"From the newspapers of course," was Franz's reply, as he looked at John in bewilderment, wondering if his friend was seriously doubting his statement, or if he was just leading up to one of his strange jokes.

They had not realised how Franz's hire of a bicycle from John's own father was to lead to such complications. All they had known was that they had wanted to explore the Island together as Franz had accompanied his enemy friend while

9

he made Feldkommandantur deliveries to the coastal fortifications.

"Wait for me, Englishman. Wait!"

John, having clambered through hedges and banks, eventually reached a familiar track, stopping to regain his breath. Franz quickly joined him, the two making a duet of their panting and rasping.

"O.K?" asked John. Franz nodded still unable to speak, his face red and soaked by perspiration.

"How about a lovely cool swim down there?" asked John, pointing into the bay, with a gleeful chuckle.

"No!" gasped Franz with horror.

"No? Why not? Can't you swim?"

"Yes I swim a little but . . ."

"'Fraid to get undressed, is it? You're going to say you haven't any bathers, eh?"

"No, it's not . . ."

John was not listening.

"You could use your underpants you know."

"I know." They both laughed.

"We could dry in the sun."

"Yes but . . ."

"Oh, don't get worried Franz, it's only a joke. I know, we haven't got time. Besides I'm not stupid. I know it's against the law to go bathing. Bloody stupid law if you ask me, eh? Bloody stupid German law, eh?"

Larry, John's father, had even been persuaded, against his better judgement, to let his son's enemy friend come to the house. Yes, even Larry, 'Jerry' hater that he was, had acquiesced, and the two youths had regressed to childhood, free from the restrictions of belligerence.

"Oh, you have a garden, yes? Can we take these cars and make some roadways?"

That had been such a good idea! John had felt a thrill that here was a kindred spirit who would enjoy such erudite activities.

10

And so, despite the nagging worry that old Gaudion would view them — he probably knew of Franz's visit anyway — they went to the high-walled garden, Gaudion's private nature reserve for snails.

As always, the walls had been clustered with snails, snails upon snails. All the low dividing walls and paths, which had once divided cultivation from carefully-tended soil, had snails and silver trails. Dandelion and long grass grew in profusion, forming jungles in which were to be found the graveyards of the thousands of discarded shells.

"Wonderful!" Franz had exclaimed. "We can cut some roads through that patch and we can make some ramps here, see?" He had run about excitedly picking up bits of broken slate and flat pebbles to use as the tools of engineering.

"Look," John had ordered as he had taken Franz to part of his territory, "see?" He had stood back with pride, knowing how Franz would appreciate such things.

"That is absolutely very good, John," Franz had uttered in amazement, as he had viewed a network of Dinky car roads John had made only months before. There were cuttings and embankments, stone bases with carefully sieved earth turned into mud and laid as macadam surfaces. True, some of the intricate structures had been broken through by weeds like some giant trees, while some roads had been eroded by rain and others badly cracked by summer's heat. There were even aliens in the form of ant colonies unaware of the dangers of being run over. That did not matter, they would both enjoy the renovations and repairs.

The two friends had walked together, talked freely and confidently with each other and had even made plans. Oh yes, Franz had been full of how they could visit the nearby islands of Herm and Sark once the Germans had won the war. They had even made plans to go to the Gaumont together to watch films of how Germany was winning. Yes, they had arranged to sit either side of the barrier which divided Germans from civilians, in order to be near each other.

Franz had been invited to John's Church Boys' Club, and both had anticipated attending a Gala arranged by the masters to perpetuate the idea that they were 'Brothers All'.

Notwithstanding Franz read out loud:

> *"Notice to all members of the civilian population and
> forces of the Reich:*
> *The German Command, with due regard for the well
> being of all its occupied territories, and as further proof
> of its care of all those for whom it claims responsibility,
> and in the continued promotion of excellent relations
> with such peoples, does invite the civilian population
> and the military to compete in a water gala of excellence,
> as brothers, on the afternoon of Thursday, 24th July at
> La Vallette pool known as the 'Ladies Pool'. For full
> details see La Gazette Officielle in your daily newspapers.*
> > *Signed*
> > *Feldkommandantur"*

*John was stunned. It could not be true! A gala? An excellent, fun-
packed, exciting gala? Just like before the Occupation? Races, diving,
clowns, cheering, laughing, swimming? A chance for John to shine
again, to be the Boys' Champion that he once was? No, surely it must
be a cruel hoax?*

*He read it for himself while Franz read the German version. They
both looked at each other for a long time then suddenly John came to
life.*

*"Yippee!" he yelled, jumping in the air like a young kid and
throwing his arms round his friend. "Franz, there's going to be a
gala! There's going to be a gala and I'm going to be a champion!"*

This period of innocent friendship had all passed so quickly,
just as any experience of true worth seems to have finished
almost before it has begun. Yet they had done so many things
together and had enjoyed such fun, neither realising that it
was going to end so abruptly.

They must have been blind in their innocence, for the
ominous signs had been there but they had chosen not to see
them, or had just repressed such concepts. If they had
analysed their short period of friendship, they would have
perceived the dangers which were building up. Franz would
have taken the angry advice from his Gestapo uncle, who
found it an anathema that any true Aryan would wish to
demean himself by mixing with the Guernsey peasants. John

might have regarded the prohibition of such an 'unhealthy friendship' from his employer, Herr Tropp, and he would have taken more notice of his mother's anxieties that he would bring trouble to their door.

There had been those wicked evil incidents too, in which John had almost lost his innocence and had been shocked and embarrassed by the behaviour of adults who, until then, he had looked up to. Franz had borne the brunt of all that unpleasantness, John felt sure of that. Somehow it had been a condition for their continued association. It had been the price poor Franz had been made to pay.

"They're queer. Or if you want the proper word for it, they're homosexuals,' said John, feeling a great relief at having finally given birth to this concept.

"Er . . . yes. Yes that is it, exactly so," agreed Franz. "How did you know?"

"I don't," said John, correcting himself. "That is, I didn't 'till I told Dad."

"You tell your father?"

"Yes."

"Why?"

"Because, oh I don't know, can't we just drop it?"

"No. Why do you tell your father? What did you say?"

"Oh, I don't know. Let's just say I didn't like what they were doing to you."

"What were they?"

"Oh come on, you know."

"No John, believe me I don't. I think I know but please tell me."

"Well, if you must know, they had their arms round you as if you were a girl."

"Oh?" said Franz, by now quite scarlet. "And?"

"Well they . . . " John paused.

"Please go on, John. I want to know."

"Well, that womanish looking one was stroking your hair and kissing you."

"Oh no! Oh, please believe me, I did not know. I think something like this but I do not know."

"And the Patrol Leader was rubbing your leg."

*"Rubbing my leg?" asked Franz involuntarily touching his calf.
"You mean like this?" rubbing his own leg.*

"No, you fool. Higher up!"

"What there?" enquired Franz, touching his own knee.

"No, up there," explained John rubbing his own thigh, at the same time laughing to hide his discomfort.

"I see," acknowledged Franz, too laughing to hide his feelings. "Well now I know, thank you. Do you believe me when I tell you it is not my wish . . ."

"Yes!" interrupted John. "Yes, yes, yes! I believe you. Now can you please shut up or I'll start rubbing you and it won't be your leg. I'll rub your nose with my fist!"

Very clear now was that conversation.

"Well, Müller," had said the Patrol Leader who, having realised his position to be so strong, had been able to be quite direct, "You may keep contact with that Britisher of yours."

Morten had watched the delight and near disbelief colour the young detainee's face.

"Sir?" Franz had been hesitant but his excitement had taken charge of his caution, "I can meet with John while I wait to go to Russia?"

"Yes, little Franz." Morten's eyes had melted slightly with amusement at the insipid wretch who had stood before him. He had felt almost good at having been able to use his authority so.

"You can go out with your dearest friend, whenever you like, so long as you tell me first."

Franz had gasped. His inclination had been to want to shake Morten's hand but he had stopped himself for the prospect of physical contact with that person had taken him back to the dark shades of reality.

"You can go out this very evening, if you so wish." Morten's intervention had prevented Franz's mind travelling further along the dark path of suspicion. "But remember to tell me where you will be and at what time I am to expect you back."

There had been a chill note in the reminder, but nevertheless Franz had anticipated more in it for him and his friendship with John than if the offer had not been made.

"So I can go now?" Franz was still expecting the words to have been just a cruel hoax.

"Yes, go, go!" Morten had gestured with mock severity, as he had

ushered Franz to the door, while his victim had not been given choice in the matter.

"Oh, and Mr. Franz Müller," had called the Patrol Leader, so forgetful that he had only thought of it, as his charge had been leaving the office. "Try to cheer yourself a bit. Try to be a little friendly, to Germans as well as to the enemy."

Franz had almost stopped at these words, as they had come at him from around the open door, but he had decided it better not to answer than to try.

"Oh, and Franz," a pause for Morten's coup de grace.

"It's Sunday Relaxation in two days, remember? We would like your friend John to attend, right?"

John, in his naive innocence, had been prepared to sacrifice his decency in order to save his friend, but he had never had to pay that supreme price. He was destined, however, to carry the guilt of what might have been and the shame of what happened to Franz, for the rest of his days.

Well, the downfall of the two friends had not been brought about by the evil perversion of S.S. Hüffmeier or Patrol Leader Morten. No, those had just been burdens they had carried, while the true and wholesome aspects of their innocent fraternization had continued.

Ironically, it was that innocent part of their friendship and not the sinister influences, which had led to their eventual downfall.

On that glorious summer's day in which the two friends had cycled together, delivering the Feldkommandantur messages to the military coastal zone, they had unwittingly stored up much evidence against themselves. These misdemeanours had culminated in an event which was to precipitate their separate fates and bring all their previous wrong-doings to light.

"Be still, you fool!" insisted Franz, more forceful now than John had ever known him. *"Look, John, don't you see, that animal was killed by a mine!"*

"Eh?" John became silent and very still as Franz excitedly explained his thesis.

"We are in a minefield John. Look, see?" He pointed to the decomposing creature in front of them. It lay in a small crater the size of an upturned dustbin lid, tiny ripples of disturbed gravel and stones radiating from it.

John did not argue. They just looked at each other in horror.

"Anyway, let us think ourselves lucky," Franz added, *"for their other plan was even worse!"* He shuddered at the prospect. *"Well, I heard them talking of two plans really . . ."*

"And?" John interrupted.

Not noticing his friend's ill manners, Franz continued.

"The first plan is to make us lie flat then they are going to fire their rifles, from where they stand, to hit the ground, every metre or so, so that we can step safely where the bullets have land."

John gave a low whistle at that idea.

"I don't like that idea one little bit," he said. *"What made them change their minds?"*

Franz replied, *"They do not want to waste their ammunition."*

At that, John was almost amused, and a faint flicker of a smile just slightly lit his pursed lips, to Franz's annoyance, as he felt he was being disbelieved.

"If you think that is funny you should have heard their other plan," he said.

"Oh?" queried John, sounding quite defensive. *"Go on."*

"They wanting me to lie down and you to walk to them."

"Why?" asked John, aghast at the thought. *"Why?"*

"Because then, if there were any mines you step on them and I am safe."

"But why me?" John shouted. *"Why not you?"*

"Because, they say you are not a German," came Franz's reply, *"therefore it not matters if you are killed, so long as I am safe, for I am a German."*

"Hell!" said John, shaking at the prospect. *"They really considered doing that?"* His fear beginning to form itself into anger.

"Don't be cross with me," Franz begged. *"It was not my idea."*

"O.K. O.K., I know," John replied. *"What stopped them?"*

"They are afraid they might get injured in the explosion. Besides they did not wish to get into trouble for wasting a land mine."

Yes, they had been rescued, but a price had needed to be paid, a price for the breaking of military law, for their trespass and wasting of the masters' time, for a disregard of the state of war by the wilful and deceptive collaboration of these two enemy friends. That was why Franz had been sent to the Eastern Front in Russia, condemned to almost certain death by his former friend's puerile selfishness. That was why John, along with all the others whose lives he had ruined, had been sent to the Police Court. That was why his father, his uncle and the fisherman Keith had all been committed for trial at the Royal Court, so that their black marketeering could be punished, that the custodians of Guernsey's ancient system of justice would be forced to do the Teutons' work for them. It was for this reason too that young John Collins and his parish priest were now to be made examples of in the Nazi court martial in the neighbouring island of Jersey.

So, John Collins, not yet sixteen years old but already having been dragged into the adult world, is now at the culmination of his short period of criminality. Soon he will be meted the swift and harsh justice of the new order, soon he is to pay the bitter price for daring to befriend an enemy. He does not mind, however, for he is stoical, it is all outside his control. In some ways, he sees the coming purging as a necessary evil, almost as welcome, for it will put him in communion with his enemy friend Franz, who must now be already paying the price in far off Russia. His punishment has to be accepted, for only then, once he has paid the price, can he begin his search for the one he has so harmed, only then can he try to make amends for all the troubles and misery he has caused his own father and his father's friends and contacts.

Chapter Three

There are times when the pain begins to surface, a pain which if not tended will fire and burn him from within, as when, semi-conscious, he had been contorted, trapped inside that tangled wreck which had been his car. He feels those slivers of glass deep inside, as unseen hands manipulate and prod him. Yes, John Collins feels that ghastly agony and he will choke and gasp, unable to communicate the fear. Always, however, at times like these, there is someone at hand. They seem to know his unspoken need, as mercifully he is returned to his past.

* * *

Well, it was all happening fast, the focus of the disdain of the mighty forces of national socialism, was having his crimes dealt with expeditiously. As John's Advocate had earlier prepared him in Guernsey, as the civilian gaolers had warned him last night in the States of Jersey prison, the trial was conducted almost exclusively in the master tongue. Not that it mattered, for all they knew he was guilty, otherwise why would he be here at all, wasting their time?

As the morning sped past, as statements were referred to by his accusers, sometimes read or partly read out but more often just accepted as good Aryan truths, as occasionally one Nazi officer and then another would confer, perhaps for the sake of the appearance of their pure justice, to question him in their incomprehensible tongue, John began to realise how damning and conclusive their case seemed.

It was all wrong, of course. All the incidents to which they referred had perfectly innocent explanations. John knew he only needed the opportunity to explain, for them to be able to understand what had really happened on the day he and

18

Franz had strayed into that German minefield, putting German lives and property and defences so much at risk. He knew too that, were he given the chance, he could explain the innocence of his friendship with Franz, and that they had not wished to harm or subvert the Nazi state. If only he could have framed the words, he could have explained how both he and Franz had detested the unknown and evil practices in Town Patrol House, and both would far rather have distanced themselves from that place. It certainly could not be said that they had entered into those wicked things willingly in order to undermine authority.

Just as during interrogation at the Gestapo, however, John was never given the opportunity to make these things clear. It was as though they had decided the outcome before they had started their interrogation and were studiously avoiding any arguments which would contradict their foregone conclusions.

"They saying you to hospital go," quizzed John's German officer, his nearest approach to a defence, his selective interpreter.

"Eh?" Out of context, this did not make sense to John.

Irritated, perhaps embarrassed that, as the most junior officer, he had been assigned the ignominious task of cosmetically appearing to defend an enemy of the Reich, the German, with his broken English, explained that John's visit to Victoria Hospital was being referred to.

What a nonsense! John's innocent visit to try to see Franz was being misconstrued as an attempt to spy!

After considering all the possibilities, John decided that Franz was most likely to be at Victoria Hospital. He made up good time on one of his Messenger errands, and by a great stroke of good fortune, his idea proved correct.

He brazened his way into the former civilian hospital to seek his friend, running the gauntlet of a ward of Germans so recently mutilated by the evil and feared R.A.F.

No, Franz was not in bed, he was not even wearing bed attire. He was, in fact, to John's surprise, working in the kitchen, peeling vegetables for the meals of those less fortunate of his compatriots.

"You cannot come here!" exploded Franz. He seemed both angry and embarrassed.

19

"Why?" asked John, surprise and shock reducing his question to little more than a whisper.

With a mixture of emotions of fear and guilt, the young German explained to John that he had already caused him a great deal of discomfort, possibly even danger. It seemed that Herr Tropp had wasted no time and had seen to it that Franz was in no doubt that he was being un-Germanic, almost unpatriotic, to be dabbling in so called friendship with a member of an inferior conquered race.

The whole group of officers seemed very animated when their senior held up a tattered piece of paper. They had obviously discussed this piece of conclusive evidence. With horror, John realised it was his route plan. After the rescue from the minefield, the Germans had confiscated it as further evidence of spying.

Well, it was a legitimate map with routes and direction signs so that John, accompanied by Franz, had been able to work his way to the various coastal fortifications to deliver messages, as was his job. John knew what was coming though, he knew the implications of the other marks they had found on his map. Yes, the Gestapo had been very interested in those too. He had tried to explain to them but they had not wanted to know the real reasons for his having marked the fortifications of Hitler's mighty Atlantic Wall. They had not believed his explanations then, just as now John was sure this court martial would not. Could any court, even a British court, be expected to believe such excuses? Was the truth always destined to sound so ridiculously improbable? Perhaps that is why democracies permit the accused to employ the services of Advocates of Defence?

Rudolphe muttered something and disappeared.

'Thank goodness!' thought John.

"Right Franz, let's go eh"

"All right, John, Rudolphe has just gone to get permission to walk with us, to our bicycles."

"What for?" asked John, not attempting to hide his annoyance.

"Well, you see, he is being punished for what happens at the Soup Kitchen. That is why he is out here . . ."

"And?" interjected John rudely.

Franz, not cognizant of any rudeness continued:

"He is been separate from his best friend who is now at another cliff place we are to visit. He want us to . . ."

"Oh no!" declared John, realising they were about to be asked to deliver a message.

"What do you mean, 'Oh no'? Why not? What is wrong with that? It won't put us out of our way. Look, here he is. Quick, John, get out your list so Rudophe can tell you where Helmut is stationed."

John felt controlled by circumstances rather than being in control. He suspected to comply with this request was the easiest way.

"Very well," he sighed, as he took out his list and map together with the route plan.

Rudolphe actually smiled at John, as Franz gave him the good news. Without waiting to be asked he eagerly snatched John's papers and scrutinised them. Without reference to John he took a pencil from his tunic pocket and marked, with a circle, one of the military zone emplacements at Jerbourg, at the other end of the south coast cliffs. John was annoyed but the matter was outside his control. He nodded. Using Franz as an interpreter, Rudolphe explained where they were at present. John knew where they were. This German must think him stupid or something! Notwithstanding he marked their present position with yet another circle. John tried to snatch the map but Rudolphe pulled away, then, to emphasise the point that they were at Pleinmont, and had to make their way several miles to Jerbourg, marked the intervening coast route with a hastily dotted line.

Rudolphe pointed to the next headland, to where a huge sandcastle, a concrete monstrosity, was springing up, an inverted cone whose layers of gun slits appeared stark like rows of smiling black teeth facing out to sea. The whole had the appearance of a fantastic schoolboy drawing of war.

Franz interpreted. "We can go along that road there instead of leaving the Military zone. Quick John, give him your map. This will save a lot of time!"

John did not resist. Rudolphe marked the lane and then, still addressing Franz, began marking symbols.

"He says he knows this lane," explained Franz. "Whatever we do, we must not leave it. Those there are mines." Rudolphe marked some patches with the letters M.

"And those are overhead wires with bombs attached to deter parachutists." Rudolphe drew a series of little poles with crisscrossed wires looking rather like a field of cultivated hops.

By now Rudolphe was getting quite carried away and on the cliff sides was making what, upon enquiry, John learned to be roll bombs, trenches and barbed wire. This was all clearly irrelevant and Franz retrieved John's papers.

More damning were John's bravado-laden, yet innocent, questions when the two friends had reached their final call at Jerbourg on the south east cliffs.

The German officers looked very serious as they discussed amongst themselves how this enemy of the Reich had skilfully tried to extract vital information from the soldier on duty.

The senior again snapped his incomprehensible questions at John, ill disguising his contempt for the traitorous peasant who stood before him. Half heartedly, his German defence officer came to the criminal's side.

"At this place called Jerbourg, you asking are many question. You say about German defences," declared the youth's defender with thinly veiled detestation in his voice.

"Not so," replied the accused, hoping to sound affronted at the very idea, but knowing full well what damning evidence was to follow.

"No," insisted John, *"come my way please. There's such a lot more to see."*

"See?" questioned the sentry puzzled. *"What do you mean 'see'?"*

"John, you can't ask these questions!" insisted Franz in his annoyance.

"That is so," interrupted the sentry. *"There are things there that you must not see and which are very dangerous. You ask too many questions!"*

He watched Franz scowl as the questions poured out.

"What are those?" he asked, indicating what appeared to be iron crosses, set in concrete, scattered across a field near the rows of

bunkers. To his surprise the soldier did not reprimand him but simply explained:

"They're anti-tank traps, not that any British tanks could get up the cliffs or even pass our guns," he said with a laugh.

"Mmm!" commented John pensively.

"What if they dropped them in by parachute though?" interjected Franz, intrigued by the thought.

"Don't be daft," said John, "they'd be shot down before they reached the ground."

"Not if it was night time!" exclaimed Franz feeling annoyed to be criticised so.

"Ah, but for the night, we have search lights, see over there. And there, see?" The sentry pointed to where there were obviously batches of lights. Franz could not see them, but not wishing to appear foolish, said he could. John, possibly more naive, said he could not make them out, to which the man was delighted at the effectiveness of their camouflage.

"Anyway," said John, "I know another method you use to stop things coming in by parachute."

"Oh, and what is that?" asked the soldier raising his eyebrows in mock curiosity.

"You have poles with wires and bombs attached so that, if anything touches a wire when landing the bomb goes off and, hey presto!"

"How you know all this?" asked the man scratching his head in amazement.

"Oh, we Guernsey people know everything," replied John, with bravado.

"That is not true," countered Franz, glad at the opportunity to get back at his friend. "We were told that only today. He is not as clever as he is pretending!"

They all three laughed and the soldier did not question them further.

Franz would have been able to tell them otherwise. He understood his friend. Franz knew that John had not intended to ask spying questions, he was just being a bit boastful, as is the way with Guernsey youth. He meant no harm, it was just a bit of innocent juvenile cheek, nothing more.

"You have making these questionings?" asked John's defence. It was more rhetorical than enquiry however, as the Teuton listed the offending catalogue.

"What does it matter?" asked John, despairing. It was true he had asked these things, so what was the point of denying?

"O.K. I asked, but . . .," he was cut off as his defence confirmed to his comrades that the criminal concurred.

There was the other matter, too. They brought up that he had persuaded Franz to carry letters from one German fortification to another. These letters were not official communiqués but were uncensored German letters sent from one Aryan to another. It was an offence against the military code, a crime encouraged by this corrupt civilian who now stood before his judges. John had known it was unwise, but circumstances had persuaded him to go along with the idea, for he been outnumbered in his protestations. Besides, how was he to have known that simply passing on a letter from one friend to another could have been misconstrued as an act against the forces of occupation?

There were many other recorded incidents, all of minor significance in themselves yet, added together, just pointed to the undoubted guilt of the young Guernseyman. So depressed was young John Collins, and so sure now that his fate was sealed that he made little attempt to protest or try to explain what he gathered from the sparse commentary his assigned German gave to him.

Well, it was inevitable that the argument of the two youths should be brought up. John supposed it must have looked like a fight from a distance, especially to German sentries, but to hear their quarrel listed as an offence against international law . . .'striking a member of the armed forces' . . . was so ludicrous.

Yes, they had argued, but don't all friends fall out sometimes? Why didn't his accusers mention that the incident had quickly mended, that they had made up? But no, that would not suit the German case!

"Bugger off can't you. Bugger off!" Franz did not understand the words but was cognizant that he was being sworn at. He retaliated in anger, using a German expletive of his own. He was not to be thwarted. He gripped the handlebars securely so that John was forced to dismount.

"How dare you speak to me like this? Me who has waited here to speak to you! What have I done that you must be so rude?"

The struggle had attracted the attention of the Feldkommandantur sentry and the Military Police guard. Both were staring in their direction. Franz was the first to observe their stares. The sentry called to him in German, to which he replied with a shrugging of his shoulders. John was now aware of their presence and looked at the two men grinning at each other, obviously sharing some joke at his and Franz's expense. Through gritted teeth he hissed.

"Let me go, Franz. We'll be reported!"

"No!" was Franz's adamant reply.

Similarly instanced was the time the two had been observed ostensibly brawling in a country lane. The court was not to know that it was just an innocent happening. How could they know that the two friends had earlier drunk too much cider, and that John had felt ill? They were not told the good side, how Franz had cycled back down the lane to wet a handkerchief at the douit, in order to freshen up his vomit-soiled friend. No, they were only told what appeared to be happening when that Feldpolizei had come across them. They would never know that what had started in anger had quickly translated into the good fun of true friendship.

"Why, you little bugger!" shouted John, by now acting anger rather than feeling the emotion. "I'll make you eat your words, mon vieux!"

He jogged up and down on Franz's abdomen, just sufficient for him to call out giggling,

"Oh, stop that, you're being stupid!"

"Stupid is it?" asked John, now grinning broadly, "I'll give you stupid."

He began to give his enemy the typewriter treatment, rapidly poking his fingers at his chest so that he dissolved into fits of laughter at the ticklish sensation.

"Stop! Stop!" screeched Franz, as he writhed in torment, while his laughter howled up into John's face.

John too, laughing, asked once more, "Submit?"

Did this court really need to be told such details? Was it so important to the German case that John had tried to give a false name and address to that member of the Feldpolizei? How was he to know the man understood English all along, as John had used interpreter Franz to give false information? That was not a crime, surely? It had been just fear-induced panic.

Just as they knew of Franz's frequent visits to the Collins' house, they were aware that the young German had had dealings with John's father, but that, it seemed, was being kept as evidence to be used in Larry's own trial. Well, they knew Franz had foolishly accompanied his enemy on that fateful day, so it stood to reason that he had needed a bicycle. It seemed perfectly legitimate to John that the young German should hire a bicycle from Larry Collins. He did operate a bicycle shop after all!

"Right, young man, let's see what we can do?"

Franz's spirits took a decided leap.

"Do you smoke?"

"No thank you, Sir."

"No, no!" snapped Larry, "I wasn't offering you one, I just want to know. What do you do with your cigarette ration?"

"Oh," replied Franz, "I usually give them away or exchange them."

"Good, then maybe we can do a deal. I'm not promising, mind!"

"Yes, yes," said Franz, taking Larry's tone as a sure promise, despite his protestation to the contrary.

"When do you need it, you say?"

"Oh, tomorrow morning, please. For the whole day"

"Hmm," murmured Larry, "yes, I might be able to help you. Come in when I open, O.K.?"

"Oh yes, thank you very much," said Franz, the delight at the prospect shining in his eyes.

"It's not a promise, mind."

"Can you tell me, please, what I am pay?"

Larry was taken aback at this. Usually he could strike a hard bargain but this time he did not feel at all inclined to make gain of this particular enemy. He felt he must be getting soft, or old, or maybe just like his son, and many others in the community, getting used to them, or to like them. He felt he would like the lad to have the opportunity to fulfil his wish at no cost to himself.

'Hell,' thought Larry, 'it's a poor thing if one has to charge a mere scrap of a lad just to use my bike for the day.'

"I'll have to think about that," he replied. *"Maybe a few of your cigarettes would do."* Then, as an afterthought adding. *"And of course you'd need to keep your mouth shut about this place."*

"Mouth shut?" asked Franz, confused.

"Yes, you know what I mean. You don't tell your friends you came here and borrowed my bike, understood?"

"Understood!"

Considering they only brought guilty people to these court martials and few ever went free from such places, the Germans certainly had built a strong case. Strange that, it seemed almost as though they wished for appearances to show justice being fairly administered, perhaps they even believed that that was what they were doing? Doubly strange, that they went to such lengths, then only denied themselves the advantage of such propaganda by not allowing press coverage. It was as though their very thoroughness and attention to detail was just an end in itself. No, for the Teutons, it seemed sufficient that the public should only be told what severe punishments had been administered to the breakers of good German order.

Many more seemingly trivial incidents were referred to, John only receiving snippets from his German defender. Such trivial incidents, yet obviously viewed with seriousness by his judges. What he was not informed directly, John was able to guess at from the odd recognisable words or place names, and was able to recall the incidents with a mixture of memory and conjecture. This was the case with the incident where, he had found himself witness to the actions of Franz and his German comrades at the civilian soup kitchen.

John smiled.

   Franz looked away.

   The foot soldier shook the table.

   John moved towards Franz.

   Two other soldiers shook the old lady.

   The last of the customers left.

   John stood by Franz.

   Franz signified the door and left.

   The old lady shouted in anger and fear.

   John followed Franz.

   The older German spat in the stew.

   Outside, Franz stood looking at the ground.

   John was aware of the dull, silent hate looks from the last of the men and women as they slowly retrieved their bicycles.

   'Go away, go away all of you,' he thought, 'Why don't you hurry up and go? I want to talk with my friend. I do not want to share him with any of you. You do not understand. You hate us.'

   The last man left. He looked at John. John thought he was almost smiling at him, as he wheeled past.

   He spat at John's feet!

   "Franz, are you well?"

   "Yes, how are you?"

   "I'm fine, me."

   There was a long awkward pause.

John had been just an innocent bystander there, and it had been a coincidence that Franz too had been on the scene. This had not been planned as one of their devious meetings, but the court was now being told how it was an ominous liaison. Further, they had records of how John's uncle Bert, in the capacity of police constable, had taken it upon himself to reprimand the youth before the matter came to the attention of the Chief. Was this not further evidence of the whole corrupt complicity between the Collins' family and certain traitorous elements within the civilian police force?

The court even heard how this suspect friendship had led the two enemies to be seen walking together as though they felt themselves in some way to be equal. Well, it might be pretentious for a youth of occupied status to seek to be equal with a member of mighty Germany's forces, but for that same inferior to encourage one of the Wehrmacht to sink to his level was tantamount to subversion.

But all this trivia was not worth the mental effort to refute, not that the accused guilty person would have been given opportunity to gainsay or call witnesses to prove his innocence. Why should an inferior be afforded such an unneccessary luxury to further waste the time of the Reich?

It was only when they mentioned John's involvement with Town Patrol House that he was pricked into participation.

"They saying you go uninvited to social gatherings, German relaxation times," said his defending German.

Uninvited! What the hell were they saying? Why were they bringing all that up again? It must be all part of their plan to break him down. Yes, that was it, they wanted to shame John Collins, they wanted it to be thought by the public that he was as degenerate as that dirty bullying S.S. Hüffmeier. If only they knew, if only that evil man had stayed in Alderney where the S.S. belonged.

He did not feel inclined to be ordered by this person of the master race.

"I'm watching a film," he replied firmly.

David did not quite understand the logic of that statement. To him it was quite obvious that John had been watching a film but now it was equally apparent that he was going to stop watching it and accompany him for he, David Hüffmeier, was a member of the S.S. To request someone to do something was to order it. His request was the velvet glove hiding the iron fist.

"You are to come with me. It has to be!"

In no way could it be said that he had gone willingly, or even contrived to go to those reprehensible gatherings!

*It was this sight which greeted John as he followed S.S. Hüffmeier
down the steps into the noisy, hot and smokey drawing room.*

*John immediately located Franz. He saw him with his food-soiled
uniform and his leaden arms weighted on to the adjoining knees of
Morten and Jules. He saw Franz with his vacant drunken stare and
inane open mouth. He observed him being cuddled by the bangled
arm of the sparkling Jules. Franz was lying back, his thigh being
caressed by the jubilant Morten.*

*"No, I will not drink, thank you, not today, not on Sunday." That
last clause had not been planned, it had just been inspirational,
perhaps a gift from Sunday itself?*

*"But you must drink!" exclaimed Hüffmeier with mock
affrontedness. "You are at the Relaxation. Drinking is part of the
fun!"*

*"He cannot," suddenly interjected Franz quite unexpectedly but
obviously controlled by the same inspiration. "It is Sunday, he has
been to Church."*

*"So?" asked Morten, jabbing Franz in the ribs with his elbow.
"Since when has going to Church stopped him?"*

*Morten was annoyed as he got up and whispered to the waiter. He
was ready to make an issue out of this. Drink would be provided and,
by the Führer, drink would be drunk!*

*The drinks were duly brought, the two youths accepted them
protestingly. Franz could have done with something to dull his racing
senses, for in his case alcohol could only have assisted him. But he
realised that to John it would have been lethal. How long before they
would be pressured into sipping the mixtures? Those first sips which
would then lubricate the resolve into being less necessary.*

There was nowhere to tip any of the potential danger.

*'Maybe just a little would be harmless?' thought John as he lifted
his glass, turning it, noticing how the mixture seemed filled with lines
like myriad cracks in ice, all swirling in their miniature currents.
Perhaps, if he took a sip, food would be brought? The two men might
be less attentive if they saw their hospitality was not refused? Maybe
they would go off to fetch food then, if requested? Could they get away
with drinking just a little and then maybe tipping some under the
seats of the sofa or onto the carpets at their side? It had, after all, a
clear water-like appearance.*

*Franz was aware of John's intention and, in his anxiety to
communicate his displeasure to the far end of the seat, knocked*

Morten out of his temporary musing lethargy.

"What's up with you now?" growled the Patrol Leader, as Franz edged forward. "Why don't you just sit back and enjoy your drink? Go on, drink it. That's an order!" He turned his attentions to his friend David once more but S.S. Hüffmeier was already busying himself with his guest.

The pushing off of the hand on knee had been taken as just a game at first, all part of the lead up. Time was on their side.

"Go on, drink," cajoled Hüffmeier. "You cannot insult good German schnapps. It is too hard to come by, these days."

John just stared ahead. He heard the words but he was determined not to take any notice. It had started, the fight for his decency and self-respect had begun. He felt justified in ignoring conversation and disregarding polite convention with such a person.

How he hated this time. All the planning in the world could not have given him the slightest insight as to how he would feel right now.

With the removal of the hand his every inclination had been to get up and move away, to rush from the building and never come near it again. The very portents of Hüffmeier's action had opened for a him a gaping hole into which he stared into a nothingness, an abhorrence of negativity. Yes, he could have left but where would that have put poor Franz? This was the beginning of the price he had to pay for friendship. This was the price and more, which Franz had already been paying for him.

Perhaps the Germans really did believe that inferior civilians of occupied status were so lacking in morals that they would enter willingly into such practices? Maybe they really did believe John was as evil and calculating as their evidence seemed to suggest? They probably honestly thought that a person of such inferior race was capable of cultivating one of their own sons in order to corrupt him, and ingratiate himself to enable his undermining of German authority.

Well, they must certainly have been aware of the accused's animation, anger almost, when those degrading incidents were brought to his attention. Was not this dejected and depressed criminal now protesting too much? Was it not just further proof of his utter deceit and guilt, if further proof were needed?

No, John Collins, this lean fifteen-year-old who, through strange contortion of coincidence looked so Ayran, yet was an enemy of the Reich, was guilty beyond doubt. Not only had he betrayed a trust put on him, when he had worked for the masters, but he had foolishly attempted to spy in a vain attempt to gather information which might be passed on to the enemy. Worse still, had been his actions to subvert a young German soldier from the course of his duty. John Collins had employed subversive talk, when, in contact with Franz Müller, for which that young German was now being punished by posting to the Eastern Front, Collins had pretended to befriend one of the Wehrmacht, and had attempted to corrupt him in many ways. It was only right and fitting that the criminal should be severely punished, for if the innocent German he had so misled was now under threat of death in action, then this civilian must also have at least part of his tender years executed from him.

The assembled officers took only minutes to reach their conclusion. Perhaps they felt they were showing mercy to such a misguided criminal? Could it be that they thought they were dealing with a mere child, that they were so lenient? Did they really have regard for the Geneva Convention, or was it just coincidental that their generosity and forbearance fell within its remit?

John was not to know their reasons any more than he could have expected to have a balanced hearing, or contemplate an appeal against his sentence. He accepted their mercy as, for his crime of friendship, his act against the state of war, this fifteen-year-old boy was only sentenced to twelve months of hard labour in a prison on the French mainland.

For John Collins, it was over. His war was finished. Not for John to see his beloved island again for an endless twelve months. Not for John to be able to say goodbye to his mother, but only to carry with him to the temporary transit of the Jersey prison, her gasp of unrelieved anguish which had filled his ears as his sentence had been read out in its Teutonic brevity.

The young criminal was manacled and led away to yet more unknowns. His time had come. Yet to be heard were the fates of those whom his puerility had brought to danger. Still to be tried in this Jersey court martial was his father confessor, that evil man of the cloth who had so conceitedly blasphemed about the saviour of mankind, the mighty Adolph Hitler, as he had preached his misguided sedition from the pulpit.

Yes, John Collins felt the prospect of his unknown terror in a French prison, surrounded by foreigners, guarded by those reputed less gentle than the benevolent liberators of these British islands, paled into insignificance compared with the guilt he was to carry alone, the guilt that it was he who had wrecked the lives of so many. Wrecked the lives of many Guernsey families, yet, worse still, had condemned one of the enemy, his only true friend, to unknown terrors or almost certain death.

Chapter Four

Half awake now, eyes closed, of course, John is aware of those around him. They talk quietly in a matter-of-fact way, almost as if he were unimportant, not there. They must be doctors and nurses. John is nothing special to them. They just do their job. Yes, that is it. They do not care that here he lies unable to move, lacking the motivation to communicate. They see him only as a job of work. They cannot know what thoughts he holds. They do not know that here lies a young man, held there in the mind of a departing senior.

Well, this is fine, for why should John share his thoughts with them? What right have they to know what he holds dear? What he sees and what he re-lives is his alone. No-one can ever know but he.

* * *

In Guernsey, it suited the masters to permit the trial of certain recalcitrants to take place in the civil courts. Yes, John's father, Larry Collings his father's best friend, Police Constable Uncle Bert Bisson and the fisherman Keith de la Haye were to be afforded the luxury of real pre-war justice.

After those initial hearings in the Police Court when, at the behest of the occupiers, John's own case and that of Father Peters, had been transferred to court martial as being of a subversive and undermining nature, the other three seniors were committed to trial by the Royal Court.

Strange how the Aryan overlords still permitted the existence of such anomalies from the past. What other country of occupied status could expect such generosity? Which other vanquished people would be permitted to keep, in its place of judgement, the Royal Coat of Arms, belonging to the head of state of the conquerors' enemy?

Yes, the Bailiff of Guernsey, head of state and Lord Chief Justice, appointed by the British Crown, still held sway in his own court, assisted by his permanently appointed Jurats.

None would ever know the behind the scenes conversations which had taken place between the Bailiff and the masters. Who would ever know the pleadings he made for this person or that to be treated leniently in that other court room? Who would ever thank him that he would sometimes agree to pass sufficiently severe sentences on his own people, for them to serve out civilian imprisonment in the Town gaol, subject to the usual waiting list for accommodation. In return the Germans would mysteriously drop charges of their own. Was that working for the Germans? Was it for them or against them?

Only this week had he found himself embroiled in such a conflict of conscience. How was he to seem convincing to the general public in his severe sentencing for what, before the Occupation, would have been just minor infringements of law and order? The secret conversations still stung his learned ears as he relived the swallowing of his professional pride and integrity.

". . . It is possible and that is how it will be! Also Mr. Bailiff, I would remind you . . ."

He had not finished his statement for even the Bailiff, conditioned as he was by more than a year of such lack of courtesy from the Teutons, had risen to his feet incensed that his authority to arbitrate in such decisions had been usurped.

"Sir!" he had almost shouted, "We know all things are possible with your new order! If you had just had the courtsey to hear me out, I was querying the administration of the matter, not your power to impose your undoubted will!"

"It is not a problem," the German had said dismissively still unaware that he had been particularly discourteous, for he had not been dealing with a German after all. "I will authorize it."

"There is the question of the Advocates of defence," the Bailiff had added smugly, proud that under this ancient democratic system the defence was independent of the will of the judiciary.

"Exactly so!" replied the German. "Have I not just said your people will alter their papers?"

How exasperating!

"What then about the newspapers?" had insisted the Bailiff, determined not to be belittled.

"Newspapers? What do you mean?" the German had asked, genuinely puzzled.

"Yes, the Advocates of defence will already have told the charges to the *Press* and the *Star*. They will report the severe sentences for just petty crime." That was telling him, smug arrogant prig that he was.

"Leave the newspapers to us," had been the answer.

"Very well, then," the Bailiff had interrupted, impatient to conclude the meeting. "So that is how it will be. Our islanders will only be tried on the charges which you approve!" He had stood ready to assert his prerogative to bring the conference to a close.

"Not exactly," the German had smiled as he had enjoyed the sense of power he experienced. It was good to see the Reich triumph over its vanquished — even those who were permitted to play their games of democracy. "You must find these people guilty and sentence them sufficiently severely to please us, in order that we do not go ahead with our own charges, in our own courts. We do not drop charges out of benevolence. We do it to save the reputation of our authority. Now please to sit down, we will review and revise before this case commences."

"What about the youth?" asked the Bailiff.

"The youth?" queried the German. Why did this old fool refer to the criminal with such a term as almost to imbue him with human attributes? He was a criminal of the worst kind, was he not? He had been trying to undermine German authority, just like that priest. He was despicable. Yes, they had quite a good case against him with spying, subversion and persuading a German national to break military law.

"Yes, John Collins. What charges can you keep against him, might I ask? All his offences are against your own authority. He is not in any way implicated in this black market nonsense."

"That is quite in order," the German had agreed with confidence. "We will go ahead with the spying charges, for it

36

will show the civilian population how astute we are in discovering and rooting out such foolishness."

The Bailiff had nodded.

"And trespass on the minefield?" he added. "I suppose it helps to prove how well defended you are against futile commando raids and such like?"

Had there been just a hint of sarcasm in the fellow's voice?

"We will pursue it," had been the terse reply.

"Even though it will inevitably bring up the question of your own young soldier's involvement with this civilian?"

"Yes, I have said, the youth will be dealt with in our own court. It is not a problem!"

And so, just as John Collins' fate, and that of Father Peters, had been set in motion and judged by the masters themselves, the lottery of Aryan logic had decided that the other three miscreants were to be given a fair trial, their crimes against the people of Guernsey exposed and their characters blackened. Yes, it had been greed which had led them to steal from the supplies of their own people and to trade in goods which should have been subject to rationing. They had dealt in scarce goods, inflated to the maximum price these wicked men could extort.

In the newspapers, the population was told just enough to know that those on trial were self-confessed criminals or had been proven to be so. This being so, the people knew the wrong-doers were to be justly and fairly punished.

None would know, and few would ponder, why the strong fisherman, hero of the pre-war sporting fraternity, had been so willing to confess, had it not been that he was exercised by guilty conscience.

Keith had stopped crying when at last he spoke. The salty tear trails shiny like the paths of snails.

"I'd have gone off to England in the boat but the blighters have impounded it, haven't they?"

Larry ignored the rhetorical question.

"I tell you, Larry, I can't go through last week's interrogation all over again, It was bad enough last time but, if they touch my face again I don't think I can take it," He shuddered and terror flashed across his eyes.

"The bastards!" mouthed Larry slowly, suddenly forgetting his fear as he watched Keith, the idol of all the girls of yesteryear. Keith of the school swimming team, Keith of the school football team, Keith who had played for Centrals. That hero now reduced to a quaking, broken bundle of fear. He became angry that they should have done this to one who was an esteemed plinth of his society. As Larry's anger grew, so his fear subsided and he felt the old fight returning. At last he became released from all tensions of the past week. He became, once more, Larry the champion of the weak, Larry the hater of injustice, Larry the politically aware.

"But they can't treat you like that!" exclaimed Larry, angry and defiant. "They're not allowed to beat you. There's the Geneva Convention to protect you!"

"The Geneva what?" sneered Keith. "The Jerries don't need any conventions to tell them how to behave. They've won this bloody war, haven't they? They can write their own damn rules!"

"Don't say that!" shouted Larry, "they haven't anywhere near won. You talk like a defeatist!"

"Wouldn't you?" demanded Keith, dramatically pointing to his face.

Perhaps there were some, maybe those others who had been implicated by Keith's confession, themselves later to face similar ordeals, who might have reasoned that it was inevitable that the fisherman would have cracked, after the gentle persuasion of the Gestapo in Room Five. They would have observed his battered visage, they would have witnessed his sobbing, pathetic state, as at night time in the Golden Lion they had willed and begged him not to divulge their names. None would really know, though, what had finally broken the man.

"Right de la Haye, you scum, you are going home to your wife now.

We will come for you when we are ready. Maybe your wife would be a little more cooperative than you? You will talk! Your friend de Carteret cracked!"

"Here is the licence you need, and here is my signature." The Major signed with a flourish, fumbled in his drawer for the appropriate rubber stamp and pad and, with great showmanship, completed the job.

"All that is needed now is for you to present this at the Feldkommandantur on Monday morning, in the usual way." The Major sat back beaming at Keith.

"Thanks."

"Is that all you have to say?" enquired Major Müller, somewhat surprised at the reaction of one to whom he purported to be so generous. *"Do you have any questions for me, concerning this?"*

Keith sighed a deep heavy sigh. This was all so ridiculous. It was not following any logical pattern. Here he was at the Gestapo headquarters, ostensibly to be interrogated and beaten up so that he might divulge his mates who were involved in anti German activities, but what was happening? Not a mention of those activities, or of his previous session. Not a single question, just kindness, consideration and, what appeared to be, a return of his livelihood. It just did not make any sense at all!

"O.K.," he said, *"so you're returning my boat. But why? That's not what I was brought here for, surely? Come on now, what's this all about? What do you expect from me?"*

Keith hated Anne, for she was a woman, she was weak and she was pregnant and he had not been able to let her suffer. Keith hated Anne because he loved her, with a love so deep that he had sold all his friends to the evil of the German tyranny. He hated her, for now she was all he had, she was the only item of value in his life, for she was everything. There was nothing else.

Anne hated Keith for he was free and she loved him and she wanted him to be free. But she knew that his freedom must have been gained at the expense of others' suffering and incarceration. And she knew that he had sold all so that she would not be harmed, and she loved him for it. But now he would have only her and she, only him. How could they look each other in the eyes again and see the betrayal?

Bert Bisson was probably thought the most reprehensible, for he had been a police constable. Few respected the police, for many were of the opinion, rightly or wrongly, that they did the Germans' work for them. That they helped the masters was reluctantly accepted as one of the facts of Occupation, but for a man to further add to his sins by betraying a trust in his own people, that was just too bad! How dare he use his position, his uniform, to work against his own people, whilst privileged, exempt from curfew controls?

Yes, Bert's complicity with the criminals of the Collins' family, was well documented. He had saved Larry from the rigors of a curfew patrol, and he, even after his suspension from duty, when he was not entitled to flout curfew, had frequently been observed visiting the Collins' household. How could he claim a bond of friendship with criminals, if in fact he were not himself a criminal? How could he defend himself by telling the real reason for his frequent visits and 'phone calls?

He had known loyalty to Larry was called for, respect for Frances who had, after all, freely chosen Larry and with Bert's blessing at the time. There was the consideration of love and constancy to his own wedding vows. He had known all this and accepted it, yet, with his heightening desires, which knew no quelling, their urgency so strong that they might self-destruct if not heeded, so did his logic give way to his animal need.

Bert the animal, as he now regarded his guilt-ridden self, had been devoid of blame while in the full flood of his sating, for his animal self had not allowed his conscience to function. All he had known, as he had taken Frances, was that it was all that had mattered in that timeless moment. They had been locked together for an instant. Yet it was eternity.

Even now, in his guilt, Bert knew that he would do it again. Theirs was for ever, the flowing of love so timeless and yet so instant had been such for them both that it had never been nor would ever be equalled.

How Larry's wife Frances, that good mother, who had

witnessed her son's harsh sentence and removal to France, listened with apprehension, as she held vigil at the trial of her two other men. How she willed Bert to defend himself more, and yet she knew she was grateful to him for sparing her so selflessly. It seemed true how their brief act of infidelity was destined to haunt them for ever.

Frances agonised as the Police Chief gave witness against his failed colleague, for that man too had it in his power to destroy her in the eyes of her husband.

"I see. Well, where does that leave me?" asked Frances, the hopelessness of her position firing her anxiety.

"You have some explaining to do, my dear, haven't you?" Despite his feeling of deep and lasting fatigue the Chief realized he was beginning to sound patronising and he regretted his words.

Frances too, was not prepared to be patronised.

"I've already told you why I came. What more do you want?"

"Well, for a start, I'd like to know your interest in Constable Bisson."

"Interest?" Frances seemed puzzled, almost angry. "My interest in Constable Bisson? What the hell is it to you?"

Even the Chief in his debilitating exhaustion and lacklustre, picked up this response and felt it interesting enough to pursue, to the end if need be.

"Yes, that is what I said Mrs. Collins. Why were you here, looking for one of my suspended Constables? And, furthermore at this hour, after curfew? Why was it so important that it could not wait?"

For a Royal Court case, involving so many, the experience was brief. It was almost as though the officials knew they had to expedite their business, as though to complete and pass sentence before the masters had time to change their minds and become involved. Indeed, little mention was made of any subversive aspects of their crimes, and the prosecution did not press its point when it referred to dealings with the Germans.

Despite the pleas of not guilty, despite all three having

genuine defence, through impartial Advocates of their own choosing, all the guilty men knew they were confounded. None put up too much of a fight, for all knew the game which was being played. Each knew he needed to be found guilty here by fair trial, to be dealt with by his own people, rather than have the matter taken up by a less impartial authority.

What hope was there, what leniency could they expect for their dire offences, when they had all learned of the Aryan severity on the Collins child, whose only crime had been his naivety? How could they expect mercy-tempered justice, when even a respected pillar of society, the parish priest Father Peters had lost one and a half years of his life for ostensibly reiterating the sentiments of Mein Kampf?

No, each was destined to serve three years of penal servitude. For their crimes, each man had to lose three summers, each was to be denied his freedom. With such lengthy sentences they, like John and Father Peters had been, were to be deported to the French mainland, there to spend their time in hard labour.

So now were sowed the further seeds of John Collins' terrible guilt. When the news was to reach the youth, already in receipt of his own punishment, he was to know that, not only had he been instrumental in his best friend's disappearance, but also he had stolen the freedom and health from his own father, he had destroyed his father's best friend in career and reputation, he had left his own mother friendless and alone and he had condemned Anne de la Haye to bear a fatherless child. The three criminals and his parish priest might have longer sentences in gaol than John Collins, but his life sentence of guilt and remorse was only just beginning.

Chapter Five

As the pain begins to grow once more, so does John's consciousness. Yes, that was it. He remembers now. From the moment of the collision, which had set him on this course towards death, he has been like the drowning man who is reputed to view his whole life in retrospect.

With an intensity and clarity, far clearer than his present circumstances, John recalls he had not been alone. No, as his machine had plunged forward to enmesh itself with that great monster of a lorry, he had been with Franz. He clearly remembered Franz's voice, which had accompanied him moments before, while he had twiddled the knob of his radio.

Yes, now as the pain intensifies, so does his picture of the friend who deserted him all those years previously. Which will John choose; to stay with Franz yet pay with pain, or be spared the agony of body but become tormented by rejection once more? He will hold on to Franz as long as he can, for Franz is still alive. Had he not heard his voice?

* * *

Often, when looking back at a traumatic period in a person's life, awfulness is smoothed and edited to some extent, while sparse moments of joy or peace, probably too insignificant to be noticed at the time, are brought to the fore and exaggerated to gild the memory or distort it, so that it does not seem as bad as once it did. What has once seemed unendurable can be transformed, in the recalling into a period almost of pleasure.

Once John accepted that his term of imprisonment was, as was its intention, a year executed from his life, that period began to move. There was little point in indulging in guilt, in self recrimination, for now he had no control over his destiny.

John Collins received the occasional letter from his mother, but he could not concern himself with such things, for she was of his past, just as Franz was. As John was excluded from his past, he did not need to be reminded of it; not yet, anyway.

The prison authorities might have control over his life, but John was still in charge of his thoughts, and he could either call people to mind or disregard them at will; his mind could be free whenever he chose.

With prison life, John learned to adapt. He expected nothing from his time in France, so was not disappointed.

John Collins, guilty youth that he was, seemed almost to welcome his time of hard labour. He cared not that his clothes were too inadequate to keep warm his half-starved body. He did not mind the rough, at times brutal, exhortations to work harder, whilst on work parties. Even the crude, only half-understood French talk and laughs at his expense were preferable to being left alone, isolated in a bare cell, with only his thoughts and conscience to keep him company.

As the young Guernseyman staggered with blocks and planks, or dug pathetically into stony earth, aching and exhausted, hungry and neglected, always cajoled to work harder, never recognized for his efforts, he knew it was preferable to the timeless nothingness of being inside. Routine, however dull or arduous, at least helped the days to pass. It was good to have his days filled and to be so tired he could hardly think.

No, John was content enough to let his labouring fill his time. He had no need for friends or comradeship outside working hours. If he needed such company, he could always conjure up Franz and bring him for some leave from Russia. Not for John Collins to bother himself to learn a foreign tongue, for why should he wish to have companionship from all those rough and common Frenchmen?

His return home had been an anti-climax. It was true his mother had greeted him with enthusiasm and had doted on him, despite the greater shortages as the Occupation had entered into its third year. He had, however, anticipated such actions from her so her generosity was already negated. Also, he had fully expected her neuroses to have increased so in this knowledge too he had been forewarned. Besides which, even the shortages of his homeland in late 1942 were, by contrast with his experiences in the French prison, luxury indeed.

What John had dreaded most, as he had contemplated returning to his island, was the reception he would receive from those he had harmed. True, his father, Bert and Keith could not reproach him directly, only through his guilty thoughts, but what of the families of those who had been harmed by his foolishness?

It seemed strange indeed that those he met or passed seemed almost unaware that he had gone away, that it had been he who had once been the focus for their hate and disdain.

Where he had dreaded reproach from those families which had been damaged by his infamy, John found none. No, the youth really began to feel quite insignificant, that he had almost ceased to exist. In his unspoken thoughts, it might almost have been better to feel their reproach than to remain so unnoticed.

There was one exception, however, one circumstance brought about by his past actions, which was to recognize his complicity and to make demands on his conscience.

Soon after his return from the continent, John met Anne, wife of Keith de la Haye, the fisherman, whose whole life had been set in turmoil thanks to the thoughtlessness of the puerile youth.

Keith still had a seemingly endless two years of sentence to complete, while Anne had learned to adapt to this tribulation, and had got on and picked up the shattered pieces of her life, neither did she appear to harbour any grudges against John, but seemed genuinely pleased to see him. How could she appear to be so tranquil and relaxed about it all?

Well, of course, Ann's brave fisherman might now be labouring in a French prison, and she missed him and longed for him with a wanting that could not be surpassed, but he had left her a gift which was a constant reminder of his enduring love, of their shared love, for she now had their child, a little boy, whom in Keith's absence she named Patrick.

John became an uncle to Patrick, poor little ailing child that he was to become.

Uncle? Well, that title certainly had the power to evoke almost forgotten memories. Had he not once been invited to be an uncle to others? Were they John's recollections or those of his friend? John could not be sure, yet to become an uncle to Patrick was such an honour, Franz would be pleased for him, and that was for sure.

"Do you know, this young Corporal is a university lecturer?" asked Franz, then correcting himself to "was" as his face clouded at the stark reality.

"Oh yes, he has a wife and three children, Anna, Clara and Bern. He say he write to his wife and tell her to get the extra bed ready for me. He say I be an uncle to his dear children after this war."

"And now this will never be!"

Oh yes, how John remembered that first day when he had met Franz, before they had even been friends. How Franz had longed to be an uncle to his corporal friend's children, but the chance had been stolen from him by that awful R.A.F. raid which had taken his friend's face away.

Perhaps, if John now became a good uncle to baby Patrick, it might in some way make up for his lost friend's devastation. He might even be able to share the responsibility with Franz.

John walked through the main doors of La Porte to be confronted by a seething activity. His attention focused on the centre of this turbulence, on a young soldier lying in a semi-conscious stupor on the floor. His short dark hair was dishevelled, his green eyes staring vacantly ahead. His uniform was soiled with blood and vomit...

"My friend was Corporal Schmidt. He died next to me in the boat. He died and I ran away! It was very bad, and I ran away because I could not bear it..."

"He was so good to me you know? They took his lovely face away. He no face has!" He groaned in his misery at the memory which he once more relived. He began to relive the scene he had called up only a

46

while before as he had stood in the hall of the Feldkommandantur. His body shook, his face contorted and he turned towards John. The skin of Franz's face was stretched so tightly over his cheek bones now, as his mouth opened wide and his eyes expanded, that it looked like waxed paper. His whole facial misery seemed fixed like that of some hideous gargoyle. He began to cry. He cried but not a tear wet his eyes or his deathly cheeks.

This was how the two boys had first been thrown together, the one a failed coward of a German, who had run away after the horror of an R.A.F. raid, only saved from speedy punishment by the influence of a Gestapo uncle, the other an unemployed Guernseyman, forced to work for the masters.

Well, that was all in the past, albeit in some ways a past more clear and rational than the present which now shaped John Collins. Now, however, despite the awful confusion the youth often suffered, it was good to be needed, especially by one such as Anne, who by rights should have despised him for the awfulness he had brought into her life.

It was a great honour to be bestowed the title 'Uncle'. Yes, John would make sure that he remained as John Collins, uncle to Patrick, while Franz could see to his own nephew and nieces.

The joy of being needed and the pleasure of having opportunity to be of use was of course offset by the fact that baby Patrick was an ailing child, but this could not affect the love which he induced in those who looked after him. Even though the little mite was destined to deteriorate in health, as precursor to his inevitable early demise, the world was a better place for his presence, for he had demanded and created love and tenderness where otherwise only bitterness and lonely remorse might have inhabited.

Yes, Uncle John was a good uncle and a great support for Anne. He took a loving interest as the baby progressed to unsteady toddler and inquisitive exploring infant. Like Anne, he pushed from thought that little Patrick was unlikely to be blessed with a future, just willing that the child's present could go on for ever.

47

Chapter Six

There have been operations, the surgeons have done their best, but even they cannot repair internal organs too damaged to survive the shock. They have worked hastily and well from the moment of the ambulance's arrival, but have been unable to save the man.

John Collins is destined to die but that has to take its course. His time will be prolonged even though the outcome is inevitable. The best of care and medical skill are at his disposal, but the end is as sure and certain as for the poor exhausted butterfly, its wings removed by ants, as symbolism of the death to come.

Well, even so, John Collins is not yet aware of his fate. He much prefers to journey to times gone by to find his real self, to indulge in his search for his friend.

* * *

When John had been sent to serve his sentence in France and Frances had been left alone, the good mother and wife, had needed to take a job. For the first time since she had married Larry, Mrs. Collins had no one to support her, nor had she needed to be at home to see to the needs of her little boy. No, anathema as it was to this good home-maker, Frances had taken work. No more for her the receiving of two wage packets from her men at the end of the week, so that she could take what was necessary for the upkeep of their comfortable home, returning to the donors what remained. No, Frances had found she had been compelled to do it all, and what was more, alone. Not only had Frances needed to labour, to keep body and soul together, but also she had been forced to experience the added indignity of working for women's rates of pay, doing the same work previously done by men yet, for all its exertion, not granted the rations due to heavy workers. No, that privilege was reserved only for the superior gender.

A further irony for John, had he been receptive to such thoughts, was that his mother now worked for the same greenhouses from which he had been dismissed, supplying vegetables for the conquerors. It had been that same dismissal which had led to his working for the Germans originally, which had led to all their downfall.

"That's enough!" said his father. "You won't be so bloody fond of the Jerries when they take your job away."

"What do you mean, take his job away?" asked his mother with a frightened look on her face, a look that would go well with wringing hands. "Why should they take his job away?"

"They haven't!"

"You just said. . . "

"Oh don't be so stupid, woman . . . .!"

What a strange and portentous coincidence it had seemed, all those years previously, that John had been ousted from his civilian job, surplus to requirements, at the same time the masters had needed the labour of a number of young men to help with the work of the Reich.

The green Major led the way to Mr. Le Prevost's own office and there, without further ado, having seated himself in the senior clerk's own chair behind the desk, produced his papers.

He had come with a requisition; to order, not to request.

"This is the first requisition of labour. The Feldkommandantur requires thirty men, aged between fifteen and twenty five years, to work forty-eight hours a week until further notice."

Mr. Le Prevost was given until four o'clock the next day to comply. No amount of protesting, would have prevailed. The fact that he had no such young men was not considered an impediment.

"Then unemploy some," he was told.

Larry, so John gathered, was surviving his sentence, as was Uncle Bert. Frances had shown John his father's letters. He had experienced strange sensations as he looked at the typed comminiqués and had wondered how many drafts, mutilated in blue, had been submitted before these final publications. He had nonchalantly flitted through the scraps of thin papers so carefully treasured by his mother who had read and re-read them. He had known how his disrespectful handling of this only link with his father must have hurt Frances, but he had been unable to stop himself, for he had found too difficult the contemplation of apology spoken or actioned.

Not only was John's conscience dogged by what he had unwittingly wreaked on the lives of all those he had contacted, including his one and only friend, albeit an enemy friend, but also by the knowledge that although he felt guilt and shame, he, puerile self-conscious youth that he was, found difficulty in translating his private remorse into actions which might have helped soothe the wounds. If only he could have told his Mum how sorry he felt, and asked her to forgive him for sending Dad away like that. If only he could have redressed some of the damage he had done. He knew a kind word or sympathetic listening would have helped. Yes, he knew that was what was needed, yet it seemed that this very knowledge forced him down a contrary path against his heartfelt wishes.

It was as some secret form of penance that he went to his mother's handbag one Thursday afternoon as she slept, exhausted from the morning of labour in her 'Turkish Bath' greenhouse, and borrowed those treasures to re-read and digest in private. He had never helped himself to the private contents of his mother's bag before, yet the guilt at not showing his father sufficient respect, that very father whom he had imprisoned, was stronger than that of betraying trust in his mother. Well, after all, he was now a grown-up, wasn't he? Besides, he was also a criminal now and criminals are unscrupulous.

It was then that he had found Uncle Bert's letter folded in as carefully as those of Dad's. He read it and he understood. He had known all the time of course. Yes, it all came back to him. He had thought all these things about Uncle Bert before, he had recalled the irrefutable proof, with memories of that man's attentions to his mother and that woman's deception of his father. But, should he really be thinking so disrespectfully of his mother? Should he really be thinking of her as 'that woman'? Hadn't Franz once, long ago, needed to correct him about such lack of respect?

"She'll be all right John, you'll see," said the great philosopher, "she is a good woman, your mother."

"Lady," corrected John.

"Pardon?"

"I said lady. She's a lady, not a woman." John sounded almost petulant.

"Oh," came Franz's non-offensive, non-offended reply. He sensed he dare not explore the esoterics of this statement.

"It's O.K., Franz. Sorry, you wouldn't know. It's just in English you call ladies ladies and women are women, you know?" He wasn't explaining very well, but damn it, he wasn't a teacher, besides he had enough worries, didn't he?

"Anyway it doesn't matter, you can call her woman, for all I care."

"No," insisted Franz, "your mother is a lady, you must not call her woman." He could not understand the difference but he realized there must be one, therefore Mrs. Collins had a choice and, in his eyes, she had to have only the best.

No that concept realised too many emotions, emotions still strong enough to transport himself wholly back to distressing times. Perhaps John was not ready yet to be transported back to that particular past. No-one should ever be thought of or spoken of as 'that' anything.

Yes, John had known of his mother's infidelity, of her deceit, they had even spoken of it, but, until now, he had not been willing to face up to it. Each time the liaison had entered his sensitivities he had pushed it from his mind and repressed it. Now, with the letter in front of him, he was forced to confront it.

"I've got problems too, you know?"

She waited for his reaction before she could steel herself to continue.

Mum? Problems? What problems could she possibly have apart from the obvious? Dad, he supposed, and the worries of the trials. What could John do about such things? He felt embarrassed at the prospect of hearing his mother's concerns. It was quite in order for him to load his matron, for that was her job, but for his own mother to have problems? No, that was not right! She was grown-up, she was not entitled to such irregularities.

He resigned himself, wishing the moment past. He would try not to look as his mother undressed her mind with the light on. . .

He never could have guessed! Uncle Bert! Bert, no, he was not worthy even of that stark title. Bisson, plain Bisson, was better for him.

His own mother?

It was then that he realized how closely he was bonded to his mother, for their two experiences were so alike. Each as living an impossibility, or at least each had and now kept the impossible alive as a memory only. He had been placed into the impossible circumstances where a choice had been required, where he had to choose between a forbidden friendship with his enemy brother, or the stability of his family life. Frances too had been required to make a choice to keep the family together and to be wed only to Larry, or to allow herself to go to Bert while the family disintegrated. Neither had been able to choose for impossible choices cannot be made freely. Neither had attempted anything except the continuation of the status quo. The result was that both had experienced events and decisions wrested from them and both had lost everything.

Now that John had been forced to acknowledge the existence of Uncle Bert, and to acknowledge that he could not edit him from consciousness any more, he accepted him and he understood his mother. With that realization, and, having used his eyes to violate Uncle Bert's tender and well chosen words to Frances, words that had strength and true love, despite their being handled by the censor's office to be read and typed by the uncaring.

John now understood Frances, resolving in some small way to support his mother, for it was now clear that this she had been doing all along with his own impossible friendship with an enemy.

Chapter Seven

There are people coming into this room. This room? Is John Collins in a room? Is he sufficiently conscious to distinguish room from ward? What do they want?

They mutter, they whisper, they are talking about John, not to him, but he cannot discern their conversation. The words come and go, as does the patient's concentration.

The Doctor and the Sister confer quickly. The relatives are here, it is unfortunate, but they have rights and must visit. Should the victim be kept from pain or should it be allowed to surface just a little, so his loved ones might be permitted to communicate with him?

* * *

John managed to get work too. At least he was spared the indignity of working again for the Germans. Twelve months before he would have felt slighted that the masters would not have accepted him as worthy enough to work for their cause, but now he was relieved. He could cope with the shame of being classified criminal against the occupying forces, for it meant that he could keep to a minimum his contact with that detested race.

The hours were convenient, too. Being a baker meant early starts. John did not mind this, for it meant his afternoons were free so that he could visit Patrick.

He was grateful to be given the job, on temporary trust at first, for there was a strict bread ration, and few would have thought a criminal, especially one who had been implicated in theft of food and supplies from his very own people, would have been given such a chance.

John quickly proved himself worthy of the trust, and even when rations at home were reduced, he did not take advantage. What little he did take to Patrick on his regular visits there came from his own 'heavy workers' rations. Yes, it was good to be classified, along with labourers and the registered prostitutes of the Germans, as a heavy worker, thereby getting a sizeable percentage extra on basic rations, even when a large percentage of very little is in fact still very little.

He had also the advantage of having at least a portion of his days, during the chill winter with its east winds, of being warm, and even at times with the luxury of feeling too hot.

John Collins learned his trade, making bread out of ever more strange ingredients. Who, before the Occupation, would ever have dreamt of making bread from whole husks, bread from potatoes, rolls with sea water for salt?

Far better such a job, surrounded by his own people, than to work in a shop with the constant reminders of virtually nothing for sale, and that which there was, for barter rather than for payment with greasy cheap German notes. Better too, than to ply a trade, such as Dad had, with his bicycle repairs, where he would have been required by law to stop whatever he was dong to tend to the needs of the masters. No, John was glad of the anonymity of his job.

And so John and his mother struggled their way through the interminable Occupation, each becoming more a support to the other, as they eked out their ever diminishing rations and as the privations of their lives increased without anyone else to bring relief.

Chapter Eight

Whose are those voices? Are they real? If only John could concentrate, he might learn who it is who sounds so familiar. It certainly is not Franz and yet, he knows the sound so well.

It is a pity really that there are some nearby who keep invading him, whose voices keep pulling him back to a time and place which is foreign to him, when really he should be about his business.

Perhaps they are doing it for the best? Maybe they are trying to save him from an impasse? And yet, they have no right to interfere. John knows he'd rather face up to the consequences of the circumstances of his very real past, while they put him close to the reality of true friendship, than to come to a present which is not really his.

Well, he only has to tell them to go away, but to speak is too much of an effort. Perhaps, if he opens his eyes, he might recognise them, and then maybe they will leave him in peace to return to his real past self, where once he had no present worth; only a future charged with the eternal hope of the very young. Better that than be drawn to a present with no prospect for future, except to distance him still further from what had once been real.

* * *

It should not be thought surprising that John Collins became confused. What boy of sixteen could have had such experiences as he had had, or felt such a loading of guilt, and have remained untouched? Who, so young, could have carried the burden that his best friend had been sentenced to, at best, an interminable period of misery, at worst, certain death? All this had materialized because John had so selfishly befriended one of the enemy.

Who else could have felt normal, having been the cause of his own father's incarceration and the imprisonment of his parish priest, and denying little Patrick his very own father? John had even sent his mother's best friend off to prison too.

If only he could have spoken to someone, if only there had been friends to share his anxieties with! But all his acquaintances were adults, and all were too absorbed in their own problems to be approached.

So at times, John took on the whole guilt for what had happened, and imagined the reproach of all he had harmed. When in these moods, with no-one around who could possibly understand, he wished he were not John Collings but could be one of the Aryan masters, for they never experienced any doubts about their status, they just knew they were always right. Yes, at times like those, John almost wished he were his best friend, Franz Müller.

At other times, John found himself detesting anything Germanic, for was it not they who had wrecked all their lives? Was it not those same wicked Germans, in the form of Patrol Leader Morten and S.S. Hüffmeier, who had stolen his childhood and offended his innocence? Yes, in those moments, John almost hated his friend, and was able to blame him for all the present troubles. But hate is a difficult emotion to sustain, especially if it is directed towards a friend. No, once a bonding of friendship has been formed, it is difficult to unlearn. Far better to keep the memory of friendship alive, and leave the hating to the adults of their respective nations.

More and more John made himself disregard reality, as ever more frequently, he encased himself in memories of happier times and pleasurable events, while his daydreams became increasingly real. Far better to dream alive a happy past than to live an unpalatable present.

He felt the same today, he had a holiday feeling. But suddenly too, he missed his freedom, he missed his friends. How were they all in England? Were they thinking of him? Were they too remembering those heady days of endless summer with swimming and dancing and picnics? Did they recall all this as the Nazi bombs rained down on them at night? What would they think if they could see him now with a German as a friend? He loved them all and he missed them so. When would this bloody war end? He wanted them back but even so he would not give them this day. No-one would take away this day with his friend Franz. His face became solemn as these thoughts raced through his mind.

"About what are you thinking, John?" asked Franz, turning to his friend.

"Who, me?" asked John, reluctant to release his dreams. "Oh, I was thinking of the days when we were free, when I had friends." He spoke the last words casually, almost unwittingly, as his old friends were transported in his mind away from his island back to their misery and the blitz in England. He did not realise the hurt he had caused Franz.

"Et tu, mon vieux? Penny for your thoughts," asked John.

Franz had not reacted to John's unintentional but hurtful statement, sensing that his friend's mind had been far away, for his too had been transported back to his home momentarily.

"Penny? What penny?"

"What were you thinking of?"

"Me? This place, this farm. It makes me feel so happy and so sad at the same time. Can you understanding what I mean?"

"Yes," replied John, knowing exactly how such a feeling could be engendered. "Tell me how."

"Well, you see John I am a farm boy and this farm so reminds me of my home. I wishing I am home with Mama and Papa and Ilsa. It is so stupid, John, I am happy to be here with you today but I wishing I am home and Papa is alive. Do you understand me?"

"Yes, of course," said John. "I was also thinking of before the war and my friends and all the good times we used to have. I wish this damn war would come to an end!"

"So do I," agreed Franz, "but what end will it be?"

When at times John Collins indulged himself in these happy aspects of his memories, and he was sure who he was, he also remembered that he must find Franz, for part of his disturbed consciousness told him that Franz was still alive, that the Bolsheviks had not crushed and killed him, that he was not even their prisoner.

At other times the youth who entered through old Gaudion's front door, felt himself to be that very same Franz Müller. In visiting the de la Haye child, had he not really been a good German uncle visiting Bern Schmidt?

Soon this war would be won, soon the foolish English would submit to the Ayran will and would help their German brothers to extinguish the communist threat.

Yes, this was it, peace would come. The mighty Führer, magnanimous in his victory, would greet the King and together they would bring peace to the world.

As these dreams of glory and peace invaded him he would wonder exactly why he was visiting his erstwhile friend's mother like this. Did he still have tales for her of his bad treatment by the cruel Patrol Leader Morten and that evil pervert S.S. Hüffmeier?

Would she understand and believe that he had not done willingly those awful things which had happened in Patrol Leader Morten's room? Would she realize that he had been forced to accompany the cruel Hüffmeier, that he had had no choice?

Could that good lady, John's mother, also be mother to him, for he so missed his own Mama back in Germany?

Franz sat on the rug, his thin tense back resting against the legs of his new mother, as Frances gently and absentmindedly smoothed his hair, as she could no longer to her other son, who was now too grown-up for such attentions.

Both were coloured now, the one by embarrassment and shame at what he had had to tell his mother, and the other with anger at what had been done to her boy. Yes, 'done to,' rather than 'done with,' was how Frances had to see what had happened.

Frances, a woman, a housewife and mother, whose role was to make the home and look after her family, as all women of her age, was not expected to understand such things as she had just heard from the helpless little victim, and yet she felt she understood. The ways of some men could be dark and strange! No wonder men never spoke to their women in detail about such things, but just alluded amongst themselves, sometimes laughing or fooling to hide their own discomfort at the wickedness.

*Franz too, still confused and in mental anguish, could not bring
himself to understand all which had happened, and yet they both
knew kindness and hugs and tender love, from his substitute mum,
had been his contact with this good lady and had enabled his feelings
of guilt and hurt to be lessened by sharing his ordeal with her.*

So was this lost and damaged youth, who now visited Frances
Collings, really Franz Müller? Was the young man, who now
came into 12, Rue Marguerite, really that young German who
had been so ill-used by his own people? Was he really here to
just pour out his own problems on the good lady, she who was
just like a mother to him? Should he not be following some
less selfish pursuit, shouldn't he be looking for his lost friend
John? No that could not be. Had not John gone to some
lengthy trial? Tried and sentenced to prison in France, along
with his father and others of his acquaintance?

Anyway, why was Franz here right now? Shouldn't he be in
Russia? Hadn't he, Franz Müller, been given the death
sentence of the Eastern Front, as surely as his uncle had been
returned to Berlin?

No, the youth sometimes John Collins, sometimes Franz
Müller, was destined to become more and more confused.
The problem did not confine itself to his time at home, when
he could not decide if it were his home or that of his friend,
his own mum or adopted mama, Mrs. Collins. Even at work,
John, or was it Franz, experienced the same misconceptions.

"John," Mr. Carré coughed delicately, "John my boy, I've
been asked to have a chat with you."

Eh? Who was this man? Who was it who could feel so
familiar that he could request a chat with one of the
Wehrmacht? This was a civilian. What right had he to keep
the young soldier standing in front of his desk like this? What
authority had he over the forces of occupation? Franz felt a
stirring, he was reminded of the days when he worked at the
Feldkommandantur and was called in by the administrator,
Herr Tropp, Herr Tropp with the kind grandfatherly smile,

Herr Tropp with the bad temper, the man who would not permit him to be a friend of John Collins! No, that was not quite right; Franz knew he as a German footsoldier had not worked for the Feldkommandant. No, that had been his friend, John Collins, and yet it all seemed so clear. It was as though he held the memories that only John could have known. It was all very confusing, just as standing here in this office was confusing. Why was he wearing a large apron? Why did he have a hat on his head instead of his peaked hat? And why were his hands covered in flour?

"John, er, Mr. Collins," continued Mr. Carré, "Your supervisor, Mr. Simon, thought I should speak to you, he's a bit worried . . ."

'Worried? Why for should he be worried? I should be worried,' thought John, 'One moment I am Franz, but I hold in my head the memories of my friend John, and now here I am, John Collins, standing in front of my employer, yet knowing that this is all wrong, for I should be in my uniform. Yes I, failed Franz Müller, should not be wearing the uniform of an inferior worker, I should not have my hands covered with flour. I should be . . . should be . . . in . . . in . . . Russia. Not flour . . . not flour . . . but . . . no . . . but blood. Blood and in Russia!'

"Pardon?" asked Mr. Carré, "Did you wish to say something, John?"

"Russia!"

The General had shouted. The General had stamped. He had clenched his fists. He smacked his sides in his temper. Swear words he had uttered, whole streams of filthy oaths, the like of which Franz had never heard before. And while all these induced histrionics had been performed, Franz's gaze had been held locked on to his verbal assailant's eyes as they sparkled with the excess moisture of fiery anger. So strong and piercing had that gaze been that Franz's fixedness had not even been momentarily broken when the General's monocle had dropped during the flicker of a twitch. All Franz could now really remember clearly were those eyes of National Socialist fervour and fanaticism. The ringing tones and the excited actions paled into insignificance as he watched still, those eyes. What he heard in his living recall was clear but almost irrelevant, as if intended for another and therefore of no great importance to him;

"You are a pervert! Yes that is what you are! You are filth, the scum, the refuse of our nation! You are not fit to be called a son of our beloved Führer. You are to Germany as a bastard of a Jew creature is to the human race . . ."

"Your bones will be crushed to make foundations for the tracks which will be used by our true German spirits, as they speed with bravery to their glorious victory, on the Eastern Front. You, loathsome coward, are to be part of our beloved Führer's victorious push into the heart of Bolshevism.

"Pardon me, I do not understand?" This was all so awkward. It really did seem right what Mr. Simon had been telling him. This young man really was a day dreamer. Perhaps it was worse? Maybe the young fellow was a bit deranged? Well, he had been to France, and one so young, too. Terrible, terrible!

No, John did not need to tolerate sessions like this. He was here to work, to do a job well and take home his wages to Mum at the end of the week. He was not here to be questioned and quizzed, that was not part of the agreement.

What was Mr. Carré on about, anyway? If he, John Collins, chose to look for his German friend, then so what? It was none of Mr. Carré's business.

Daydreaming indeed! John would soon see about that. How dare the man interfere? This civilian was obviously getting ideas above his station when he felt he could address one of the Führer's men so. No, Franz knew he would think about the missing John as often as he liked. It would not prevent his shaping the dough or working the ovens, so there was no real problem. The man should be grateful to have one of the master race deigning to show him how to organise a bakery.

Well, it certainly was more comfortable than being in Russia right now, that was for sure!

"Quite so!" agreed John. He was glad Franz agreed with him.

Yes, these moods were John's constant companions now. He could be so quickly transformed from his arrogant Aryan self-assuredness to be plunged into bouts of inferiority and fear, almost to the point of self-imposed persecution. In this, as in most matters of late, he was so like the friend he had known so long ago.

He looked at John, now seeming to have forgotten his pain. His mouth tightened, his lips narrowing into a thin cold line. A sneer grew across his ashen face.

"You English murderers! You fools! My friend you killed today!"

John did not know what to do or say. He recognised that here was his new friend changing so rapidly in mood from fear to fury, from insecurity to extreme confidence. He realised that Franz was not well and, although he had no great experiences of life upon which to draw, he accepted that this present was not the real Franz. He knew in his heart that the real Franz was his friend present and friend to be.

John said nothing and did nothing. He sat. He waited, waited for Franz to change once more as surely he must.

Down Franz plummeted from the exalted heights of his master race, with Hitler in all his glory, to the depths of fear and despondency with him a tiny creature, ready to be ground in under the heel of the Gestapo and the shadowy, sinister, ever-expected, just behind the scenes, S.S.

Yes, such fears were all so real to John Collins. John was convinced that all the evils of this world were seeking him out. He knew that when he came into a room where a group of his fellow workers were talking, that their words were about him. Oh yes, he was aware with trailing-off conversations or contrived jollity, that he was the subject of their debate. Why else would they look at him so and with such puzzled stares? Why did they go out of their way to patronize him? Was it just the uniform? Could that be it; they just wanted to get in with him to be collaborators or quislings? Oh yes, Dad had been right, the place was rotten with their type! Dad? Whose Dad?

63

Papa had died in Poland. What could Franz be thinking of, he was for a moment thinking he was John Collins again!

Every time a stranger would come into the bakery, John knew it was the Gestapo coming for him. He almost willed them to come and take him away. Oh yes, he watched them go up to Mr. Carré's office, and then he waited. He knew it was to be only a matter of minutes before his employer would bring them over to him and he would be taken away to Grange Lodge once more. And when his employer did come down with the two strangers, chattering to them and smiling as if he knew them, and did not bring them to John, the youth then felt sure it was all part of the plot. Yes, indeed, Mr. Carré also was a collaborator, and had agreed to keep careful watch on young Collins. That was why they had not taken John away yet, they wanted to lull him into a false sense of security.

John knew his workmates kept a careful watch. They were all longing to catch him out. When he saw his supervisor writing, he knew it was something about him, especially when Mr. Simon would stop the scribbling if John approached. That was why the man was always so friendly, and engaged in such small talk, asking him how he was today or if he felt well. Oh yes, John knew the type!

Walking home, the young baker would often alter his route, just in case he was followed. In case? No, John was positive they trailed him. Up flights of steps he would go, doubling back, waiting in recesses. Oh yes, he had watched them pass his opening. He might be a failed German, but he was astute. John would have been proud of him.

Even his mother seemed to view him with suspicion.

"You are very late, dear, I thought you would be finishing at twelve today. I . . ."

Damn the woman, what did she mean? Why was she quizzing him like this? Was she not his adopted mother? Did she give her own son, John, such a going over, checking up on him? Perhaps she too had turned against him? Yet she used to be kind, very kind indeed. Hadn't John said she should be referred to as a lady, not as a woman? So why did she want to know why he was late? Perhaps she knew he was being followed home from work? Yes, that would explain it, the Gestapo had involved Frances Collins. That was how they knew what time he would leave work each day, so they could follow him.

"Mrs. Collins," began Franz, "I must say . . ."

"You what, John?" Frances interrupted, "Mrs. Collins? What do you mean, Mrs. Collins? I'm your mum! What the hell are you playing at, John?"

'So I'm John, am I?' thought the youth. 'Well, let them think that if it pleases them, then perhaps they won't send me back to Russia.'

Chapter Nine

Old Frances sits there. She seems confused as she holds her son's hand. She thought she felt it tighten slightly. Yes, that was it, John is getting better. Her little boy is in hospital, but he will be all right.

She smiles to herself, she has many memories. It seems she has only memories now as once again her little boy needs his mum. She is young again as she feels needed. Old Frances, in communion with her only son, is taken back to times long ago. Harsh and cruel those times might have seemed, but the passage of time has smoothed and gilded them, so that the present reliving has made them palatable, divested of their trauma.

Another sits here with the old lady. She waits her turn to take the dear man's hand, but she must be patient for she does not yet exist, she is not yet young John's friend.

* * *

John spent many hours during the remainder of the Occupation trying to gather information about his friend. When he was not working and when he was not concerning himself with little Patrick and his more and more frequent visits to the States' Emergency Hospital, and when he was sure that he really was John Collins, not in fact Franz Müller, he was thinking about the fate of his friend and trying in vain to gather information.

When he tried to make enquiries, or just imagined that he had, he experienced rebuffs and threats. Did he really try to visit his former work place at the Felkommandantur, or had he just thought he should, in order to make his futile search? Well, the anger such a visit would have induced in the authorities seemed real enough, but had they really hammered on his door late at night? Had he really been taken back to Grange Lodge to the awful interrogation of Room Five? Did these things happen, or had John just conjured them, as an inevitable consequence if he were in fact brave enough to seek out his missing friend?

Was the youth really able to contemplate the implications for his friend's mother, working as she did to grow vegetables for the masters? Could he really put Mrs. Collins' job in jeopardy like that? Similarly, what would happen to Mr. Collins, now only half way through his prison sentence in France, if Franz now selfishly pursued his quest for information about John?

It was all so complicated and all so confusing!

No, the only avenues of enquiry that remained available to John's research were through the ordinary German soldiers, if there was such a thing as an ordinary one. He had to find young soldiers of his own age. There had to be some Germans who, like Franz, still had the attributes of humanity.

It was not easy, however, for this failed Guernseyman to accomplish his wish. Whereas before, in his innocence, John had at first adulated the master race, as witness his studious observation of their ceremonies, uniform, music and aura of timeless history and glory, now he was seasoned, and had experience of life, beyond his years, and illusions had been shattered.

Whereas before it had seemed the most natural and innocent of actions to take up the companionship of one of the foe, untainted by the evils of war and, like himself, young and lonely, now John had bitter experience of life. Since the time of adventure and sharing with Franz, when both had been children, unaware of the traps and snares of the adult world, John Collins had been forced to grow up over-night. He had moved on from sharing the toys and games of his childhood with his friend, from rolling and fighting together like young kittens, from laughing and guffawing at the ridiculousnesses of the grown-up world, to having spent his sixteenth birthday cold and hungry in an austere French prison.

Since his days of innocent fraternization, young John had tasted many experiences which had speeded his metamorphosis. Had he not had his very decency threatened by those same uniforms which he had once admired? Had not his best and only friend been forced into such abhorrent filthy actions in order to keep alive that very contact, which in its innocence was deemed evil and a crime against war? Had he not stood in court rooms, judged by the elders of his own people and the representatives of their Teutonic overlords, and been condemned as a despicable criminal and traitor? And had not this young man now to bear the guilt that his own father, his uncle, his parish priest, the young fisherman or poor fatherless little Patrick and countless others, were now suffering, and would continue to do so, all because he had been so selfish and indulged himself in comradeship with one of the enemy?

Whereas prior to eating the apple of truth, John would have welcomed the opportunity, or the excuse, to be able to speak with the self-assured young Aryans, now the concept was abhorrent. The prospect of having to make contact with any but Franz Müller was anathema to him.

When seeking out a potential German who might spare a moment to discuss the fate of Franz, or news of his whereabouts, John could no longer find any young soldiers with whom to confer. They all seemed older than Franz somehow. Was this because he had been brought to the Island too young by his uncle, or was it perhaps that John still remembered his friend as he had been, more than a year previously? Perhaps Franz was destined not to age?

Also, had not the youngest and fittest, for the most part, been removed to battle fronts to help reinforce young Franz? Were there not rumours that the Reich was now under threat? Had not the Americans sought to turn the tide in Europe?

Each time John plucked up courage to approach one of these soldiers, that same Teuton would become either his prison guard in cold, cold France, or else he would be one of the Gestapo about to shake and hit him once more, to smack his face, bruise his lips and loosen his teeth.

"Excuse me, mein Herr . . ." John's voice trailed, his courage replaced by fear and disgust as the young soldier turned, his uniform transforming from green to black. It was David Hüffmeier, that awful S.S. Pervert.

"Ja? was?" The S.S. leered for he knew he now had John

Collins in his power, soon he would have his evil way with him.

All John's attempts failed. Never could he find a straightforward ordinary, decent German. Perhaps they no longer exited?

If he came upon a group, he knew, should he approach them, they would make fun of him, for he was sure they all knew how he and Franz had been embroiled with Patrol Leader Morten and his friends. Yes, it must be common knowledge what that wicked man did with boys at Town Patrol House. If John were to try to speak with these men, they would be able to tell he was not quite right, they would know his innocence had been invaded, and he was no longer completely normal. No, they would laugh at him, they would deride and hold their private jokes and he would feel more excluded than if he had not tried.

"Oh Franz, I'm so glad to see you. Is everything all right? Did it work?"

"Yes." He paused. "Thank you very much." From behind John came an echo.

"Yes. Thank you very much." Then it was repeated by the second giggly German.

They went up to Franz giggling and chattering.

"Oh Franz, I'm so glad to see you." They were derisory and degenerated into fits of laughter and German chatter.

Franz looked embarrassed. He shrugged his shoulders and tried to laugh too.

John was unable to speak. Two more Germans joined the group with loud talk and guffaws. The older German went up to Franz and theatrically put his arm around him.

"My little Englander," he said. They all laughed. Franz laughed. John had to laugh.

The taller giggly one's face set hard. He did not like John to laugh with them. He put a hand on John's shoulder and, scowling into his face, pushed him away.

69

What about the Jerry-bags? Could he not ingratiate himself with one of those ladies? Surely they got on well with the Germans, or they'd not have wanted to go out with them night after night? They must have seen something in the masters, or they would not have put up with the nasty comments and jibes from their fellow Islanders. Perhaps John Collins should get to know a Jerry-bag, then possibly he could mix in with her soldier friends? But no, John might be low enough, with his criminal and prison record, to feel an affinity with these women who knew their place was the gutter, but even they would look down on him, for they would know what he had been up to at those Relaxations. Yes, John Collins was aware that women had a knack of knowing when someone was not quite right, and had experienced things which were not normal.

He was startled when a girl from further along his row touched his arm and said;

"Here mate, your friend over there wants to speak to you." She could hardly contain her mirth, as she imparted this message, covering her mouth to prevent her splutterings of hilarity, while pointing in the general direction of the German side of the cinema.

John, who had been completely taken by surprise, reacted with puzzlement.

"Eh? What did your friend say?"

"Your friend, 'im over there, 'im with the black uniform." Again she giggled and laughed.

John looked in the direction to which she pointed. Just the other side of the rail he saw a smart soldier in dark uniform isolated from the rest of his crowded compatriots by a sea of vacant seats.

The man was looking John's way. He had a broad smile which was the same colour as his water flattened hair. Realising John had at last received the message, he slowly, almost hesitantly, raised his hand in greeting.

John was aware of a second girl looking his way. She was also laughing. He did not know this man but the man seemed to know him. The girl who had passed on the message started her clumsy return towards the dividing rail, casually asking as she went, "You funny or something, mate?"

70

John blushed to the roots of his blonde hair. He felt the whole of the civilian side must be penetrating him with their eyes and thoughts. He heard their thoughts. 'Is he funny or something?'

On one occasion, John thought he saw Helmut in the distance. Yes, he was sure it was the young German he and Franz had been trying to deliver Rudolphe's message to on that fateful day both boys found they had trespassed into a minefield. It had been that message and those routes, so scrawled upon John's map by Rudolphe, which had been so misconstrued as an attempt to spy, when John had faced his trial.

So sure was John Collins that here was a link with his missing friend that he suppressed his aversion to anything Germanic and broke into a run down the cobbled High Street of Town. It seemed as though the civilians, carrying their empty shopping bags, as they moved from empty shop to empty shop in the forlorn hope of finding something upon which to spend their ration coupons, conspired to prevent this meeting. Every move John took seemed to be thwarted, as the milling individuals kept stepping in his way. His panic told him that he would lose Helmut, and that at any moment the German would disappear into one of the myriad side streets and alleyways.

He had almost reached his goal, having upset several old ladies and gentlemen, who clicked their tongues in annoyance at the brusque manners of this hurried young man, and mothers, who held their infants to them in fear that they might be trampled.

As John went to rush his last few paces, out from a shop doorway sauntered three uniformed Teutons, so that the youth's collision was unavoidable.

"Helmut!" cried John, partly in frustration at this impediment, partly in anger induced by the adrenalin of the collision. "Helmut, stop! I want to speak to you!"

So violent had been the collision that two of the soldiers had been pushed hard against the shop window, and one had knocked a passer-by, who muttered to herself, looking angry at the antics of the young and foolhardy.

Everything after that happened so quickly, from John's being angrily pushed from one to the other of the offended soldiers, to the small crowd which gathered, the annoyed shop-keeper and the very predictable arrival of two Feldpolizie attracted by such an illegal assembly of civilians.

The rapid dispersal of the witnesses, the transformation of the ruffled soldiers back to smart upholders of the dignity of a superior nation, the disappearance of the shop-keeper and the angry barked demands of the Feldpolizie was all accomplished in seconds, and John Collins tried to apologize and explained he had meant no harm.

But Helmut had gone. While concerned at his present plight, John was nevertheless aware that recognition had flickered across that German's face as he had involuntarily turned to see who had called his name. Yes, recognition but also another emotion. Had it been disdain or perhaps disgust or even fear? Well, John was not to know, for Helmut had evaporated from the scene.

So even those who had been mutual contacts with John and Franz now wished to dissociate themselves from this pariah. It was hopeless for John to continue to make enquiries of the conquerors.

And so John Collins, confused and insecure, derided and persecuted, with all avenues of enquiry either closed or imagined to be so, was one of the first to greet Father Peters, on his return from France, in the bleak February of 1943. Well, at least the priest would listen to him, he would turn the proverbial cheek and love his enemy, be he failed Guernseyman or distressed Aryan. The Father Confessor of the two youths would know how to sort out the problem.

"John, it's you," the priest emitted, trying to sound enthusiastic, but it was difficult to be so about anything at present.

Just back after eighteen cold and hungry months in France, a year and a half of being treated as a common criminal, and no communication at all with the outside world. This priest, all but broken by the hard labour and the nights of interrupted sleep, the dearth of news from his wife and boys

72

in England, the anxiety for his flock, left to fend for themselves in Guernsey, was now having to pick up the pieces of his wrecked routine. And so soon to be confronted by the very one who had contributed to his ordeal.

"Father Peters." John was stiff and formal. He held out his hand in the manner of an Aryan. He had being going to enquire after his lost friend, John Collins, but he did not feel easy with this enquiry, somehow it was not right.

The priest stepped forward. Now was the time to turn the other cheek, now he had to reconcile to the youth who stood before him. John Collins must also be feeling awkward, why else the stilted formality?

Ignoring the proffered hand, summoning up all his stifled emotion and his priestly calling, Thomas Peters pulled the lad to him and hugged him as though he were the embodiment of his parish. Little did the priest realise that in this physical contact with Franz Müller he was fraternizing with the enemy.

With the conversation which followed, Thomas felt he was back in that warm period in his life. He had returned to two Summers previously. He had not been to prison, he had not been cold, hungry or deprived of human dignity. No, all that was as yet unknown, and lay before him. Father Peters had no problems or misgivings of his own. He had once more to give himself over completely to the well-being of this strayed sheep. Yet again he had to disavow John Collins and tell him plainly that Franz was no more, for the duration of the war that was, and perhaps for ever.

John, you will not meet up with Franz again until the war is over."

"Why?"

"Because . . ." This was so difficult. How could the priest enforce starkly the finality of Franz's departure, probably for ever, to speak of the inevitable with his posting to the Eastern Front?

"Because, John, your friend is on his way to Russia. You knew this was to happen, surely you must accept that?"

Russia? How silly! Of course Franz was destined for Russia! Franz knew that, John knew it, the priest also. Of course his friend was going to Russia.

73

It did feel strange to Franz to be told he had to be forgotten and that he was back in Russia once more and would not be heard of while this war continued through yet another chapter, perhaps even to be lost for ever? The priest was clearly confused, his time in France had really unbalanced him, just as it had for his friend John. Yes, the man even expected him to be that same John. Ah well, he would try. It would have to be whatever the priest required, for the youth wanted to please. After all, had he not been brought up and educated to follow orders without question?

And so John became John once more, if only to please this adult. It was quite comforting to play this adult game for a while. Yes, he could even go home to his own Mum and help her while she so missed Dad still languishing in France. Yes, John Collins would go about being man of the house once more, and would continue to support Anne de la Haye and visit his little nephew Patrick. Yes, that was it, he would go to see Patrick today, not Bern. Bern was Franz's nephew but Patrick was John's. Today, John, tomorrow . . . well, who knew, perhaps he would be Franz again? Well, one thing was for sure, he did not have to worry about his friend, for he knew at any time of his choosing, he could return the Aryan to Guernsey. Yes, John and Franz could exchange places any time they chose and that was good, really good.

Chapter Ten

Here he is again, this policeman is so persistent. What is the point of his trying to take a statement? Has not the hospital already told him so?

"No, I'm sorry," says the doctor, "I already told you, constable, you don't stand a chance."

The Doctor is weary, does he really have to explain the whole prognosis to the man? Does he have to spell it out in words of one syllable that Mr. Collins is not in a fit state to comprehend, let alone reason or make any form of statement?

"I only need a minute," persists the constable. He does not enjoy this task any more than the doctor. He has seen the state of the victim cut from what had once been a car. He has guessed that nothing worthwhile can come from such a visit, but he has to try.

"The man is barely conscious," the doctors's voice ill-hides his irritation. "He doesn't know what time of day it is, besides he's got to save himself for his family."

The policeman understands. He would not have been so persistent if it had not been for his sergeant. Besides, what about that poor sod of a lorry driver, it could make a lot of difference to him, with no witnesses and all?

"Can you let us know if there's any change?"

"There won't be."

"But if there is . . ."

The crass impudence of the man!

* * *

In later years, when John was to look back on this period of Occupation, from his time in prison to the eventual Allied liberation in 1945, the whole period was to be relegated to confusion and distortion. It was to be viewed as a period of distrust and rejection, misery and self-doubt, anxiety and fear.

There were, however, certain events which remained clear, etched into his mind, never to be replaced or changed by the passage of time.

Naturally, John Collins was for ever to hold poor little Patrick in his memory, for was he not uncle to the poor fatherless child, and did not seeing to the little one's needs in some way atone for the guilt he felt?

Despite his confusion and lack of identity, regardless as to whether he held the Germans friend or foe, or the attempts of the allies to liberate Europe as cause for hope or concern, John could not disregard the 'D-Day' landings in nearby Normandy knowing that it was only a question of time before the liberation would come. He would always remember the roaring hum of that June day when, high above at mid-day, rather like etchings on the pale blue glass dome which was the mid-summer sky, formations of tiny black crosses edged their way almost imperceptibly as they moved from England towards that great battle for victory. The realization, as it dawned on the tired and dejected Islanders, had transmuted itself into cheers for those R.A.F. and U.S.A.F. aeroplanes far above viewing those below as only large sun glinted maps.

It was this same event in June 1944, regarded by all the long-suffering Islanders as a prelude for peace, which caused the Collins family the awful realisation that Larry had been caught up in the belligerence. What timing! Larry, Keith and Bert, all due for release in August 1944, would be incapable of return to their homeland. Had they been moved on ahead of the liberating forces to Nazi Germany itself or had they been released by the allies?

It was a very bad time for John and his mother, that period of uncertainty. For Frances the denied reunion was both misery and relief. The misery was that the longed-for individual contacts so anticipated, so wished, so unthought out, were now rendered impossible dreams, the relief; that she would not yet again have to make those impossible decisions, between Bert and Larry, or both.

Eventually, news was received of the fate of Larry, Bert and Keith. It was a great relief for Frances and Anne to know their men were safe.

John was unable to share in their anxieties, for he felt little sympathy. Why should the two women mope and moan so? At least they knew their men still existed, they would live, they would return, but for him there was no such confirmation that his friend was safe and well. John Collins was unable to afford himself the luxury of sharing his load, he had to carry it alone.

The three prisoners had been sent to Germany ahead of the Allies' advance. A Red Cross letter eventually confirmed this in July 1944.

The following month, when all three were due for release, but of course all their friends and relatives knew that such a happening was now impossible, Frances Collins and Anne de la Haye were called to the Police Station. They had not met since the trial of their respective husbands, yet each had been kept informed of the other by Uncle John.

Anne had been grateful for John's unstinting attention to her little Patrick. Frances too, was thankful that her son had maintained one enduring interest.

The sadness of the little child's rapidly failing health, despite all the love and attention he received, and the best medical treatment available from both civilian and German doctors during the ever more stringent shortages of the siege, had at least one blessing in that it had given John a sense of purpose. That, together with his passing on of information from one lady to another, had made this new meeting between Anne and Frances more natural.

The Chief of Police himself interviewed the two ladies. He could easily have left this purely informative task to a lesser being, but he had felt the portents of the news he had been ordered to deliver merited the need for as much courtesy as he could muster.

Perhaps the Chief was also aware of the changing tides of war? Could it be that this man, this victim, puppet to the will of the Nazis, was now feeling the wind of change? Did he also wonder if the eventual outcome would reverse the status quo, that perhaps he would be deemed to have taken the wrong side? The Germans were certainly more defensive these days in their dealings with the Islanders. They now felt outnumbered as the Allies controlled the seas around this prison.

As they took the seats indicated, Frances felt strangely vital, she felt a combination of anxious anticipation tinged with embarrassment and discomfort. Which was the stronger emotion she was not sure; could it be that she was about to hear awful news, or was it that she remembered how she had bared her infidelity in front of this same man, in this very room, all those years previously?

"I came here to ask if Bert was being held," she said with a deep sigh. "He left me ages ago and didn't come back." Frances now hung her head bending her shoulders in her disgrace.

"Yes, well," the Chief coughed delicately. "Yes, I see."

After a brief pause, in which he looked at his pocketwatch he added;

"Where did he leave you from, Mrs. Collins?"

"From his house, from his bedroom, if you must damned well know!"

"And your husband? Do you know where he is?" enquired the Chief kindly,

"No, I don't know, but you can rest assured he wasn't with us," she said with bitter bravado.

The silence lengthened.

Eventually the Chief cut into the hiatus.

"Ladies, you have probably guessed that the reason for this meeting concerns both your husbands." He coughed delicately, looking up from the document he had been toying with, to give an exaggerated nervous smile which he involuntarily extinguished.

His remark was so obvious. Even he realized how foolish it was.

"I have news for you," he continued. "It concerns your men. It is very momentous."

Anne was suddenly clutched by almost uncontrollable fear. Keith was dead! The Chief of Police had called them in to inform them that the two men were no more! Those Germans did not have the guts to impart their own evil news but pushed it on to the civilian Police Chief. That was it, the prison had been hit in an allied air raid! Yes, the two had tried to escape and had been shot by the guards. Or they had escaped and then, in prison uniform, had been shot in error, by Americans thinking they were Jerries. Maybe the bomb on the prison had scored a direct hit on their cells?

Perhaps the Germans, frightened of the advancing armies had taken them out and shot them? Perhaps they were using them as hostages and had tied them on the front of their tanks to prevent their being fired at? Oh yes, she had heard of such atrocities from listening to the B.B.C.

She had no time to indulge this flood of evil conjecture for the Chief continued;

"As you know, the Germans have made a temporary retreat in northern France in order to regroup to make a victorious advance and drive the Allies out once more."

The Chief had certainly read his *Press* and absorbed the Teutonic propaganda. Whether he believed it, was another matter.

"The prison in which your men folk were held has now fallen into the hands of the allies and, as far as I can ascertain, all political detainees have been released."

Frances' consciousness gave a leap. Had then, Larry been released? Was he now a free man? Why was the Chief telling them all this news? Surely the three men were now in Germany? Had there been a mistake though? Had they been given the wrong information last month? Such errors can easily occur during the rigours of war. Maybe all along they were free? Probably they were at that very moment in England? Perhaps they had been enlisted into the British forces and were now preparing to free the islands from their evil domination? Why then, had they not written? Surely Red Cross letters could still get through, despite the siege?

He continued;

"Your men are now held in a prison in Berlin." He had almost completed his task. Both women were disavowed of their thoughts.

"I have to tell you that, despite the ending of their sentences, present circumstances make their return home impossible, as you will appreciate . . ."

"What then?" interrupted Frances. "What will happen?" Her voice was shrill yet heavy with the disappointment of the dashed hopes so recently raised.

"That is why I have asked you to come," proceeded the Chief, wearily. "They will be transferred from their prison to internment camps for British subjects, until the war is over."

"You mean Biberach?" whispered Anne, relieved that Keith was in fact still alive. She could hardly believe the reprieve from her self-imposed misgivings. Biberach was all right! She knew several whose friends and relatives had been deported there from the Island before the siege. Those British nationals, not Guernsey born, had gone off in the ships with fear and foreboding, to the black continent of no return, imagining their fate to be that of the Jews, so ruthlessly exterminated. Yet they had all survived, witness their letters, which had been published in the newspapers. They actually seemed to be faring quite well if all that she had heard was to be believed. It seemed they had formed their own council and ran their own affairs, were given work, for which they were paid, and were allowed time to go out into the local towns for amusement and shopping. She had even heard that they had started a register of marriages and births, which was to be legitimized by the Guernsey Greffe. So it could not be too bad when the internees were able to contemplate such normalities. If Keith were there then he would be safe.

"Biberach, Mrs. de la Haye?" asked the Chief, almost incoherently, as if stalling for time to be able to phrase his reply to her pathetic question. "Well not exactly. You see Mrs. de la Haye, your husband is Guernsey born . . ."

"And?" interrupted Frances, "And what is is that to do with anything? My Larry was born in England. He was not Guernsey born! What are you telling us?"

"Dear Lady, precisely. That is what I wish to say." He addressed himself to Anne once more.

"Mrs. de la Haye, by rights, by International Law that is, your husband does not need to be interned, therefore Biberach is not for him."

"What is then?" demanded Anne.

"I am not too certain, he probably will go there, with ex. P.C. Bisson, for a while, but I believe they are both the subject of activity by the International Red Cross." He stopped, as though he had imparted more than a sufficiency for them both to draw their own conclusions.

"Excuse me," interjected Frances, "but are you telling me that my husband, who is English born will be treated differently from the others, that he is to go to Biberach?" She was holding back the relief ready for confirmation.

"Yes, Mrs. Collins, as I understand it, but . . ."

"Well what of my man then?" urged Anne.

"There are moves," added the Chief timorously, "only moves I would have you know, to have your husbands repatriated, along with Mr. Bisson, to Great Britain."

Both women gasped.

"What do you mean exactly?" asked Anne, not sure whether she should feel anxiety or elation.

"I mean your husband could well be free in England before Christmas, as he is not a member of a belligerent nation."

"Oh," Anne understood but could not yet allow herself the appropriate emotion. She was delighted that her dear Keith was likely to be free, yet it was to be a freedom without her. She felt strangely jealous. She should have been selfless yet all she could think was that Keith would be fine but she would then have the double torment of knowing that what was right for Keith was bad for her.

"So what about Larry?" asked Frances, then adding, almost as an after-thought, "and Bert?"

"Sorry?" the Chief was puzzled. Was he querying her interest in Bert?

"Yes, I mean no. Oh I don't bloody well know anything any more! Can I see Bert, please?"

"What about your husband, don't you want to see him too?"

What was this? Was he trying to trap her into confessions of adultery? Well, so what if he was!

Perhaps he had already made Larry's fate clear but she had not understood?

"Tell me about my man." This time she studiously avoided mention of Bert.

"Well Mrs. Collins, as I am given to understand, the diplomats dealing with such matters would like all three treated the same. As for Mr. Bisson, I've already explained his position, as a born Guernseyman he has a greater claim to being repatriated, as has Mr. de la Haye."

Frances blushed to the roots of her hairs. She felt the Chief had laboured his point too much and was enjoying her discomfort. Her embarrassment was interrupted as Anne asked;

"Why have you brought us here? Is it just out of kindness to keep us informed? The Germans aren't usually so considerate."

"Quite so," agreed the Chief casually, not really intending any disrespect to their masters. "No, we do, that is the German authorities, do require your help in this. Let me explain."

The Chief of Police continued to explain that repatriation could only be entered into with the willingness of the subject to be treated in this way. He did not put it into words but it was implicit in his logic that for British subjects to refuse repatriation was unheard of.

However, it seemed, both Larry and Keith had been dilatory about agreeing to the scheme and would not go without the wishes of their wives being known to them.

Times certainly were strange when criminals like Collins and de la Haye could pick and choose and almost tell the Germans what they would or would not do. Yes, indeed it all pointed to one certainty, that they had lost the war. It was only a matter of time now. Why else would they begin to show considerations such as these to this tiny group of British subjects, if they were not in awe of the revenge which was coming?

This was why the Island, despite the hunger-sapped fatigue of its inhabitants, was awash with rumours. Was it true that the British government had initiated discussions with the Germans to repatriate the whole population of all the islands? Or was it a German idea, in order to conserve the dwindling stocks of food? Some had said that Churchill himself had scuppered any such ideas, for it suited his purposes that the enemy would have less food by having to keep the civil population alive.

Whether these were just rumours, or had elements of truth, was of no consequence to the two women, for the outcome of their meeting with the Chief was inevitable.

Larry, Keith and Bert were duly transferred to Britain. Keith joined the Royal Navy, Larry volunteered for the army but instead was directed to a munitions factory, whereas Bert was assigned police duties.

As the eleven months of siege progressed, with its misery and isolation, both Anne and Frances at least knew their loved ones were safe and free. As surely as Red Cross parcels got through, there were the occasional Red Cross letters, their twenty five words confirming the new status of their men. These few words, assuring that their loved ones missed them and longed for reunion, sustained the two women in that long winter of hunger and privation.

Chapter Eleven

Well, perhaps now he'll believe the Doctor? No, the Houseman should not be feeling so irritable, the constable was only trying to do his job. It is a pity, though, that he will not take the Doctor's word; it is a shame that the relatives have been required to move from the bedside for a while, not that they have made any fuss. Well, perhaps they are not as overworked and tired as the doctor.

"Mr. Collins . . . John," asks the constable self-consciously, aware that the Doctor is hovering with unsaid 'I told you so' pervading the atmosphere.

Whose is that voice? It is not Dad's. No, it cannot be, Dad is still exiled. It certainly isn't Franz's voice, for it is too authoritative.

The policeman begins again. "Mr. Collins, I'm from the local police station."

Bert! It must be Uncle Bert! The dirty old bugger is looking for his mother again! But no, he too has not yet returned.

"I'd like to ask you a few questions if I may . . ."

No way! John is not about to go through any more interrogation, this dream has gone too far! Why should John contemplate yet more pain when at will he can go to look for Franz instead?

* * *

As the siege progressed, John felt more and more isolated, and withdrew into his own private thoughts.

No, John Collins felt aloof from the cold and hungry sufferings of that period, and yet he observed, mainly from a detached viewpoint, but at times touched by the misery experienced by his mother and that of Anne de la Haye and little Patrick.

Even Auntie Rita was not so well blessed with food as once she had been. No, the Potato Board had put a stop to all the extras which had once come from that source. The garden which had once provided vegetables, with some to spare, was now requisitioned by The Board. Estimates of crop yield per vergee were made, and those who did not come up to expectation of provision for the common good were to expect frequent raids, in which plants would be pulled and examined and houses thoroughly searched for hoarded roots. As if that were not enough, with the attendant anxiety that at the time of search other crimes might be uncovered, perhaps as illegal crystal set for picking up the proscribed B.B.C., or a camera which should have been handed in long ago, there was also the threat of the withholding of seed potatoes, purchased from France, or fertilizer on the rare occasions it was available, or the purchase of vraic from the beaches when at times the masters sanctioned its harvest.

The highlight of Christmas in 1944 was a meat dinner in which they ate the two pet rabbits Uncle Tom had fed with dandelions each day. It was strange to be invited into the home of his best friend's Aunt and Uncle like this once more. Franz remembered how he had once left that same table feeling over full.

The whole week's fish ration used in one serving or the second helpings of vegetables, or the pudding with sauce which could almost have passed for custard, as host and hostess tried to make welcome their unexpected guest.

Rationing was so severe in that final Winter, and yet still supplies became exhausted. First potatoes became completely depleted and then flour. It seemed the population was destined to live on roots and beans.

Some of the Germans and their forced labourers had meat, however–well, it explained the rapidly dwindling cat and dog population. John heard that, at night, the fortunate country dwellers, who still had chickens, would take these valuable creatures into their houses.

The Islanders had to resort to the crafts of bygone times, necessity became the mother of invention once more. Shoes were fashioned from the old tyres of lorries, and clogs became quite common. Little Patrick even had a pair of shoes made from his mother's old kid gloves. Salt was made by evaporating sea water, and vendors would sell sea water in which to cook vegetables for anyone still fortunate enough to have such supplies.

John was not concerned at the dearth of food in that final winter of 1945. He was beyond the selfish interest of the needs of his body physical. He had been given good training in his French prison but, even so, it was not an active spurning of material acquisitions and luxury, it was more a passive acceptance that all was outside his control and nothing appertaining to himself was important any more.

Yes, John could understand his mother's longing for Larry, and could even accept her illicit thoughts about Bert, just as he was aware of Anne de la Haye's need for Keith, but it was with that same unspoken bitterness and resentment which would not go away.

Both the women had letters, both had proof that their men existed and one day were sure to return, but what did John have? His only friend had gone without trace. Not for him the luxury of twenty-five typed words. John could not even discuss his thoughts, for who would understand his need and longing to wish to be with his enemy once more? Who would understand the guilt he felt that his friend had been taken away as a result of John's own treacherous selfishness?

The only thing which kept John from complete absorption in his own miseries was his concern for little Patrick. He loved that little boy with an intensity in proportion to his own increased misery and complete hopelessness, combined with the infant's failing health.

It was not through lack of food that the little child had languished, for all had sacrificed to see that he had plenty. There was always someone to spare a drop of precious milk or a treat from a Red Cross Parcel. He had chocolate and biscuits, jam and honey. It was not through neglect that he had lost weight, but just through ailing.

In that final winter of the siege, at a time when the east winds were at their coldest, blowing from nearby liberated northern France, the little child contracted pneumonia and died. Part of the good uncle died with him, as John mourned inwardly, not sharing his grief with anyone. Nobody knew how deeply John felt, just as no-one was aware how he still so missed Franz.

Chapter Twelve

They have gone now, those two Feldpolizie. John is glad he had not opened his eyes. Why should he spend so much energy on their like? He does not even afford such courtesies to his own mother or the friend who has come with her.

Hospital indeed! They have told him he is in hospital, as if he does not know that. Hasn't he had enough experience of hospitals in his time?

No, he had heard the one tell the other that to conduct an interview was a hopeless prospect and that he should forget about it. They do not usually give up so easily, but then, of course, that is why they have lost the war.

*   *   *

When liberation came on 9th May 1945 John attended the celebrations, more out of duty as some necessary medication that had to be endured in order to pass to a further state of well being.

He witnessed the unusual sights, he witnessed but did not partake, observed but did not share or enjoy.

John was always to be haunted by that sense of eerieness with the sudden absence of all German personnel first felt when the liberators had disarmed them and ordered them to their billets. The island without its familiar, almost rusticated Aryans was a strange place indeed. The effect, almost of loss, was made even more strange by the unfamiliar appearance and the unmilitary behaviour of the smiling-faced Mr. Bountifuls of the British Forces.

John watched two lean and hungry parents, as they coaxed their perambulated infant to sample his very first sweet, which had been given by a passing sailor.

Everywhere he went on that day, either with Frances or

88

alone or with the still grieving Anne, he saw the generosity of the liberators, with their handouts of packets of biscuits, bars of chocolate, sweets and cigarettes. He noticed the restrained greed on the faces of the hungry, as they managed not to snatch and not to rip off the wrappers with too unseemly a haste, yet relieved that they had not been passed by and the person next to them had not got more than their share.

He watched the circling Red Cross vans on Cambridge Park, he saw everywhere the human walls of hearty waving civilians anxious to cheer and prove their Britishness. Everywhere were hastily discovered Union Jacks and the crosses of St. George, with myriad other pennants which had long ago gone into hiding, awaiting the very day.

The town of St. Peter Port was festooned with flags and streamers the like of which he had never seen before, not even on the King's birthday.

The shops opened, the Church bells rang incessantly and the ships of the harbour added to the constant euphoria with their jubilant sirens.

In the afternoon John went with his mother and Anne to Candie Gardens and had listened to the speeches by the liberating heroes, and the replies from the various members of the civil administration who now considered themselves and their efforts as noteworthy.

In the evening the streets of the capital were thronged with people from all over the Island, from its far reaches. In they came in droves, in horse buses, ponies and traps, on bicycles and even with the odd motor-car or motor-bike which miraculously still worked and for which, even more surprisingly, there was fuel.

Restrictions were lifted, as life returned to normal. No longer did the Islanders have the indignity of a curfew. To have been able to increase their siege-time rationing to the level of that enjoyed by the United Kingdom would have been luxury indeed, but to have a period completely without rationing at all, was beyond imagining.

All were happy, everyone danced and sang and got out those long treasured luxuries. Wirelesses were listened to openly and people began to pester the telephone exchange to enquire when they could telephone the British mainland. The forces of liberation were indeed honoured guests and were freely invited into the Islanders' homes.

Yet, there must have been many like Frances, like Anne, who had observed the symbolism of this new freedom and noted the removal of tyranny, who nevertheless, could not settle and be at peace. How long would it be before they could be reunited with their loved ones and their families? Would it be only hours, days, weeks or even months? No-one could give an answer. There were urgent priorities of food and supplies and the place had to be restored to safety. The regalia of war had to be dismantled and the German prisoners removed. All these matters were far more important and urgent than setting dates for such mundane things as the niceties of freedom.

Yes, there were many who found the hours and the days dragging endlessly, like an indeterminate sentence, as they hoped and prayed for a quick return of their separated loved ones. There were those also who anticipated the event with some nervous consternation as if they had premonitions that the years of separation would have caused old bondings to have weakened and new bondings to have formed. Not least of these was Frances who was now forced to face up to the fact that both her men would soon return.

Anne had the prospect of facing her man with the awful burden which she alone had carried. She knew it, and she dreaded it. She longed to share it with her dear fisherman, for then the agony would become halved, and yet she dreaded the moment of revelation with such foreboding that she just wished she could run away and that their re-union should never have to happen.

How could she tell her man that his only son was no more? How could she murder the child which Keith must, at this very moment, be holding alive still, anticipating his first meeting?

Oh yes, she had written to Keith when his little son was alive, and she had told him what a wonderful child he was, not mentioning that he was in poor health. What would have been the point to worrying her darling, who would not have been able to do anything about it from his cell in France? No, she had been able to bear the worry of that, for it was the least she could do to compensate for Keith's incarcerated absence. Besides, hadn't she had the help and support of young John Collins?

Anne was not even sure if her darling had received the news that he was a Daddy, it all seemed so long ago now, and Red Cross letters had been few and far between, not always reaching the recipient, and oh so brief. Yes, he must have known that. Yes, Anne felt sure that Keith must have had the good news, and yet, she could not recollect his reply. But then, with only twenty-five words, albeit carefully chosen, perhaps he had not thought to acknowledge? That was strange though, Anne had felt uneasy about it at the time, but had needed to push the thoughts from her mind.

When Patrick had died, she had intended to let Keith know, but the longer she had left it, the harder it had become. With the siege, too, it was almost impossible to communicate, but at least she could have tried, and not used the difficulty as an excuse. Perhaps she felt glad that maybe Keith, did not have to be disavowed of his parenthood, that he did not even known of the existence of his child? But she knew that this was just delusion, that the guilty truth had to be faced. Perhaps it was true that they were being punished for their lustfulness before the cruel parting all those years ago?

Keith had been fearful that their love violence, with all the inventiveness of insatiable teenagers, would harm their unborn child. Somewhere in the far reaches of his mind he remembered the playground talk of sex and passion and of intercourse with pregnant women which would cause birthmarks on the visages of the unborn innocents. But Keith could not help himself for that all belonged to a past and forgotten world of dirty and furtive talk and guilt-ridden actions in the secluded parts of his boyhood education. None of that could be associated with his darling Anne who was clean and strong and beautiful and, like his angel, that she was, responded to his every pressure, welding herself round him so that their two bodies had become one, neither knowing where the one ended and the other began but both delighting in the feelings and sensations of the other. No, Keith and Anne, in their love making, were perfect and clean and

very very beautiful. Their unborn child could be nothing but blessed
by their emission of love, time after time, through that long, short
night.

Both were guilty, and both must now be condemned to suffer
for it.

John Collins must surely have been unique in those early days
after the Liberation. There can have been few who actually
missed the former masters with all their Teutonic glory, as he
at first did. Now they were only to be observed marching past
as squads of prisoners busy about the work of dismantling the
trappings of the former Führer's Atlantic Wall, its bombs, its
minefields, its camouflage netting and its barbed wire. No
music accompanied them now, no jolly singing or proud
stamping of boots, just the stony faces of the vanquished and
the hunched shoulders of the defeated with occasional
greetings of a boo or two from some children full of bravado.
Mostly these erstwhile masters were disregarded by the locals.

John missed their authority with an unthought-out
nostalgia. They had after all, been present for a quarter of his
life and had witnessed his change from boy to man. Amongst
their sons too, he had numbered his greatest friend.

The Islanders, true to their nature, did not conduct a self-
destructive witch hunt, as did some of the their neighbours in
Jersey and on the French mainland. There were no incidents
of revenge-seeking, there was no haircutting or tarring,
against lamp posts, of those who had provided creature
comforts for the enemy. The people did not need to prove
their loyalty and gratitude to the British liberators; their lean
figures and threadbare clothing testified to that. The British
Tommies were invited into islanders' homes as the Teutons
had never been.

Instead of revenge and recrimination against their own
people who had adapted to the masters, the population set
about dismantling the signs of Occupation. With great
fervour, everything Nazi which could be removed was

removed. Vehicles, furnishings, machines and paraphernalia of war were hurriedly removed by the shipload, an action which was perhaps to be rued by some in years to come, when that period would be viewed not as real and emotional, but just as history. For the people at the time however, it was right and it was therapeutic.

Parents for the first time, without fear of recrimination, could imbue their children with ideas that anything German was unwholesome and tainted.

The British Government, to the chagrin of many, the honest members of the island community, honoured and exchanged the worthless German currency which had been forced upon the hapless people. There was no upper limit to the amounts exchanged, thereby a missed opportunity to ask how certain people had amassed such huge quantities of Reichsmarks. Perhaps to proscribe exchange to some would later have been seen as anomalous when those same people were to be honoured and decorated for wartime services? Thus life quickly returned to normal with first one reinstatement of privilege and then another, while the temporary and removable evidence of their recent over-stayed guests was removed.

The concrete and the trenches were not so easily taken care of and remained, as did the brightly coloured direction signs, their black gothic set against lurid backgrounds, as ghosts from the past to remind all that they really had existed, they really had been there and had held the power of life and death, captivity and freedom.

John was not derided nor disdained, not that he would have minded. He had reasoned that such behaviour on the part of his peers might have been a real possibility but it had been of little concern to him for nothing could outmatch the loss of his friend which had now become his one and all pervading obsession.

They received telephone calls from Larry, and the letters, now came more quickly, long letters hungry for news, full of love, uncensored letters. Wirelesses were restored and the people became au fait with the outside world once more. Even the newspapers had a more real ring about them. Frances even received a 'phone call from Bert.

It was not too long before the telegram came to say that

Larry was returning and could be expected at the airport within days. Frances became a nervous wreck, she gave up her job, she did not know what to do. Should she go to the airport and wait until the 'plane arrived? Should she just wait at home for the telephone to ring? If she went to the airport would she be permitted to enter or would she be turned away? If she waited at home would Larry take that as a sign that she did not care enough to go out there to meet him?

John elected to make enquiries and made his way to the competent department of the British liberating forces. He was surprised at the animosity he felt within himself at having to deal with these foreigners in their foreign and frumpy uniforms. They were not as smart and efficient as their German counterparts had been. No, there was nothing military about their bearing or their procedures. He felt full of contempt for these forces which belonged to and had liberated his friend John Collins, that friend who, with passage of time, and because he had not succeeded soon enough, had been prepared to sit back and give up the search for him.

"Yes, sonny?"

"Eh?" John woke from his daydream, that recurring dream in which he was never quite sure whether he was John Collins looking for Franz Müller or if he were Franz whom John could not, or would not, find.

"What you want, mate?" demanded the British Corporal wearing the uniform of a British soldier.

John shrugged.

"What's your name, lad?" The Corporal sighed as the vestige of his smile drained from his face and he began to look business-like.

John muttered but was incomprehensible as he fumbled in his jacket pocket for the telegram.

It was too much for the Corporal. He had been pleasant and uncharacteristically full of bon ami far too long with these people. It was true they had put up with a lot but they just couldn't expect to be treated like royalty in this way for ever. A lad of this one's age should be in military service not lounging around looking sorry for himself like this.

John was nearly home now. He had been told he need not wear a helmet any more for there were no more air raids now that peace had come. He looked down at his polished jackboots and could literally see his face in them.

As he passed a British sailor he impressed him by doing the goose step.

It was a British soldier who stopped him at the sentry post in the Grange. When John showed him his papers and turned, so that the other would notice his Iron Cross, the tommy saluted and shouted.

"Heil Hitler!"

The Corporal snapped,
  "Name, I said, damn you!"
  John recovered himself, and as quickly fired back.
  "Müller, Franz Müller!"
  "Bloody heck!" retorted the Corporal. Here was a pretty kettle of fish!

At first the liberating authorities were puzzled by John Collins. Their concern ranged from the possibility that he really was a German national who had somehow escaped the net, through the possibility that he was a local who had been converted to nazism by the Germans, to the likelihood that he was a deranged young man. Perhaps his experiences had put him off balance? Possibly he had always been unbalanced?

The British forces quickly established that John was a bonafide Islander and that he could not possibly have been a quisling for he had spent a year in a French prison, so young too, for such an experience as that. Well, the youth might appear a bit odd right now, and lifeless and lethargic into the bargain, but he must once have had something about him to have been so viciously treated by the Nazis.

Those who dealt with his enquiry felt that he was in need of some help which was not at their disposal either to give or to advise. Theirs was not to provide for the health of the inhabitants, either physical or mental.

Despite the anomaly and the inability to help him, John was nevertheless endearing enough and co-operative to their questions when he was in fact John Collins. At times, when he was Franz Müller, they just disregarded him.

Some good came out of this accidental liaison for not only did John discover the object of his mission, the date and time of his father's arrival, receiving permits to enter the aerodrome, but also he was spoken to by an army chaplain who in turn contacted Father Peters.

The priest was only too aware of his young parishioner's growing psychological problems. Had he not spent hours trying to sort out young John? He knew how the youth had previously found great difficulty in accepting the loss of his enemy friend, and of the unspoken guilt young John felt for what had befallen the young Aryan.

Were there not indications of problems to come? Was not this latest episode indicative of the seeds of some serious personality disorder? Was John destined to an eventual life of confusion, identifying with one person and then another, never to be truly himself? Was this just a temporary understandable aberration of one of Father Peter's flock, or did it prelude a deeper involvement, so that John might not only identify with but become the very person he was emulating?

Well, it was true. The priest could see all the signs, but despite caring, he was not a doctor, and he did have other souls who needed his care, souls who had not sent him to France. Besides, Father Peters was so very very tired, and young John Collins was so very stubborn.

No, the priest could not persuade the youth to any action against his will. After all, the young man did have youth on his side, and with the ending of hostilities, things could only improve for him. Yes, John Collins would mend, Father Peters felt sure of it.

Not that John would have taken too much notice of his confessor anyway. He might be temporarily unbalanced, but he was certainly still a very wilful young man; John Collins still knew what he wanted, and would always determine to get his way.

Out of his contact with the army chaplain and Father Peters, and, having established his wilfulness, it seemed no time at all that John gained another permit. Not this time papers for his mother and he to greet the returning Larry at the airport, but his very own papers to leave the Island. So quickly was this rigorous formality effected that it might almost have seemed there were those in authority glad to see him on his way. So rapidly indeed did John leave Guernsey that he had left before his father's return.

Chapter Thirteen

Frances does not really seem to accept that she is soon to lose her only son. How can she? How can this old lady, now without her dear husband, divested of Bert too, contemplate that the only other man in her life is soon to be removed.

No, of course he is getting better! Frances has heard some strange news in her time, but she is not so old and foolish now that she would take notice of the silly talk that white-coated man had tried to tell her on arrival at the hospital.

It might be all right for her companion to take notice of it, but not she, for she is too wise and too old to be so misled. She had known John far too long for that, more than three times as long as the girl who now sits with her and calls her 'Mum'.

* * *

For one who had never left his homeland island except for short holidays, and an enforced stay in France, John adapted rapidly to his new surroundings. He was not concerned to make friends, to set down roots, to build a life for himself out of the rubble and destruction that he found on the mainland. Bodily comfort was not his aim, he remained non-materialistic.

Post-war Britain was not the easiest of places from which to carry out a private search and post-war Europe did not lend itself to being visited.

John tried hard. He went through correct procedures, filled out many forms, attended offices, waited for hours culminating in short non-productive interviews. Always he was moved on to yet another department, still another building, more letters to write, more 'phone calls to make.

He was oblivious to comments and to the prying curiosity of those he met. All he needed, he knew, was to go to

Germany itself and there all would be revealed. This was not so easy however and John Collins was forced to remain for some while in England, to conduct his mission by the unproductive proxy of letter writing.

John's first job was as a lowly clerk with a small shipping company which traded with his island. However, he was no more excited by this connection than bothered by his humble employment.

John would arrive at his desk, always punctual conscientiously work through his day, then in the evening return to his digs. All attempts by his fellow office workers to involve him in their gossips and their lives failed, and he was quickly almost disregarded, first by the ladies and then by the other men, as they drifted back from the war to take up their ledger keeping, filing and shuffling of papers.

Such jobs have an innate tedium which is often only alleviated by the comradeship of the workplace, but for John the very monotony of his working day was his shield from reality, from realizing that the quality of his young life was very poor, far worse than the time in which he was imprisoned in his island of occupation, for then he had known the freedom of friendship.

Yes indeed, these English people, whose reputation was of shyness and diffidence, really tried hard, but seemingly, to no effect.

"Good morning, Mr. Collins, or might I call you John, now?" enquired the pretty young receptionist who doubled as wages clerk. "Did you have a good week-end? We went to . . ."

"Yes," cut in John curtly, neither offended by the girl's attempts at familiarity nor flattered that someone was concerned enough to quiz him and try to make him feel he belonged. "The week-end is over now. Excuse me, please, I must get on with this," indicating the day's chores which were to anaesthetise him.

"John, my lad," one of his fellows would say, "how about joining us for a pint tonight? There's a darts match on, don't you know? Do you play?" The stark, "No" was guaranteed to end conversation.

"Mr. Collins er . . . John, my parents went on holiday to Guernsey before the war. They had a lovely time there, such happy memories. We were wondering if . . ."

"No . . . sorry," said John, anticipating an invitation to share his private life with people he did not know, nor could hope to understand. "I am very busy in the evenings and at weekends, I . . ."

It was put down to shyness, of course. Why else would such a good-looking fellow not want to socialise with people of his own age? Who in their right minds would live only for work and the solitude of sparse lodgings?

Even his landlady tried in her own way. John was one of several lodgers, most of whom took up the invitations to sit in the front room of an evening and listen to the wireless, while taking turns to poke the fire and fill the scuttle. John heard them all right, as they laughed at Archie Andrews and Arthur Askey. He knew they were having a good time, and he knew he had only to tap on the door to be included, to drink endless cups of tea and cocoa and to join in their games of Snap and Housey Housey. But no, he chose to sit in his cold room writing his letters, carrying out his search for his friend of yester-year. He even, on one occasion, asked that the wireless volume be turned down, as its joyfulness, accompanied by short wave whistle and whine, disturbed his lonely quest.

No, John Collins was considered very odd, aloof even, by all those whose offers of friendship and kindness he spurned.

"John, if you're late coming in dear, this window here lifts up," explained his landlady, who did not really feel the necessity to have more than one key for one house.

"That won't be necessary," he replied, "I don't intend to be late ever."

No, curfew rules were intended to be kept. Were they not, after all, invented and imposed by the master race? Was it not obligatory to obey without question?

No, the frantic letter writing, enquiring, searching, went on. Those receiving such communications, so thorough in every detail, could not have imagined they eminated from such a shy and introverted person as bland John Collins, self-imposed exile from his homeland.

He in turn, became the focus of a search and frantic letter writing by his mother and father but even when the letters reached him and when he allowed himself to be telephoned, he had remained untouched by their pleading or their concern. Whereas in the past an absence from his mother, or an anxiety expressed by her would have struck a chord in him, he was now quite impassive. Nothing they could write or say would move him to change his course.

It was hardly to be expected that one so anxious to leave the Island years before, even before the return of his father, one who had been separated from his family for years, was likely to be moved by his mother's pleading, or her passing on that Larry had forgiven his errant son and a fresh start would contain no recrimination. No, they just did not understand, they still believed that he had left the Island as some sort of misplaced atonement for the troubles he had caused. How could they be expected to understand that he was seeking his lost friend, his only friend, his enemy friend?

The fact that Larry had taken over the shop and was beginning to expand his trade to include motor-cycles and motor-cycle repairs and that he had room for an assistant did not persuade John to return.

Nor was he impressed that old Gaudion had died and that his parents were trying to purchase the whole house to turn it into a guest house for the rapidly increasing visitor trade from post-war Britain.

He was not too concerned that Uncle Bert might be selling his own house, that he had turned down an offer of reinstatement in the Island Police force and was seriously contemplating going in with the Collins family and their exciting venture.

Lost to John was his erstwhile uncle's brave stand against the temptation of reinstatement. No, despite the previous blackening of his character in the eyes of the whole population, that man remained cynically aloof, not seeking to clear his name, for his conscience was clear. If people wished to think ill of him, that was their problem. Bert did not need to protest his innocence. Oh yes, he had tales he could tell, and might one day, but not yet. No, it amused failed police constable Bisson to see those who were in no way whiter than white receiving, after the Occupation, their decorations for services rendered. They really seemed to believe in themselves too, so that the hypocrisy of their circumstances was lessened. No, Bert could do without their acclaim, he could wait his moment, just as brave postmen, who had opened Gestapo-destined letters of denunciation would wait, not telling the world of their bravery and service to fellow Islanders, for fear of having been in breach of contract by interfering with the post.

Uncle Bert was from his past, as were his mother and father. It did not really concern him any more what they did.

Maybe one day, when he had found Franz, then he might return to Guernsey. Maybe then he and Franz would help with the visitor trade, possibly set up their own business? But Franz had to be found first. That was what was important!

John almost wavered at the news of the de la Hayes. Anne was to have another baby. Yes, Keith had returned but he had been unable to settle either. He had remained in the Navy, getting home on leave from time to time.

The thought of being 'Uncle' once more was very powerful for John, but not strong enough to deflect him from his mission. John Collins had to cut himself off from the living and the new life in order to search for the old and . . . dead? Well, to others, Franz might be presumed dead, but certainly not to John.

John could not be expected to empathise with the fisherman and his wife and their expected new child. How could John Collins, now in England, expect to know, or bother even, why the fisherman did not return to his boat to ply the trade which had been his whole life before the Teutons had come to enhance all their lives? He did not concern himself that Keith, a Guernsey Donkey to the core, agonised over his absence from home and family, that he longed desperately for his beloved island, and only stayed with the Royal Navy because he could not face those he had been tricked into betraying.

In it was requested the legalising of the removal to France, to a house of correction, at least 10km from the coast, of one Anne de la Haye, spouse of Keith de la Haye, withholder of the Reich's information; there to be kept indefinitely at the Führer's pleasure.

No, Keith had to do Judas' work now and do it quickly. He had no time for further soul-searching. All that had been done already.

He complied. One after another he sold his friends to prison, he gave the families of friends to anxiety and fear. He let their wives die over and over as they waited for non-existent news from the French mainland, where their fated loved ones served indeterminate sentences. He gave the children of his friends bitter salt-sobbed night-time pillows for comfort and hungry bed-time bellies. He gave himself over to doors slammed as he passed by, unseen bearers of rude calls in the street, to an exclusion by all at the Golden Lion, to vandalism on his boat, abusive 'phone calls and anonymous letters. In return he kept his Anne and his unborn son.

Well, at least Keith and Anne had become united once more, albeit a unity with long breaks. Their state was far better than John's, he had no such luxury; still he had to find Franz.

John was almost tempted to return to Guernsey to become uncle to the expected child, especially if the little one was destined to need the presence of a man during its father's frequent absences. But no, this unknown child could not possibly take the place of the Schmidt children; it would mean nothing to Franz.

Chapter Fourteen

The younger woman speaks.

"Mum, let's go and get a cup of coffee, we've got time . . ."

Old Frances is glad to do what is suggested. Yes, of course they have time, plenty of time. John can rest now while they are away, rest and get better.

The younger woman gently takes the arm of this old lady, who has been Mum to many in her time. This girl is different, however. She has been really good for her boy, and had stood by him through lots of troubles, she is glad to have a daughter like her.

*   *   *

John did not intend to remain a lowly office worker, but became a bank clerk. Having nothing much to do with his spare time, except to wait for the day that he could travel freely to the continent, he used it wisely studying for appropriate exams to help him attain his goal. Not only did he take a great interest in the growing trade with the newly born Western Germany, but he also taught himself German and studied with great intensity, fanaticism almost, the geography and the war history of Germany and its surrounding nations, including that part of Russia relevant to his search.

In fact, all this hard work was good for John, for it kept his mind fully occupied, and had the effect of keeping his other personality in its correct perspective. It was good indeed, at times such as these to know that he was John Collins, ex-patriot Guernseyman first, Britisher second, and that he was working towards his self-set goal of finding his enemy brother and friend. How difficult it would have been if, at these intense moments of preparation and search, he had lapsed for one moment and let slip his dogged tunnel vision, to become distracted by any other influences surrounding his life. No, it would have been impossible to search for Franz if in fact he allowed himself the luxury of becoming Franz, even if only for a while. These cross-personality expeditions had to be saved only for his free moments, which fortunately, were few. Mostly they were relegated to his dreams.

Those in contact with John Collins at work, at the bank or in evening classes, had no way of knowing that sometimes here was a member of the Wehrmacht successfully disguised as a clerk. No-one knew of his bravery on the Eastern Front nor of his continuous search for that naive young Sarnian from all those years previously on that beautiful little island, that microcosm of paradise. No, all they saw was a rather aloof, slightly odd and very hard working Englishman. And Franz did not even feel the need to explain that to emanate from Guernsey was not to be imbued with such a title, as once his friend had told him in those far off days when, in captivity, they had known such freedom. No, those unseeing and unknowing, unfeeling faceless people who worked near John, but not with him, saw him as just a very cold person, and as such, chose not to communicate. Well, this suited the two youths just fine!

John's rapid advancement did not go unnoticed so that early in 1948 he received his great break. Because of his progress, and the high esteem in which his work record was held, he was invited to talk with someone in one of the higher echelons of his bank. Seizing this opportunity, and realising its great potential, John turned it to his advantage.

Before the year was out he was established in a mission of commerce in the West German Federal Republic.

It was not as easy as he had imagined, to get the co-operation of the ordinary German citizen or the new order of German authorities. He was there on a personal mission of friendship and reunification but of course such information could not be discerned from the look of him and no-one would realise from his accent that he actually felt warmth to the memory of many Germans in general and one in particular.

At times he had wanted to shout out;

'You are not all bad! I saw the good in your people as well

as the evil! I should know, I lived with Germans for five years!'
He wanted to tell them sometimes that he had a German
name, that he was Franz Müller, one of them. However, he
was never allowed to get close enough to any Germans to be
able to call them acquaintance, let alone friends. It was never,
it seemed, to be possible to explain his quest. At times he
even began to doubt the viability himself. To observe these
people here and now, picking up the pieces of their ruined
and divided nation, determined to be successful without his
aid or interference, he wondered if his past had been all a
dream, just a figment of his imagination.

And then it happened. Early in 1949, he fell in love! Well
not exactly, he allowed himself to be fallen in love with.
Gerda it was, a slightly older woman who had come to work
with him.

Gerda had been working with him for some time before he
noticed her. It was only on reflection that he realized she had
been actively interested in him and had almost set herself this
target. It seemed she was spurred on by his apparent
complete lack of interest, almost unawareness, of all her
advances.

He only became aware of her when she began to mother
him. She then stood out from all the rest of her German
colleagues and came across as warm and human. At last he
realized that it had not all been a hopeless dream. He had
not imagined it, there had been real and human Germans in
his past. Franz had existed and, in Gerda's presence, he was
still held alive.

It was just the little things that first got noticed. Gerda
would always fetch his coffee, she even stirred it for him just
like his Mum had. Then there were the little treats, the small
slice of apple cake, baked at home and slipped onto his
saucer, almost surreptitiously, or the little wrapped paper
package bearing perhaps a piece of chocolate or a sweet one
day, or an apple another. No message, not even a hint from
where it had come. Well, John had not intended to notice or
to find someone to thank, for if someone wished to be nice to
him, who was he to stop them? No, thanks were no more
appropriate for such actions than gratitude would have been
due to his own mother—after all, were not people like his
mother pleased to do such things, did it not give them a

feeling of pleasure or satisfaction? And yet, the Aryan upbringing in himself brought courtesy to the fore, so that some acknowledgement had to be given.

Yes, this woman was no ordinary person. Like his Mum, she recognised the importance of fussing over him, and John Collins began to like it. Yes, it was good to be John Collins and to receive the attentions of, and dare he hope friendship from, a German once more, albeit not Franz.

John had been no great imbiber of alcohol in his youth, apart, perhaps, for one dream-like day when he and his German friend had consumed too much Guernsey cider for their own good. True, he had accompanied his father and mother on the odd occasion to the Golden Lion, where he had sampled, more out of filial duty than enjoyment, the imported French cider. Before the Occupation, in the days of plenty, before rationing had been invented — well, John had been far too young, a mere boy.

To drink beer, and good German beer at that, had been almost a virgin experience for the young Guernseyman. How often he sat with his new companion (dare he think of her as friend?) watching with frustrated amusement as the German brew was frothed into tankards taking almost ten minutes of topping up and settling before it was ready to pass on to the customer. John found himself almost critical of this Teutonic ritual, and almost permitted himself to jibe at Gerda, his new friend. Yes, it was true, Gerda was his new friend.

The alcohol loosened the tongue too, and neither had to contrive to fill in the feared hiatuses. The two acquaintances slipped into friendship without consciously abetting the process, or aware of how silences could be as comfortable and naturally complete as excited conversation.

Their mid-day breaks became a focus of their working day, and at last John was beginning to feel joy in his life, and to have things to look forward to with anticipation. The more they met and walked and talked together, the quicker the time went.

The walks in the parks were a delight, for here the reminders of the ravages of war were less. Here they need not be reminded that they represented enemies who had each sought to destroy the other. No, here in the parks, scented by the Spring hyacinths or coloured by the haphazard patches of daffodils and tulips and orchestrated by the birdsong, they did not have to see the stark, hollow-eyed skeletons of burnt-out buildings, or listen to the crashing of demolition, as the injured ants scurried round to rebuild their nests. Even the bomb craters had become landscape features, and had grassed themselves over to become exquisite fairytale dells. It was good to sit here and allow time to speed. It was even good, when returning to work, for all the drudgery was being drained out of their lives. Everything was good, life was good.

No, Franz was relegated to John's dreams. Franz was of the past, but Gerda was the present and was real, oh so very real. John Collins was glad that he was truly himself once more, for as much as he liked Franz, he did not really feel he needed to share Gerda with him for Gerda was his alone. Besides, why worry Franz with all these things? Surely, he had enough problems of his own, there in Russia? Franz did not bother to make contact or search for his brother, so why should John bother? Well, not at present anyway, especially not right now.

John responded to the hints of evening liaisons, and between them they managed to find venues for their meetings. What started as a Monday evening walk and visit to a beer cellar, in celebration that the weekend had at last passed and he was with his new friend once more, rapidly extended to the middle of the week and then to Friday evenings because 'they would not see each other for two whole days!'

Before long it was every evening. Gerda would not have gone back to John's flat, not that he would have asked her anyway. She might have refused or declined, then where would he have been? He would have lost his new friend. If she had accepted she might have become more than just a friend. Perhaps that was what she really wanted, what he really wanted? No, he respected her too much to spoil it all that way. Besides, it was up to her to make the moves, she was after all, almost a mother to John, and he knew that all mothers were very experienced in such things. It was therefore her duty to make the first move.

Franz was often not held alive at all. He was not made dead or mourned, he just did not exist, apart from momentary glimpses of conscience, quickly repulsed or repressed subconsciously. It is not possible to hold two absolute thoughts simultaneously, if both are to be treasured.

A new and exciting departure came when Gerda invited John to accompany her, one weekend, to visit her grandparents in Bremen. This was the first time they had spent together not legitimised by work contact. It was good that Gerda had done the asking, for it was, after all, her country, and such behaviour could only be construed as hospitality on her part. John would have been churlish in the extreme to refuse to go with her and protect her as was the manly thing to do.

John had been overawed by the medieval cathedral, grim and grimy stone lace on the outside with its twin green spires, while sparkling like a jewel through its stained windows once inside, darkness and shadowy expanses softened and warmed by the gentle comfort of flickering candles, and sounds muffled and echoed through its vast aisles and myriad chapels. There was a mustiness which reminded him of his youth at incense-cured St. Lukes, but there the comparison ceased, and he permitted himself to feel part of history.

It was very moving that, by some sort of divine coincidence, this great edifice to faith through the centuries had not been destroyed, while all around the streets had been ravaged by the Allies' campaign of revenge.

Here in the cathedral was peace and continuity, while outside was frantic energy pulling down and building up, creating replicas of what had been destroyed and repairing that which had been damaged. Both John and Gerda, although they did not speak, knew that the other was feeling close to the answer to life. They both knew it to be inevitable, as John asked, just as Gerda knew he would. Gerda accepted, just as he was confident she would. Here in the peace of history, surrounded outside by the striving for revival, they pledged each other to become one, the symbolism of enduring continuity inspiring them to similar ideals.

Chapter Fifteen

He sits there, crying. A grown man, crying? A Lorry driver, knight of the road, and here in hospital, tended to by pretty nurses, yet crying!

They have told him he is in shock. What pathetic sort of talk is that? Men like him do not get laid up for something as wimpish as shock!

They say he will be out in a day or two, they need the bed, he's just in for observation.

But what will he go out to? Will he have a lorry to drive? He doubts it. Why does he cry, though? Surely his Company will sort that out, they'll provide another?

No, it's not the lorry, it's not the anxiety of being off the road. He knows, also, he has nothing to fear of the coming court case. Court case? Inquest? That policeman had been very nice, very understanding. He had accepted the lorry driver's word, he felt sure that the other vehicle had disregarded the traffic lights.

No, it is not for personal reasons that this man puts aside his tabloid paper and cries unashamedly. It is not through shock that he forgets the expected role of a British male. The grown man, who should have been chatting-up the nurses, taking advantage of this chance to recharge his store of macho anecdotes to impress his mates later, just sobs, as he recalls the body retrieved from that wreck which had once been a vehicle, which had dared to attack the man's superior craft.

* * *

Well, it happened! The slow preamble to a long courtship led to eventual marriage. The very slowness of progress meant that firm foundations were laid upon which to build a lasting and caring life together. John gained confidence and learned his lessons. In retrospect he realized that it had all been easy, all comfortable and meant to happen.

The marriage was blessed very rapidly with its first child, a boy. Looking back this must have been the start of the eventual rift. John could not, or would not, understand at the time.

During the pregnancy, as with all expectancies, the time came to choose a name. Gerda was reticent about the matter, wishing rather to put if off. John too was relieved, for such searching through the mind for appropriate labels was likely to disturb the relative peace he had felt in recent months. There came a time, however, when Gerda, who was almost a second mother to John, and was about to become a mother in her own right, could shelve the subject no longer.

"John my darling, we have not yet chosen a name for our little light. This we must do, yes?"

John concurred, just wishing Gerda would take her usual initiative so that he could either agree or disagree, so that she could then think again.

"What then, if it is a boy?" she urged cautiously. John was not going to be allowed to abdicate completely from his responsibilities.

"Of course it will be a boy!" he snapped, almost irritably.

"Oh, so you English can arrange such things," Gerda taunted in fun.

Was there not an arrogance in her tone? Did not her taunt possess the ability to stir and bring back half forgotten memories of another Aryan with whom it had been impossible to hold a decent argument?

"Exactly!" John's excitement was complete.

"What do you mean, John? What for you say exactly? What is this exactly?" Franz sounded annoyed now for he was not sure if John was making fun of him or if he was being genuinely critical of the Germans.

"They said," announced John, with laborious patience, "that Germany had conquered Britain and their soldiers were in London playing their stupid Jerry music. Now do you understand?"

111

Franz was puzzled.

"But that is silly, John, you know it is. You know we have not won this war yet. We are still fighting your English people."

"That's what I said," was John's exasperated response, "and not so much of this, 'when we've won this bloody war' business, O.K.?"

"John, I think sometimes you are a very silly boy, yes?" replied Franz. "You say such strange things that I do not know if you have much sense!" He was not really angry but more petulant and puzzled.

"Come off it! It's not me who's silly. You're the one. You just don't have enough sense to see what I'm telling you."

"I don't care," replied Franz. "I don't want to talk any more about it. . ."

"Oh yes, I get it," cut in John, a voice exaggerated with sarcasm. "You always say that when you're losing an argument, eh?"

"No."

"Yes!"

"No!"

"Oh shut up, you stupid bugger! You argue like a little kid."

"O.K., then, it is a boy. What is his name?" She sat back waiting in anticipation.

"You decide, Gerda," prompted John, anxious to change the subject, for he felt disturbed. "You've always got lots of ideas."

Gerda laughed. She had expected this.

"Very well, then. Do you wish your son, or may I be permitted to call him 'our son', to be given a German name or an English name?" A smile was carried on her words. "Or perhaps a, how would you say, Guernseyish name?"

John was shocked into participation.

"He must be given a German name," he insisted. His words sounded very definite, very full of finality.

Gerda was surprised but she took it as a compliment.

"Very well, then. Now what name would you Englishman think is right for a German; and please don't say Hans!"

She laughed, but it seemed that the joy in her voice was stifled, as her humour met with no reciprocation from her beloved. On the contrary, John's face darkened; Gerda sensed that he had left her.

'Englishman? I'm not an Englishman, I'm Guernsey.' This needed explanation. Hans? 'What's his name, this German? Hans or something?' No, not Hans, Franz. No, not Franz, Hans. What was this? This was all very familiar. His own father had recounted this conversation once long ago.

"Yes, I know the prison." Franz turned away again.

Larry realised now that, by some contrivance of coincidence, this young lad, this first German he had ever considered human, was in fact his son's friend. What the hell was the boy's name, Hans or something?

"Have a good time, then," and as an after thought, "What's your name, by the way?"

"Müller, Sir."

"Müller, eh? I suppose your first name is Hans?"

"Hans? No my name in Franz."

'That's it!' thought Larry, 'Franz Müller.'

'You're not going out with that German!' his mother was saying. 'You'll be the death of your poor father!'

"He's not that German! He is a German, he is my friend! Not that German, not a bloody German. Don't you understand? He's my friend! Franz is my friend!"

"Sorry?" Gerda was taken aback. "What is this Franz? You wish our son to be called Franz?"

John was pricked back to full consciousness. Did he detect a slight cooling in the atmosphere? Was his mother displeased and yet making great effort for it not to show, so that the aura of displeasure was still greater? Pricked too was his guilt, for he had forgotten Franz. No, worse still, he had actively hidden him from thought. He had sold his friend cheap, he had almost allowed him to be edited from his existence for the sake of a new friend, to please his mother.

So, this temporary pause, the respite from feelings of guilt at having forgotten his friend, was removed and John Collins was exercised once more with conscious and subconscious misgivings.

Chapter Sixteen

Still shielded from the truth, unable to accept what she has been told, old Frances sits there calmly, knowing that her boy will recover. It is only a question of time.

The doctor has told Frances, and Gerda has reiterated it, but the poor old lady has not been able to take in such news, not yet.

So for Gerda, John's wife and friend, it is doubly hard, for now she has to grieve alone as prelude to mourning, but she still has to keep a cheerful facade for Frances' sake. She so needs to share her turmoil with someone, but there is no-one who would understand.

If only Little Franz were here, if only he would be quick, in time to see Papa before it is too late!

*   *   *

Gerda was very patient as John's nightmares were forced on to her. Yes, she felt she knew of Franz Müller, despite John's trying to keep him from her. Who could but know, when his memory rocked and disturbed her night time peace, while her loved one writhed in his secret torment beside her?

All Gerda was permitted to know were the signs of John's nocturnal torment. She was not able to experience the terrible guilt and desertion dreamed by her man, night after night, as he wrestled with the knowledge that it was he who had condemned Franz to the horrors of the Eastern Front. No, all she felt was his restlessness, his tossing and turning and his crying out. Not for Gerda the pictures of re-living and holding alive, followed by the death and misery, the worst her darling could invent.

But it was Gerda who had to soothe and reassure, to say that all was all right really, that her dear man had just had

114

one of his recurring nightmares. Gerda was the one always there to mop the soaking brow and to talk to John, just as any mother would, to a sick child. She it was who would repeat that it had all been a bad dream and she it was who would cuddle him back to sleep, the father of her child. And all the time, as she gently eased her husband back to normality, she felt rejected and left out while John would not share his deepest anxieties with her.

No, for Gerda it had to be just the shout or the push, the shudders and the whimpering, the tangled sheets and the cold cold sweat of the one who lay next to her, with the unintelligible streams of words just occasionally recognizable with the title 'Franz'. John could not share it with this, his newest friend, the mother of his child, his own new mother, for she would not have understood, any more than his other friends could have understood all those years previously.

Was he destined for eternity to feel the guilt of what he had recklessly and unwittingly caused to happen to his enemy friend? Was that to be, just as forever he was to be burdened with the imagined reproach from the friends of his school days? The one would reproach him for not doing enough to save friendship, the others for doing too much, thereby giving comfort to the enemy.

Why had he stopped thinking of them all, once Franz had become his friend? Did it make him a traitor, a quisling, a collaborator or a Jerry-bag? What would he tell them all after the war? Would they understand?

'Hello Vernon, how did you get on in England, eh?'

'Me? Oh, I stayed here and faced the Germans me!'

'What's happened to Cooky?'

'Cooky got killed fighting the bastards!'

'And Johnny?'

'They took him prisoner. No-one knows what happened to him.'

'What about you, John? Did you resist, did you give those Jerries a rough time?'

'Me? Oh, I learned to hate them.'

'How many telephone wires did you cut at night? How many road signs did you paint over?'

115

'Oh, that's stupid. All it caused was reprisals.'

'Reprisals? What did they do for those?'

'Well they took our wirelesses for a start and sometimes made our fathers stand sentry duty at night.'

'Big deal! Do you know what they did to prisoners who gave obstruction?'

'No, tell me.'

'No you couldn't take it, you like the Jerries too much!'

'That's not true!'

'Where's Brian?'

'He's around but he doesn't want to see you!'

'Why so?'

'He won't meet anyone. He got shot down fighting the buggers. His face is like a melted blancmange he's so badly burned.'

'Beryl? How did she get on? I know she was going to be a nun like Jane . . .'

'She's O.K. now. She went to France you know. The S.S. raped her!'

'Who's this, John? Who's your friend?'

'Oh yes . . ., I'll introduce you. This is my friend Franz. Franz, meet Vernon, we call him the Colonel, and Cooky, Terry to you. This is Egg Head, Allan really and this hyer's Johnny. Here's Brian, and David. Oh yes, and of course you'll want to know who these birds are. Well this is Jane, this one Joan, here's Beryl and this one is June, she's the shy one . . .'

'Wait a minute. Did you say Franz?'

'Eh?'

'Is your mate called Franz? That's a queer name, eh?'

'Why so?'

'Franz, it sounds like Jerry to me, eh, you chaps?'

'Yes, Franz is German, he's my friend . . .'

No, Gerda was the patient and ever-loving wife. She was always there, always ready to soothe, to reassure. She knew that her John was driven by some deep and strong secret trauma, just as she was aware he was not ready to confide in her, to divulge and share the problem.

The good wife and mother learned to cope with John's dark moods and melancholy in their waking hours, as surely as she was at hand in his troubled night-time excursions.

Not only did Gerda, the ever patient, ever loving wife and mother, support her husband during his deep dark moods, but she had to be prepared for his moments of intense enthusiasm, which would take him over just as suddenly as his lethargy and introspection. She could never know when his mood would change from its terrible depths to celestial heights, or plummet once more from heaven to hell, but she remained constant, ever prepared to adapt.

In holidays and at weekends it was never a surprise to find long made plans suddenly dropped and for John to declare that they were off to the countryside to look at farms.

"Come, Gerda. We must take a ride into the countryside. I want to see more of this beautiful country of yours," John insisted. Protests were not in order. No, Little Franz would enjoy it too. Hadn't he enjoyed last weekend? Didn't the little fellow laugh and gurgle with delight as their old car had bumped and rattled along mile after mile of cobbled road? And what about the week before, when they had all watched the farmers and their children lifting the hay with their pitchforks onto the timeless horses and carts? Had that not been fun?

No, Gerda had to love this treat, she could not fail to enjoy the pleasure, week after week after week. Why should she worry about using all their petrol coupons so? When the ration ran out, then would be the time to worry, not now, while the summer lasted and they could all be close to Franz once more. No, John would bring his friend back from Russia, Franz Müller would live again for it was only a matter of time before they would find his farm. How foolish of his mother to look for troubles where there were none! No, John could take the trams to work, the car was for weekends and their journey was into the past.

The sun always shone, the hay and corn fields were permanently golden, Little Franz was always happy and Gerda was resigned. Oh yes, it could have been worse, and perhaps, some day, it might get better? One day her darling might share with her his night time traumas which were leading him to these weekend expeditions.

Over the period, they must have visited every little farmstead within thirty kilometres of Hamburg. So many family farmsteads did they visit, John felt he had known their like all his life. The huge barn constructions, with family quarters dwarfed and enclosed at the road end of the edifices, giving them the appearance of huge tortoises, and in some ways reminiscent of Nazi helmets, became as familiar to John as once had been the solid granite cubes and tiled prisms of the Guernsey farmhouses. These rustic German farms and rural houses with their red brick and red tiles, or rustic thatch, were as much part of him as were the timber-framed houses with their brick in-filling and tiny windows. He knew, when he came to cross-roads at hamlets, where no signs existed to tell which tiny roman road, complete with camber and side ditches, led to which remote forgotten place, that he had always known these places. John, in the timelessness of such places, untouched by the wars of modern times, knew that he had come home; Franz had returned.

But, of course, with Franz now by his side, John Collins too thought of that far off place in location and time. Had they not, long ago, experienced another farm?

Passing the cows Franz suddenly left the path and made his way to the nearest herbivore

"Come, town boy. Let's have something to drink."

"Eh?" asked John.

"I suppose you town boys don't know that milk comes from cows?"

"Of course I do," proclaimed John.

"Have you ever milked a cow?" asked Franz.

"No."

"Then you must have your first lesson."

"What do you mean?" asked John, thinking he knew what Franz had in mind, but hoping he was wrong.

"Well, we'll milk this cow."

"No," said John, "You can't."

"Why not?"

"Because. . . ." replied John.

"Because, what?"

"Well, the farmer," said John, feeling decidedly uncomfortable at

the prospect of the transgression. "Besides, you've nothing to put it in and it is a terrible waste."

"We don't need anything to put the milk in," explained Franz. "We can squirt it straight into our mouths."

"Ugh, No!"

"Why? You silly town boy."

"Well, it's unhygienic."

"What is this 'unhygienic'?"

"It's not clean, it's dirty!"

Franz laughed. "It is not dirty. All the milk you drink comes this way, doesn't it?"

"I know," said John still wishing himself anywhere but there, "but . ."

"Come, John, quick, come here please," interrupted Franz, as he knelt by the placid animal who seemed quite unperturbed by all the attention being paid to her. John reluctantly stepped forward whilst pondering how best to protest.

Franz touched the cow's udder so that she turned her neck and looked towards him, licking her lips as though with pleasure. As he took one of her teets deftly in his fingers, she let out a lazy moo. John was looking around guiltily, seeking the appearance of an angry farmer who would surely come running at the sound of the lowing.

"There!" exclaimed Franz with satisfaction. As Franz let out the word John felt the noise, rather than heard it, as he looked down to see his friend skilfully directing a tiny but powerful white jet on to his mud splattered boots. "There John, that your boots will polish for you."

Had there not been sadness then, and insecurity as to where it would all end? But now, that was replaced with hope and expectation. The war had ended and no-one had really lost or won. It had all come true what Franz had said, Britain and Germany had united, and now were brothers.

"I wish this damn war would come to an end," said John.

"So do I," agreed Franz, "but what end will it be?"

"Well, that's funny, coming from you!" exclaimed John in surprise. "I thought you Germans expect to win this war before the end of this year."

"This is true, John, but what then?"

"I just don't know," said John. "I really dread to think."

"Tell me one thing, John, whoever wins this war, will we still be friends?"

"I don't see why not, do you? If we can manage to be friends while we're really enemies, why shouldn't we manage it in peace time, eh?"

Yes, at times like these, while visiting farms, John felt close to his friend. One of these, he knew, would one day be discovered to be Franz's very own. It was good for John to feel so close to the friend he had lost, so good that he was almost lost to his newest friend. Gerda, the ever patient, ever indulgent, was almost disregarded, nearly forgotten, during these excursions, but she was uncomplaining.

This long-suffering wife played her part and supported her man, even though he was not yet ready to share his other friend with her. All she knew was, it was that same name, Franz, Franz Müller, which was repeated again and again at the Inns and villages, that same name which she heard mouthed by John in his nightmares.

It is always easier to talk with or to ask questions of strangers when sitting at a bar, particularly a German bar in some ancient and welcoming Inn. Where normally a person, through his nervousness or shyness or the fact that he was an English speaker, might withdraw or remain introverted, not so in such surroundings. Once the froth had settled and the cool liquid was being imbibed, while the next tankard was already being prepared, inhibitions would lessen.

Those who might at first have been seen as suspicious of strangers or exclusive only to their own kith and kin, would take on friendly aspects.

John found this experience repeatedly as potential protagonists transformed to friends and companions. Gerda too, with Little Franz on her knee, could not fail to warm to the friendly conversations and well-meaning intentions of these gentle and generous rural folk, who were prepared to let the former animosities of war be relegated and turned into lessons of vocabulary for the two respective languages.

Beer would be followed by throat-burning schnapps, and

that in turn would require more ale to cool and quench the thirst, which would remain as complementary to the good comradeship.

It was then, once all were merry around her and she kept the discipline of a clear head, ready to drive her man and her little son home to their beds, that Gerda would hear the name. It was then that Franz Müller was almost shared with her, as John quizzed those around him for news.

Myriad Müllers there were, but nowhere was the name Franz among them.

Chapter Seventeen

He pays the taxi driver. He thinks he has given too large a tip for such a short journey, but why does he bother himself with such trivial thoughts? It is almost as though he is indulging himself in such pointless musings to put off having to face the very seriousness of his mission.

The young man is tired, he has travelled most of the night. From the moment of receiving that awful 'phone call, the hurried packing of his small travel bag, the frantic rush to the airport and then the train, the young German has thought of nothing but to reach his father's bedside in time. He has to be there to be with Papa. He has to be in time to share the awfulness with Mama and Grandmama.

* * *

Following his sessions of searching German farms, John went through a period of relative stability. To all intents and purposes, John's search had been without success, but it had left him with a personal sense of well-being that he had been in some secret communion with his friend while so doing. This period of calm was, of course, greatly assisted and induced by the growing personality of his infant son.

Yes, Herr Collins was a good father, and his little boy was in good hands. When John was with the infant Franz, he felt young again. He experienced the blessing of the temporary falling away of life's cares, as the child responded to his love. When John was with Little Franz, he was truly John Collins, and confusion was kept at bay. As he dandled the infant and played cars with him or built thrilling toy brick edifices, set out his clockwork Hornby set in imaginative layouts or read to him from his favourite Rupert stories, he could no more confuse the little one with his long-missing friend of the same name, than mistake his darling Gerda, mother of their only child, with his own mother Frances.

The family was truly one and, with the absence of the long-missed friend, the night time disturbances too began to be less frequent. If a graph had been plotted, Gerda would clearly have equated happy days with peaceful nights. It was good for John also to realize that here, at home with his wife and son, he could be himself. Yes, John enjoyed being John for great stretches of time, for he no longer had to contemplate returning east, to who he knew not what. He was so glad he was not Franz Müller now, but could stay with Gerda and their Little Franz.

So, for quite a while, the sense of search and urgency went out of their lives. John no longer felt driven to move on, to search, but was able to stay still, to savour each passing moment, enjoying it for its own sake.

There were lapses, of course, well, certainly lapses into the past, but more the inward felt emotions, and not shared with his family or burdening them, for often they were fleeting moments, sometimes so short that John could not even hold them in his consciousness long enough to stimulate a memory, but they just left him with an impression which might colour his mood for a while, just as the forgotten dream can still influence the dreamer with a feeling of well-being, whilst going about his waking chores.

These regressions did not concern his friend or his former self, as when he had previously confused himself with that same Franz. No, often they would be triggered by his little son, who reminded him of Patrick as that little one had grown and then, through failing health had died so tragically.

"Papa, will you tell me the story about little Red Riding Hood?" pleaded Little Franz.

"Eh?"

Papa seemed a bit absent minded.

"John, my love, were you falling asleep?" asked Gerda kindly, almost amused at the thought. "Little Franz wants his favourite story again."

Gerda laughed. She had a seductive laugh which almost coughed out, when her voice hoarsened in this way. John always responded to her when she was like this.

"Go on, John dear," said Anne. "Please tell Patrick a story. He says he won't go to sleep until his Uncle has done so." She smiled weakly, imploringly almost. She had a lot to be grateful for to this youth. She knew he would do what was necessary.

"Yes, yes of course I will," replied the good uncle. "Come on, Patrick, do up your dressing gown now and you can sit on my knee."

"Patrick?" Gerda looked puzzled, "What do you mean, my love?"

"Come on, Patrick, come to Uncle John, I'm ready."

Little Franz turned to his mother. He was confused, but Mama would clear the matter up. Mama would know why Papa was saying such silly things, for it must be all part of the story he was about to enjoy.

This was new. Gerda had not heard this name before. She had to know, she needed to find out, if only for the sake of their little child. To her surprise, John was ready to tell her all, as in the telling the years slipped away and she was allowed to share the tragedy of little Patrick's untimely death.

Involvement with Patrick, yes, but still not for her to be included with Franz. John was not yet ready to share his friend with anyone, but there was no rush, Gerda was ever-patient.

Well, whatever that other secret was which was kept from her by her darling man it did not matter, for John was so much better now. With the devotion of his loving wife and his interest in Little Franz, John's daytime depressions lessened, and even the night time excursions, which occasionally happened, would take on a happier aspect.

"Pardon, love," Gerda muttered, as she pulled herself out of sleep. "What did you say?"

As she accustomed herself to the dark, Gerda realised that it was just a dream. Well, what she was experiencing was real enough, but John was not in conversation with her, he was the one dreaming.

She listened. No, her darling was in deep sleep, the bedclothes were not disturbed. She gently touched his brow.

No, he was cool and very still, this was not her husband in nightmare torment. She must just have imagined his voice had broken into her peace.

"Let's put you to the test then, eh?" It was John. Well, perhaps it had all started again? Perhaps it would only be a matter of seconds before he was writhing and twitching and his body would become soaked with sweat. Gerda hoped not, but she was resigned. She hoped not, for such night-time sessions had become so rare of late, but if it had to be, then so be it.

She waited.

"Right then, say after me, 'God Save the King!'"

"Say it, say it, I tell you." His voice was very insistent, but he was smiling.

Then the dear man beside her subsided into peace once more, as with a deep sigh his slumbers returned.

There was no need to ask, not yet. Still John kept his private friend, still Gerda was not permitted to share, but she did not feel threatened by this. Yes, she might at present be excluded, but one day she knew she too would be permitted to know that other person. Besides, her darling was so much happier now, she was not totally excluded from his love, witness the joy that Little Franz was soon to have a little sister or brother.

Chapter Eighteen

Flowers? The nurse smiles as she tells the two ladies that all
ladies like flowers. These can only give comfort.

But why flowers? Who has sent them flowers?

Old Frances knows; yes, they must be wedding flowers.
That's it, flowers from a wedding, a bouquet. John's new
bride has sent her own flowers to her new Mum.

Flowers? Gerda frowns. She is not aware she is frowning.
The nurse goes to take the bouquet, to find water. She does
not need to speak.

Wait! Who has sent us flowers? Gerda has to know. Is it
their friend perhaps? Is it their good neighbour who has
rushed them to the hospital?

Why flowers, though? Are they celebrating?

Have they come from Little Franz? No, surely he will be
here, he would not just send flowers, Little Franz must come.

The flowers, they must be a wreath! From whom, though,
has this ghastly symbolism come?

*   *   *

Occasionally John made contact with his parents in Guernsey.
His mother was in the habit of writing and once in a while,
encouraged by Gerda, he would pen a reply. The tone of his
mother's news was that of drudgery. He sensed an edge of
misery, tragedy almost. The purchase of 12, Rue Marguerite
had gone ahead and the building was now a thriving Guest
House with Larry continuing at the shop, which had
expanded, so that it now boasted two fellow-workers.

Frances' tone was recriminatory in that John, who had
married without their knowledge had not yet taken his new
wife to visit them, let alone their only grandchild. She had,
however, other trauma in her life, for Uncle Bert, who had

gone into the Guest House venture with them, had also married again.

It seemed that after the Occupation, when all parties came to be reunited, his wife, who had spent five years as an evacuée and had not even been searched for by Bert after his repatriation, had found another man. Frances, although she did not actively put it into words, had felt some relief at this, but had then been doubly shocked and hurt to learn that Bert too had found a new partner when he had been in England. Once he was ensconced in the Guest House he had made arrangements for her to join him. But that was all in the past, and Frances was, after all, in her fifties now and by rights should not be affected by such youthful feelings.

She remembered, soon after they had undressed in the dark and he had begun stroking her sides and brushing his hands up under her breasts pulling them apart, as if revelling in their firmness, and then brushing them gently towards the nipples which stood out firm like buds of sensitivity, how she had longed for him to enter her. She had not asked for all that stroking and fondling. She had wanted him right inside her. She had wanted once more that throbbing and pulsing. She had wanted to groan and cry out and to feel his increased ardour with each moan that signified her pain and pleasure were playing with each other, sometimes rough and sometimes gentle.

Frances threatened that she and Larry would come to Germany to visit the family if the family would not come to them. This was to have taken place one quiet winter period when Frances would have no visitors to look after. John disregarded it and two winters passed without the plan coming to fruition.

Towards the end of the Summer, in which Gerda and John delighted in the news of their second fertility, they received another of Frances' letters. It was the usual catalogue of gossip, slight recrimination, over-work, with a few fresh pieces of information. A sort of matter-of-fact duty letter a mother

127

writes to a son who rarely replies and has not had sufficient concern to visit his parents for the greater part of a decade.

Larry was giving up the shop. It was too much for him as his health was not its best; three years in the grim French prison had taken their toll. Uncle Bert was now a father, at his age! Couldn't he face up to the fact that he was well into middle age? Why do such men fancy themselves so? Frances could not see what possible attraction he had been to and sustained for that English woman so much younger than he!

Then almost as an afterthought, an aside even, she casually mentioned in passing.

> . . . 'Do you remember that friend of yours, Franz? Well, a strange thing the other day. I was out at the time, but Mrs. de Garis who cleans for me said a German woman and her family called, asking after Franz. Wasn't that strange after all these years? I thought he must be dead and gone. Anyway they never did come back so I can't tell you more than that.' . . . .

That did it! There was no holding back anymore, either conscious or involuntary, not from himself, not for his wife. Franz was real. He really had existed, someone else was witness to that!

Gerda was acquainted with the whole story amidst urgent telephone calls, letter writing, travel arrangements and requests for leave. In no time at all a frantic and yet revitalized John was on his way with expectant wife and son to his homeland, to his mother, to the place where Franz was still real.

It was not until they got to Guernsey to meet his parents, who had aged though his memory had kept them still young, that Gerda found opportunity to pledge herself to her husband's dream and to declare that if only he had told her from the outset she could have been helping him in his quest all these years. John was hardly aware of his wife's generosity of spirit and, as with his brusque and apparently feelingless dealings with his parents, was almost oblivious to her presence and support, so urgent was his search.

Mrs de Garis, foolish woman that she was, had not taken any information about the German enquirer. She did not know the woman's name, where she had been staying, what her interest had been in Franz or even where she came from. All she could recall was that the woman had been young, about Gerda's age. Well, that made some sense anyway, and if Mrs. de Garis was correct, it would have made her Franz's elder sister.

What could it mean? Did it mean that his family too had no trace of Franz and were also trying still to seek his whereabouts? Surely that was a bad sign? It was difficult enough to accept that his own exhaustive searches and enquiries with relevant authorities had led John nowhere, but for his own kin to have had similar lack of success indeed boded ill. Perhaps, worse, they did have definitive news of Franz's fate and now, after such a lapse of time, were just trying to find out where he had spent his last months of happiness. Maybe they had only come out of a sense of nostalgia? No, it could not be that bad!

Gerda remained calm and rational. Now that she was involved, she was able to take control.

Of course, Gerda had not met her in-laws, and those people too had yet to come to terms with their new status of Grandparents.

It was not always easy for this Aryan lady to come into a home which still harboured such hatred for her race, where at times the very bitterness which had exuded from Larry Collins seemed to come out of the very walls at her.

Frances took straight away to her new daughter, and within minutes of meeting, Gerda had to call the good matron 'Mum'. After all, any friend of John's had to be a friend of hers, and this German girl represented the ultimate in friendship, for had not she and her boy created the greatest gift she and Larry could ever expect to receive, a little grandson of their very own?

At first, Larry kept well clear of his son, for had he not been a Jerry lover? Larry was bitter; each time his bouts of coughing took his breath away and he remembered his cold, damp, non-existence in France, he loathed his son for the way his selfishness had brought about his misfortune.

Perhaps it was fortunate that John was so taken up with his

129

quest to track down whoever it was who had been enquiring after his friend, that he did not perceive the animosity of his father. No, to John, Dad just seemed quieter than he remembered him from the days of his youth, but then, of course, he was not a young man any more.

And so there were no sparks to ignite the long-stored tinder which might have caused a holocaust that would then have destroyed them all.

Besides, even Larry, bitter angry Larry, so wronged by having to have a German in his very house, could not help but warm to Little Franz, his very own grandson. At times the man could almost forget the child was German, and thereby tainted. Had he not once felt such similar feelings, and was there not a coincidence of feelings and names?

"What do you want?" asked Larry.

"I wish a bicycle to buy."

"A what!" mouthed Larry incredulously, as bicycles were currently said to be 'worth their weight in gold'.

"A bicycle. I wish to buy a bicycle. This is a bicycle shop, no?"

"No . . . I mean yes. You can't buy a bicycle, mate. We haven't got any bikes for sale."

"But this is a bicycle shop. I have money. I can pay."

"That's not the point, my son. We have none for sale."

"This is very stupid," replied Franz, in frustration. "How then do you make a living with no bicycles in a bicycle shop?"

"Look, young lad, we've got no bikes for sale because there's a bloody war on and we can't get any supplies. Do you understand?"

"Yes," replied Franz, subdued at the realisation of his own silliness.

Larry was now fully wound up and decided to follow with another statement.

"We still have to repair those we've got though, haven't we? British bikes do wear out, we're not perfect like Germans, you know."

"I know," replied Franz, "but even our bicycles wear out."

Larry could not suppress his amusement at this.

Franz could not understand why Larry smiled to himself, but took it as a good sign, making himself laugh too.

"Well, Sir, I understand you but have you just a bicycle I could use for one day, for tomorrow?"

"Look, I'm not in the hire trade, lad," said Larry with a shrug.

"Even if I wanted to help you, I've nothing to help you with. I've only got my own bike and that's too precious to part with."

"I pay you well."

"What's pay? You couldn't get me another bike if anything happened to mine could you?"

"But nothing happen. Please trust me, Mr. Collins," pleaded Franz.

They calculated the dates of the visit and then, using the States of Guernsey Tourist Board's not inconsiderable list of hotels and guest houses, set about checking every one. Their task was not to be helped by the fact that in all likelihood Franz's sister Ilsa, now a mother, would have changed her name from Müller to that of her husband. This was, however, compensated for by the fact that few Germans were yet in the habit of visiting the islands. It was only to be hoped that Ilsa had at least married a German and that he was one possessing a distinctive German surname.

They split the task between them so that each travelled alone to the addresses listed. This was partly Gerda's plan to halve the work and partly John's insistence, for he was not prepared to explore the Island with any German except his lost Franz or at least Franz's memory.

Between them, as they wended their way down the narrow road they effected a compromise using neither right nor left but settling for the centre.

Both dismounted on the steep hills and there was much back-slapping and pushing. They seemed to have the whole island to themselves.

What fun it was, trying to force each other's bicycle into the hedge. How hilarious, when they splashed through the puddles of a bankside spring which had trespassed onto the roadway.

How they laughed and screamed when coming suddenly upon some old and rustic farm yard which seemed to become part of the road itself, they were taken by surprise and forced to ride through a mire of cow dung. All over John's trousers it splashed. Franz was laughing so much his front wheel skidded and he had to save himself with his foot which sank beneath the sludge. To make matters worse he dismounted and then, clown like, plodded his way to the side of the road. John could not go on. He lay prostrate against the grassy bank and howled in mirth at his friend's discomfort. Franz, at first concerned at the state of his boots, looked terribly worried but then he reasoned the day was too special to hold anxiety. And 18.00 patrol line-up was years away. He too joined in the hilarity and threw himself down next to his friend.

John had been brushing his trousers then, without thinking, wiped the tears from his eyes. His face now looked like that of a commando. Franz pointed to it unable to speak for his guffaws.

"Eh?" asked John in the familiar diction he reserved only for family and close friends.

"Your face, John, look at your face!"

"What about it?" asked John, rubbing it and making it worse, much to Franz's amusement.

"Schizer! Shit face!"

"Eh?" said John, looking down at his hands and at last realising the reason for Franz's reaction.

"Oh hell! Have I got that bloody boozette all over my face?"

"Yes, John. Oh she won't kiss you tonight!" and with that Franz once more lost control of his sanity.

Gerda was the successful one, for she came across the hotel where the family had been staying. She was even delighted to be able to come away with their address.

Gerda could never be quite sure why, but she kept this information hidden from her husband. She had not intended to be devious at first, and had been waiting her moment to pass on the news, but that moment had not offered itself, and the longer the delay in recounting, the greater the feeling of guilt she felt.

Was it perhaps that she feared this news might tip the uneasy equilibrium they were now experiencing? Maybe the information would be bad, or so inconclusive that John would slip back into his former depressions. Did she dread the possibility of the nocturnal traumas? Was it that she could not face yet another hurried rush away and frantic search in Germany? Perhaps she was too happy here, too settled with her new mum and with her father-in-law daily warming towards them, thanks to Little Franz. Such upheavals were not good to contemplate, especially in her present state. Or was it just that, subconsciously, she was not prepared to share her man again, not now that things were so good between them? Instead she went along with the charade of looking each day until they had exhausted all possibilities.

John even advertised in the *Press*. It was with trepidation that Gerda waited for a possible answer for not only would it have imbued her with guilty deceit in John's eyes but would also have prevented the seeds of an idea which she wished to carry out on return to Germany.

It took great fortitude to keep the independence of her ideas from her husband, especially when his lack of success seemed to be bringing back a return of his depression and inertia. She was, however, determined that her course was for his eventual benefit.

And so Gerda had stuck to her plan, for she would personally and secretly continue John's search for him. If it led to nothing, then his hopes would not have to be dashed. In this way, Gerda felt her deceit was justified, and took on the aspect of a white lie. She was doing it for him and for Little Franz, and, she had to admit, for herself, for them, for their marriage. If she gathered positive information about the missing friend . . . well, she would have to face that when it happened.

Chapter Nineteen

Gerda cries. She is not crying for John, she does not let her anguish show. She cannot, not yet, anyway. Why does she cry? Is it relief, is it the joy that Little Franz has come, that he too can share and enjoy this celebration of death?

Frances seems unaware that her grandson has arrived, as she remains seated next to John, holding his chill hand. She is unaware, detached, all her thoughts willing her boy to get better. She wants him out of hospital as soon as possible.

Gerda's vision is distorted by her tears. She sees Frances and John as though far off, a jigsaw puzzle of pieces, their scale mixed by the watery refraction and not fitting properly together. Little Franz comforts his mother. It was kind of the lorry driver to have sent flowers, even though it was he who has murdered Papa. It is good for Gerda to cry, whatever the reason.

* * *

On returning home to Germany, John's behaviour became so grim and Gerda, who contrasted it with his recent, albeit temporary, respite occasioned by hope, decided that she must quickly sort out and enact her plan using the information which only she held.

Gerda agonised at the prospect of leaving her man so, while he was in such a state, but she knew that it was for his good, for their mutual well-being. She felt really dreadful at the prospect of lying to her poor depressed man, but she felt compelled to do so in order to excuse her proposed absence.

John accepted Gerda's excuse for leaving him for the few days it would be necessary to search out Franz's sister. It seemed almost that he did not care.

Franz's sister Ilsa was found without difficulty. She was

pleased to welcome Gerda into their home. They quickly exchanged information so that before long these two complete strangers felt they knew each other really well.

As in one of John's conjectures, Ilsa had reached the conclusion that younger brother Franz had gone missing without trace whilst on active service in Russia in the winter of 1942. She and her husband had gone to Guernsey as an act of remembrance and in completion of her elderly mother's pleadings.

Even as she spoke with Gerda, Ilsa felt the shock-still coldness of the loss of her brother, that same chill cold that had gripped the whole of Europe those many years previously, when she and her mother had received the stark information that Franz Müller was missing in action, missing without trace.

The starkness of the message, months out of date from the event it conveyed, had combined with the desolation of winter and the fear in their hearts, and had frozen it for ever in the young girl's mind. Even now it still had the capacity to chill her, as she remembered her mother's shrill cry of anguish and her tearless eyes;

"My God, My God! First Paul in Poland, and now my little Franz!"

Germany had taken and used both Ilsa's father and her brother and had given them nothing in return.

They had enquired and tried to reach comrades for news and confirmation, for it is difficult to mourn if there are no remains. Perhaps for Papa it might have been possible to exist with the emptiness, for he had gone with glory, as the Fatherland had been expanding and consolidating in victory, but with little Franz, he had been taken from them at the start of their country's shame, as the first defeats and retreats had been ceded.

Authority had not wished to assist them. Perhaps it was policy not to acknowledge that so many were missing? Possibly Ilsa and her mother were being unpatriotic by enquiring? It might be that it was their duty to suppress their feelings and not to cause embarrassment to the Führer in this way?

Ilsa's eyes brimmed with tears as the intervening decade fell away, unreal like the icicle it represented.

"We never did learn of his end, you know . . ."

Gerda hugged her. She understood.

"Not one of his friends could we trace, it was as though he had no friends. . ."

Gerda knew better, but she kept her counsel.

"It could be that all his comrades also died. . ."

"Perhaps," said her new friend. "Will we ever know, I wonder?"

Franz's mother had never really accepted that her son was dead. It could be that he was just a prisoner now in Russia. Well, perhaps not a prisoner, perhaps just a communist working for the Bolsheviks now that the war was ended. She even wondered if he had been repatriated to the enslaved eastern part of Germany. Yes, she felt sure that must be the case. Mothers have feelings about such things. She knew her Franz was still alive somewhere, even if it was in the G.D.R. and so lost to his family for ever. One day though, one day . . .

Ilsa and her husband had gone to Guernsey, more to placate her mother's pleadings than to discover any hope. Well, one thing had come out of it, for Gerda had been found as a consequence. Both women now knew that Franz had at least had a friend. And so, some could now mourn with more peace while others would still search with hope, however misplaced.

Gerda was pleased she had kept her discovery from John for the evidence seemed so irrefutable that his friend had met a wintry end without trace that she was sure the knowledge would have destroyed him at that particular time.

On her return home Gerda found John still in deep depression. She found her guilt at having left him so and of carrying the burden of the secret, which she would surely have to let out piece by piece, almost as great as the fact that he neither seemed to have missed her nor to be pleased to welcome her back. He neither queried her absence nor her return. She seemed not to exist in his eyes.

It was in this unloving and unendurable atmosphere that Gerda had her miscarriage, losing their second child. John did not appear to notice, so unconcerned did he seem.

"I don't understand you!" she cried out.

She understood all right. Oh yes, she knew what it was like for him. Was it not the same for her in her misery? She felt so hurt, so damaged. Part of her had just died. To know this, the death of their unborn child, who had been the creation of her man and herself, just emphasised their own falling apart.

Gerda knew now what it was to exist, timeless in this living death. She knew that in this instant of her suffering, she was to be trapped for ever, while observing the passage of present and future all around her yet unattainable, as though she were solidified, destined only to watch and not to partake.

In her misery Gerda was at one with John, and yet they could not share. If only he were able to comfort her, if only to share her misery, which was theirs. But no, so trapped was he in his own deep gloom that he could think only of himself, and dwell only on his own misery. It was not malicious or deliberate, but just part of the cross each had to bear.

"I've lost my child, our child!" she shouted, her voice pitched near to hysterical desperation. "Our little girl is dead, but you don't care! She was alive, she was part of us, but you do not care! God in heaven!"

John heard her; he knew what she was saying. He heard and he knew, but he was incapable of responding. When a person is at his lowest depths, how can he appear to sink lower? How can more distress have the capacity to move or hurt? It can only smother and cover even more the need to reach out and communicate.

It was too much to bear for Gerda. Her anger had fired her and, just momentarily, had dispelled her introversion. She needed to react to that which was stifling her, she needed to use the energy which had been created by her outburst. Gerda had to shake her man from his self-centredness just as surely as she felt the need to take him physically and shake him by the throat. She had to hurt. Yes, Gerda, in this brief instant, had to hurt as she was being hurt.

"She's as dead as your precious Franz!"

"Eh?"

"Franz died in Russia in the winter of 1942!" she shouted, almost gleefully.

Just as she had been, John too was pricked into life, just momentarily.

"What you say?" he enquired, slipping back two decades into the diction of his Guernsey childhood, while his face enlivened and his senses electrified as though he had never been absent.

Gerda poured out her gospel of despair as John, aghast, had no way of stopping her. On and on came the cruel words as each cut caused the one she loved so much pain, while for her they were the gift of exhilaration, albeit temporary.

This was not true! What she was telling him had no substance! The woman was mad! How could his best friend have married such an insane woman? Why had John Collins bothered with this evil person? Why had he spent so much energy to achieve so little? Why had he not continued his search and brought him back from Russia, to Guernsey, where they both belonged?

It was fortunate that Franz had returned at this very moment, or the deranged woman might have turned John completely against him. Franz had to stop her saying these terrible things, if only for John's sake.

The young Teuton, arm upraised, stepped towards the object of his loathing.

He knew, from his own experiences, how brute force could be stronger than argument.

How he would enjoy himself! Caring not that Franz was accompanied by that little rat of a stubborn civilian boy, the one probably who had put Franz against him in the first place, in view of the sentry he proceeded. Morten, in his roused and belligerent state, could not temper his mood with moderation.

"Little scum!" he shouted as his forearm hit Franz across the side of the jaw, the meaning of the words lost on John but not their ferocity, and the sickening sound of flesh upon flesh.

Franz staggered under the blow, crying out as he clutched towards John. His brother instinctively stepped as a shield between Franz and Morten, cradling the young German's head against further assault.

Chapter Twenty

Little Franz joins the ladies. Now he can keep vigil, for they need their rest. This is not a time for happy reunion, and he almost spurns his mother's greeting, her outstretched arms not taken, her eyes, set to brim with tears, not met. The son, oblivious almost, to anything except his own horror and distress, gives all his attention to that heap which was once his father.

Yes, Little Franz is in time. He has reached his father's bedside before the end. He will do the right and dutiful thing.

* * *

With the rapid deterioration of their marriage which followed, John reverted to his early post-war behaviour before he had met Gerda. He found it easier to steep himself in his work than to face up to the barren desolation of his home. Far better to work on late, where loneliness and guilt would be replaced by absorption in the drudgery of other people's business transactions than to enjoy the chill reproachful company of his wife and son, where he would be reminded of the shortcomings in his responsibilities. John did not need such reminders; he needed to forget his family and to take up once more his true responsibilities and complete his mission.

Added to this distancing of wife and son, or perhaps complementary to it, John Collins began to drink heavily. When he was not at his work, he would find solace in alcohol. Not that he would indulge at home. No, he had to keep away from that place. No, John would seek the consolation of beer cellars and bars where he could forget all that was wrong with his life, and find some company, good companionship which would not accuse him, by not accusing him, and would not

139

reproach him by referring to the shortcomings which he knew they held unspoken in their thoughts.

Far better for John and Franz to spend time together like this, away from the prying curiosity of family, than to take up their family responsibilities. After all, why should boys be expected to take on the cares of the world? Such worries were for grown-ups. This was not their war!

And so, the misery continued interminably, each adult effectively shut off from the other, both suffering in their own way, but unable to open up and allow comfort from each other.

Little Franz started at kindergarten and seemed to be doing well, but reacted to his own father as if he were an unknown intruder. Gerda tried to make allowances. Many times she waited up for John to see to his needs, to try to coax him to eat, to help hold him and their marriage together. Even when things got worse and he stayed out more she often went out to look for him and, once found, brought him home by taxi, such was her love and concern. The more hardened a drinker he became though, the less easily he was persuaded to leave the late night cellars and she was humiliated and abused in front of his acquaintances.

It seemed particularly hard to Gerda that her man, when in the state of drunkenness, would feel a greater loyalty to those around him, than to his own wife. This was especially so when they were merely acquaintances and probably hardly knew him, apart from drinking sessions.

It was bad enough for a woman to be seen in such places, mid-week and after dark, but to have to go into this and that building in her search, a woman alone—well, it just had to be love.

As though that feeling of humiliation, were not enough she felt all the male eyes turned her way, and she heard the muttered comments, or imagined she heard what they were thinking about her. Then to find John buying yet more beer for himself and his comrades was just so awful.

To make matters worse, it seemed to her that John would use his friends to protect himself from her, as though she were some dubious stranger, a wicked person or even an enemy.

"John," her voice was gentle and kind, as though the

140

rebuff which would surely follow could not be further from her mind. "There's a car waiting outside."

"So there is," he would say, edging towards hardly recognisable, sarcasm as his words began to slur and his friends, one by one, turned away, "so there is, my love, so there is."

"John, I've brought a taxi . . .," her voice trailed, she knew what to expect. Oh God, yes, she knew what was coming.

"A taxi, is it? Oh, that's good!" A pause, then, "Why for a taxi, eh? Tell me, why a bloody taxi?"

It was futile to try to explain. It would just be the same old routine. He would declare he was fit to drive his own damned car, (when he was fit and ready!) while she would plead with him to leave it behind and come home with her, if only for Little Franz's sake.

She knew she would end up staying with him while he had just one more. Gerda knew she would have to pretend to enjoy the prospect of 'just one' herself, while all the time knotted up and hopeless inside. She would have to go along with this charade in order to humour her man, while all the time in nightmare of guilt about their little child left all alone.

There was the taxi, too. Should she go and pay the man off and send him away, either to have him call back later, or just to try to order another, once the moment was right? If she took the moment to go and tell the fellow, would John then get more deeply embroiled with his companions? Would it be even harder to take him away?

Oh yes, and he would insist he wanted to drive himself home.

"I'll just have one more for the road, Mine host!"

It seemed he took a sadistic delight in propounding such ideas, just to hear Gerda's anxious protestations.

And then, at last, perhaps after several more nightmarish delays, just as he was standing up, tottering into a stagger, ready to go with his 'Bloody nagging wife,' just as a kind friend, more considerate than his selfish spouse, was fetching his coat for him, he would think of yet another reason for delaying.

It was always a nightmare for Frau Collins. She came to expect that each time she had nearly saved her man, as surely as beer followed schnapps, he would thwart her of her desire, 'just once more.'

What wasted hours she spent talking to John's friends, futile worthless talk, as they would try to draw her into deep philosophical discussions, which she knew they would not hold in their minds once the night had erased all memory of the intercourse! But she had to do it. She knew it was all a waste of effort, but in her depleted state, to bring the nonsense to a close would have required even more effort, and poor Gerda was drained.

If only, poor woman, she had had a mother to turn to, but the only Mum she had was also John's, and so far away that she might as well be unattainable.

And when at last the long-suffering wife would get her man into the taxi, bracing herself for the predictable change of mood from bon homie with his friends, to bitter recrimination at the shame and embarrassment she had caused him by arriving like that, she would know that her troubles had not ended.

Not that John ever hit her again, for that had been a far-off and once only assault. Often Gerda felt physical violence would have been preferable to the relentless, miserable verbal and mental abuse to which she was subjected.

There would be the next morning's remorse when John would feel too ill to contemplate going to work. Yes, Gerda would listen to her dear man's apologies for offences which he could not quite remember, but which he knew he must have caused. She would take in the promises that he would never do it again, always wanting to believe them, but knowing that John was not ready yet to carry out such resolve. Yet she still hoped, she hoped and prayed while inside she still died a little, as their love was stifled a bit more each time such episodes repeated themselves.

After night-time sessions, John was reduced, childlike, to a sobbing wreck. Then he needed his Gerda, he needed her to mother him and tell him that it would be all right again. Those were not the times when she could cut him off or remove him from her life. No, Gerda had to take it completely alone, she had no one with whom to share. Not for Gerda a chance to pour out her misery, but just to listen to John. She was ever there, ever reliable, always predictable but slowly dying inside.

Weakened by the alcohol and bared by his remorse, John Collins, remained unaware that his actions were wholly self-centred and that perhaps it was he who should be listening and comforting, not for ever receiving and taking.

In his sobbing, childlike moments, John would disgorge himself of all the jumbled thoughts which were so hurting and disturbing him. John would almost share his poor lost friend Franz with his new friend Gerda. At times, in his misery, John was almost willing to concede that Franz, at best, had deserted him, had not played fair or kept to their youthful pledge, at worst had died, never to be seen again. Yes, John was almost ready to accept what seemed to be a logical explanation for his friend's prolonged absence. Gerda too was almost ready to try to disavow her darling of his false hope once more. Neither, however, could quite bring each other to wholly bridge that credibility gap.

It was hard for Gerda to share her man with a ghost from the past. It had been difficult when they had been deeply in love, but love had made allowances for the difficulties. Now that love was dying it seemed almost impossible willingly to subjugate her life to two men, one of whom did not exist, and the other directed and driven by the non-existent one.

Predictably, John's work suffered. Where once his efforts were held in high esteem, now moves were afoot for his transfer and return to Britain. Inevitably that day came, just as inevitably the marriage of the two friends was destined to dissolve. It seemed appropriate that, with John's transfer to his mother country, the union should end. It was agreed that they would part company, that John's departure should symbolise that greater break.

So, with the initiation of divorce proceedings, where there was ample evidence to be drawn for neglect and mental cruelty, John added to the demise of the marital state by leaving Germany and deserting Gerda and Little Franz.

Chapter Twenty-one

Someone is not happy. Who is it in this place, so near to John, who must spoil their time together by being miserable?

John knows. It must be Gerda. It must be the one he has deserted, or is perhaps about to leave once more. Possibly she is right to reproach him with her distress, for she has suffered much. She has good reason to be sad. And that son of hers, that Little Franz, is he too, here to recriminate? Has Little Franz come also to fill his father with guilt?

John could open his eyes to check his hypothesis, but no, that would be too much effort. Anyway, why should he bother with them? They are from his past. No, John will not go where he feels only shame and guilt. He will go to Mum. Mum understands, she will put things right.

* * *

Once away from Germany and with more time at his disposal, John's thoughts began to invade him once more. He might successfully have expunged Gerda and Little Franz from his mind, or at least, blocked them out and pushed them away, but now there was more time for other introspection. John Collins, his life seemingly in ruins, was plagued by guilt. But this time he had no one to share with him, no-one on whom to off-load this emotion.

It seemed a very natural progression to return home to Guernsey to his original Mum.

It was easy for Frances to accept her boy's return, for they both needed each other. John needed to be mothered and to feel secure, and the good lady, her youthful energy now gone was glad of some help.

Larry was no longer the man that he had been. Since the last visit to his parents, when John had been too full of his own thoughts and enquiries really to involve himself with his original family, except to accept their hospitality as of right, Larry had aged prematurely. He had been ill and had been forced to give up the shop, helping Frances and Bert with his new wife instead. Yes, Larry Collins too had become part of the team servicing the needs of the ever more demanding Guest House.

Well, Larry was officially part of the team, and it gave him self-respect to feel he was helping with the effort, although rapidly his contribution dwindled, as he spent more and more time confined to bed.

This was the Larry John discovered on his return, a man broken in health and bitter at the reinstatement of a son who had deserted his family and only came home when he was in need.

Larry was sick. Larry was angry inside. Here was this person whom once he had thought of as son, whose very mother had doted on him during his upbringing, and what had he done? He had not been content to ruin his own life, but had devastated the lives of so many others all those years previously, and then, instead of trying to make amends, had disappeared off to England and then to Germany of all places!

He had only returned once, and then only because it had suited his purposes, not in response to any of Frances' pleading requests in all those unanswered letters after the Occupation.

The only good thing the boy had ever done was to produce a child, Little Franz, a child who might have bridged the reconciliation gap between father and son. And now, even that had been taken away. Even that joy had been stolen, and Larry was to be denied the little bit of pleasure which had come into his recent years!

It was little wonder the atmosphere was frosty at first. Perhaps it was a fortunate lesson for John to see that he could have such an effect on the feelings of others. Perhaps now, for the first time in his life, young John became aware that his actions did not limit themselves to only affecting his own life.

In perceiving the need in his own father, John was able to concentrate on giving, and trying to mend the damage. In return, slowly but surely, deteriorating in health as he was,

Larry was able to respond, to support his son who also had problems.

Between them, Frances, Larry and John effected a reconciliation, and between them, with careful nurturing and a willingness for it to succeed, John gradually brought his excessive drinking under control.

It was good that John was there in Guernsey, himself fit and well in body once more, his mental aberrations kept temporarily at bay through his conscientious hard work at the Guest House, when Larry died.

John's prematurely-aged parent passed away, but in the knowledge that once more they were the Collins' family. His death was the culmination of much painful and miserable time in hospital, but his passing was a relief and a blessing, and he departed this life feeling almost complete.

John was able to continue to be a comfort and a support for his mother as she recovered from her grief, but with his own renewed health and the shaking off of the drinking scourge of previous years, he began to be exercised by wanderlust once more.

When John's divorce became absolute he felt a great burden lifted from him, a freedom from the shackles of the past. Despite his mother's and Uncle Bert and new wife's protestations that the business needed him, he was impervious to their reasoning, and any thought of the feelings or sensitivities of others had no place in his emotion.

Aged thirty-nine, John returned to mainland Britain to start a new life for himself.

Chapter Twenty-two

So here he sits; sits and waits. Little Franz has not time yet to feel tired. He must just stay here for as long as it takes.

His hurried journey has welded two days into one, so that his exhaustion is transformed into confusion, as he does his duty.

Papa has not stirred since the two ladies left. Little Franz presumes he is asleep. Well, at least the poor man looks comfortable.

Little Franz now fights his own tiredness. He is glad he got here in time, but it is all so distressing. What did he really expect while he had journeyed through the night? Had he really expected it to be any different? Had he really expected Papa to be as he had last seen him?

Surely he should have anticipated what he now sees, a wreck of a human being, not anything like the dear man of recent years?

No, the person this dutiful son now keeps company with is so changed. He is changed, just as in those days long since past, when he had withdrawn from his only son and deserted his child's mother.

As he sits here, exhausted, and as the past grips his mind, Little Franz senses the awful rejection that, although he has come, his father would have wished he were another. Little Franz knows he is to be relegated to being a Patrick once more, that soon his father will desert once more.

* * *

For several years, John Collins made a very reasonable livelihood as a business representative. He was good at his job and appreciated by the Company he worked for. John enjoyed his work, and by steeping himself in it, avoided having to make friends or needing to acknowledge his conscience for those who might make or think demands of him.

John did not seek advancement, but inevitably it was gradually forced upon him, in recognition of the value he was to his employer. He neither minded nor resisted these accolades, for he had no-one with whom to share his success. John's material needs were few, his emotional needs even less, and he liked it that way.

He was not consciously aware of the fact, but all his advancements led interminably towards some secret aim, which although relegated to the far reaches of his mind, was nevertheless working away at his conscious self.

It was a long time later, after ten years of steady, almost satisfying, work, in which he found himself in a comfortable non-thinking routine of daily and annual life, that his noticeable change of direction, (or was it defining of direction?) came. He had by then a comfortable modern house in a fairly exclusive Hampshire village, near Winchester, a house too large for one person but nevertheless convenient for his work and requiring little attention or maintenance, being newly-constructed.

He treated his home exactly as a dormitory, rarely communicating with his neighbours. He was regular in his habits, leaving early each day and rarely returning before seven in the evening. However, he liked it that way, making no demands on the community and the community unable to make demands of him.

It was shortly after setting up his new home that he noticed in the bulletin of his Company, for which he was now a senior representative, that there was an item inviting applicants to advance themselves, catching his eye and triggering his memories. Despite himself, the notice bothered him for days. He was not in the habit of applying for promotion but this was different for a representative of proven ability was required to undertake a six month tour of duty in Moscow, of all places!

It was a silly idea, of course, and John knew it, for he was far too old to be taken seriously. Besides, he did not speak one word of Russian. Well, he had learned German surely enough, for was he not fluent in that tongue? So why not Russian? No, the thought was preposterous.

But the idea would not go away. No matter where John's daily tasks took him, no matter what meeting he attended or interviews he conducted, whether he was sifting his paper work or dictating to his secretary, that notice would come into his thoughts. It was more a demand than a notice. But no, he was too old. How could a man of forty-eight be expected to give up all his established routines, learn another language, enter into a completely different system and put himself at risk by volunteering to fight in the Cold War? Who would look after his house, too? It was not as if he had wife and family to keep things going while he was away. On the other hand, of course, he had no ties of family and friends either. But no, it was too stupid an idea to be entertained.

Despite the irrefutable logic of not applying for the tour of duty, John could not help continually finding himself walking past that notice-board and stealing furtive glances once more. Each time, he felt a stirring of excitement, an emotion quite foreign to him for oh so long. How was it that a piece of typed paper had such ability to stir?

> *Notice to all members of the civilian population and*
> *forces of the Reich:*
> *The German Command, ...*
> *.... does invite the civilian population*
> *and the military to compete in a water gala ...*

No, middle-aged John Collins felt the stirrings of his youth once more. Day by day, hour by hour, minute by minute, he felt the years dropping away. As he struggled with the ridiculous thoughts and emotions which that bland announcement forced upon him, so did, one by one, all his cares disperse. The cares of his quiet comfortable home and his unknown neighbours went, his time as respectable, reliable, hard-working company representative slipped away, his shameful period in Germany with the wife and child he had almost successfully erased from his mind, came to the fore once more and were as quickly dismissed. John's lonely time spent in England just after the war was eradicated, the miserable shameful period of the cold and hungry siege, and his bleak sojourn in the French prison, were removed, and all to allow him to become himself once more.

John Collins became once more the hurt and lonely John. He was the confused youth, fearful for his own future and guilty for the non-future to which he had unwittingly, yet selfishly, condemned his enemy friend.

No, John now remembered with shame how he had failed in the promise he had made all those years previously, to search out and find his friend. It had to be. He had to take up the challenge and go to Russia to find Franz, once and for all.

Of course, as far as his Company was concerned, the job was his. John Collins, with his steady record and rise with the business, his dedication to hard work, proven ability and, above all, seniority and maturity of years, presented him tailor-made for the assignment. Added to this was the fact that he had no visible ties of family, for it was hard enough in these days to get a representative through the Iron Curtain, let alone wife and family.

The job was his for the asking. Well, not quite!

The Foreign Office had to become involved. No-one in those days of heightened Cold War could expect to enter the territory of the potential arch-enemy without a thorough vetting, and this job had to be so thorough that there would be not the slightest risk of Whitehall's opposite numbers in the Kremlin reversing what the British Government had ordained and endorsed.

"Mr. Collins, pleased to meet you, I'm Stripe, and this is my colleague, Dr. Mayes," introduced the civil servant.

The irony of name and pin-striped suit was not lost on young Collins, but he kept it to himself, suppressing a smile. He felt sure these Civil Service types were used to their interviewees feeling over-awed, but not he. No, John Collins was well used to such meetings.

"John, I'm afraid we have no ordinary work for you. There are no vacancies for young men of your age either in commerce or on the land." She took a slight pause. She was finding this more difficult than she had imagined. She had planned to give him the news that he was about to be conscripted compulsorily into the German labour force, coldly and briefly, and then comfort him in his devastation. And now she was ready to continue, to tell this young lad of his awful fate but to sugar the pill with reassurances that his hours would be regular, his pay the same as for any other job in Guernsey, and that he would go home at night, have Thursday afternoons and Sundays off, as in any other job, and would keep his ration book. She gulped, looked down at her feet, took a breath and began.

"I . . ."

"Oh . . ." said John simultaneously.

"Sorry!" apologised both together, and both laughed. It was the sort of laugh of relief experienced at the end of an ordeal. They both laughed a little too loud and a little too long. Dawn took the opportunity.

"We ourselves cannot supply you with work but there is work to be done. We have to give your name to the Germans as part of their compulsory labour requisition."

Introductions were quickly made, and John, and his senior colleague from the Company were quickly put at their ease.

"We have considered your application to represent the United Kingdom in the U.S.S.R.," continued Mr. Stripe, "and we have been in contact with our opposites at the Russian Embassy. . ." He paused and looked towards his colleague, as though needing encouragement to continue, as if he had something awkward to announce.

"Well. . .," a polite cough punctuated his words, "your, er . . . how should I say . . . record, Mr. Collins . . . yes, that certainly should help."

Record? What was the man talking about? Momentarily, John absorbed the questioning doubt exuding from his company colleague, as that other man sat impassively by his side.

All was made clear.

"Yes, the fact that you are a British national, always a tricky one to put over on the Comrades, don't you know, has been greatly helped by the fact that you suffered personally under the Nazis. You were occupied by the enemy for five years, so I believe, is that not so?''

Dr. Mayes, who had so far not uttered a word, since the formalities of introduction, confirmed that his colleague was correct, and that detailed research had produced such information.

Enemy? What was this man talking about?

John, on the other hand, inwardly thrilled at the word 'Germans'. Although he was not consciously aware of his own feelings in the matter, the mention of the master race filled him with a variety of feelings. He thought of their smartness, their colourfulness, manliness, the loud powerful hammer of their jackboots on the cobbled streets, the heavy square helmets which filled him with an almost primitive fear as though in the presence of some totem.

He was fascinated by their ceremony and their symbolism. The swastika flags with their stark black growths, contrasted by white and blood-red hung everywhere. The bright direction signs were painted on walls and trees at all road junctions, their gothic symbols lending both mystery and a sense of permanence. The music and their singing, as they marched about the Island, filled him with a secret joy. Their happy singing faces delighted him. He loved to attend their concerts in Candie Gardens. He enjoyed watching their films at the Gaumont, showing how they were winning the war for Europe.

"We note also . . ." John was drawn back almost a third of a century.

Oh yes, the Russians were happy to accept someone who had suffered under their Fascist enemy. It was not for them to know that young John had at one time adulated and admired this same foe. They did not need to know the true purpose of his mission. Soon John Collins would be coming to look for him, and Franz would be rescued. Yes, Franz could not wait for this interview to draw to a close. Why did they have to go on so? Why did they keep referring to him as Mr. Collins?

Could they not recognise the uniform of the Wehrmacht when they saw it? No wonder the English were losing this war!

"Now, we have noted you spent time in Germany after the war. This is not usually acceptable to our counterparts," continued Mr. Stripe. "However . . ."

Not usual? Surely it is very usual to return to one's Fatherland? But no, this was all wrong. They had it all wrong, the fools! How could he have returned to the Fatherland? He was caught in Russia, for God's sake! Why else was his friend John Collins going there to look for him?

"The comrades have also noted your divorce and, to all intents and purposes, a complete break with that land. They are prepared, all things considered, to endorse your application. The Russians have given their permission for you to go to their territory, subject to the usual terms and conditions, for six months, possibly renewable . . ."

She waited, words of explanation, words of compulsion, words of comfort at the ready, but John gave no response. She thought he must be shocked or stunned by the news. The wait seemed interminable. Not a sound, not a movement. The silence interpreted as a hiatus by Miss Le Huray was suddenly dismissed by John who, rising to his feet and changing his cap from right to left hand, announced.

"Thank you, when can I start?"

Dawn was taken aback at his smiling countenance, his eager expression, his look almost of excitement, of gratitude and confidence.

There was the other matter, hence the presence of Dr. Mayes, Civil Servant psychiatrist, attached to both Foreign Office and one-time War Office, now re-named Ministry of Defence.

Yes indeed, the British bureaucracy had been very thorough in its research. All the tiny pieces of information, each trivial on its own, had been compiled into a dossier, where their union had formed a stark statement about John's mental state and his observed expeditions into cross-personality. There was an enigma, however, for despite observations and statements from those with whom John (or was it Franz?) had been in contact during his post-war period, there was no medical proof to substantiate suspicions.

As with all applicants, John had needed to sign his agreement for police and medical records to become available. Well, the first had certainly uncovered his 'criminal' past, but the second had revealed nothing, for Herr Collins and Mr. Müller had never once confided their lives and aspirations with any known member of the medical profession. Why should they have needed to have discussed their mental health with such people? People only speak to doctors when they are unwell, and both knew that the other was perfectly all right. They had to be; good Germans are never ill. Neither Franz nor John would want it though they were such weak failures.

Franz thought he was going to be sick again. He tried to remember what they had taught him at youth camp when they watched those terrible films.

'Take deep breaths,' they had said. 'Take deep breaths and think of something else. The Führer has no use for weaklings.'

Franz supposed now he was a weakling. This was whey he now stood chained to a guard, outside the door of the Feldkommandant's office.

Hence the presence of Dr. Mayes. Between them, the two civil servants had to ascertain if Mr. Collins was in fact ill, therefore unable to take up the sensitive posting to a potential enemy state where, if his problem were to manifest, it might cause an unnecessary diplomatic incident. Alternatively, they had to decide whether the information they had gathered about the man was just so much gossip, and did not represent an impediment to their endorsement. It had to be decided at this meeting, for their recommendation would be accepted, right or wrong.

Throughout the interview, neither could quite bring himself to quite frame the right question to Mr. Collins. They hedged about with weak enquiries, each hoping the other would take up the point they had introduced.

"Mr. Collins, would you say you are a solitary person?" asked Dr. Mayes, hoping honest testimony would confirm his information.

Solitary? What an idea! No, John and Franz were almost as inseparable as brothers. They both knew the implication of such a question.

"I would hardly think so," said John, with a smile at the very nonsense of the idea, while turning to his Company colleague to elicit his confirmation.

Franz was pleased with that, John could tell.

"Tell me," asked Dr. Mayes, "don't you wonder if you might get a little bored when you are in Russia?" adding as an afterthought almost, "That is, won't you miss your friends?"

Nearly! John nearly fell into that little trap. "Almost gave me away then," whispered Franz.

Well, the time allotted to the interview had almost run out, and still the question had not been answered adequately. There was just one more avenue to pursue before John's application could be endorsed.

"Thank you, Mr. Collins. I think that is all we need to discuss with you for the time being," suggested Mr. Stripe, while rising, ready to see the client on his way.

"We would be grateful, however, if you would take a seat outside in the waiting area, while we have a confidential word with your Company colleague. This is quite a normal procedure, and we will be able to call you back in just a moment, don't you know?"

Why did they want Franz on his own? Well, not to worry. Franz could handle it. They had made good plans, and Franz would keep to them. He had to, everything depended on it.

"What we'll do then, Franz, is to stay together all evening. We'll never go away from each other's side. Do you understand?"

"Yes, of course, John," Franz replied to the very obvious course of action.

"Yes, but I really do mean all the time," reiterated John forcefully. "You don't go off with any of them for any reason at all. Do you understand? You don't go off and leave me alone."

"Yes, yes, I understand." Franz's voice sounded a little exasperated.

John had to be sure, he pressed the point even though he could tell his friend's tolerance was being severely stretched:

"You don't even go off to the lavatory without me, eh?"

Franz stopped walking and turned full face towards his friend. He was about to laugh but the humour left him when he saw the pale intensity in the other.

"Yes, if you say so, John."

"It's not if I say so, mate, it's deadly bloody serious!"

"I said yes," repeated Franz, "I said yes, and I mean it."

"Well so long as you remember it," John found himself nagging. "It's just that your place is full of very strange people, as you know."

Franz's countenance darkened. He did not need to be reminded. It was all right for John. He did not have to live there. He felt the waves of misery sweeping over him again. He wished he could change the subject. Tomorrow evening would come soon enough.

"And there's another thing," added John. Yes, he was definitely becoming grown-up now. He even droned on like an adult. He was the adult and Franz his child. "We don't touch a drink, eh?"

"Touch a drink? What is this, please?" Franz was puzzled. What was John about to embark on now?

"We don't touch alcohol at all. Surely you can see the sense of that, Franz?"

"Yes," replied Franz hesitantly, but he was not quite sure to what negative action he was committing himself.

"Well, don't sound so sure, old son." John's voice was getting angry again. But why should he be annoyed? Franz was saying yes to all his demands, wasn't he?

"You just see to it then. We can't afford for you to get in that bad state you got in last time, can we?"

Yes, now Franz knew what he meant. He shuddered.

"Yes," he affirmed. "I will not hold this alcohol."

"Touch, you stupid bugger! Touch it, not hold it. You can't hold it, that's your damned trouble."

Well, the two civil servants tried to fill in the missing piece of enigma by discussions with John's Company colleague, but were unsuccessful.

With the absence of John and with the confidentiality the

meeting now afforded, Dr. Mayes was able to be blunt and to the point. It was necessary to tip the balance of his report one way or the other.

"Would you say in your opinion," he asked, "that your colleague in any way displays the symptoms of schizophrenia. That is, does he sometimes . . ."

Yes, the man knew the implications of the term. But why Mr. Collins? This was all rather ridiculous! Why would anyone suggest such an idea? Did the Foreign Office honestly believe his Company would want to be represented, in these potential new markets, by anyone who was not in tip-top condition?

"I really think you should ask him that," suggested the man, his irritation barely hidden from the two officials.

Well, both Mr. Stripe and Doctor Mayes had failed, either to confirm their suspicions or to dismiss the idea. They had missed their opportunity and now had to write their report. Were they to put that they had felt reason to believe certain matters, but had failed in their attempts to confirm? Or would it be easier for them to diminish the perceived problem so that it would be too insignificant to mention at all?

Whatever their private deliberations were, one thing was for sure; within days John Collins had his posting confirmed. Now was only for John to attend briefings, put his affairs in order and teach himself yet another language in the six weeks prior to his departure.

Chapter Twenty-three

How long have they been in this hospital? Is this their second night? Everything seems so familiar, as if they have been here before. Perhaps they have, perhaps they have just been here too long?

The hospital truly is a caring place; not only do they tend the sick and the dying, but also they have regard for the living.

How kind, this little flat, these little extras provided for their comfort. Someone somewhere has really thought out the needs of devastated relatives who need to be at hand for the demise of a loved one, and yet must also have their rest and privacy.

Gerda is familiar with the tiny alcove where there waits an electric kettle, tea bags, a jar of instant coffee and sachets of powdered milk and sugar. She busies herself, as old Frances gets ready for bed.

* * *

Furnished with his thorough briefings by the Foreign Office, Ministry of Defence and Department of Trade, John Collins set off to represent his country and to develop trade for the Fatherland.

He had equipped himself with more than a modicum of the Russian tongue, and quickly settled into his accommodation at the British Embassy in Moscow.

John was good at his job, and predictably, a man such as he, with no worries or ties, was able to immerse himself in his mission, which he did. He impressed his diplomatic colleagues and contacts, and was respected by the Russians with whom he dealt daily. Yes, single men, through their dedication and application, for to all intents and purposes that was what John was, certainly brought something to such posts.

Well, single he might be, but there was more to Mr. Collins than might meet the eye, the British diplomatic eye, that is.

It was a convention, a requirement almost, in these fragile days of friendly exploration into the enemy market, that Britons kept to a very stringent routine. For their own safety and reputation, they were expected to work in pairs, the one always to witness the other, in case there were ever a suggestion of illegal or suspicious actions.

All were well aware of the ever watchful Russian eyes who ghosted their every move.

Similarly, all British passport holders were expected to live within the Embassy compound, and to keep to a minimum, excursions into Russia itself, and then only when business transactions made that absolutely necessary. In their briefings, they had been made all too aware of dangers and temptations which could come their way should they attempt to stray from this course.

They were discouraged from making social contact with any communists, unless, of course, they really wanted that incriminating photograph sent to their families, or to appear before a court, at best to be returned to Mother Britain as persona-non-grata; at worst, to cool off for a few years in Siberia.

John was aware of all this. He knew the advantages of complying and being confined to that building. It was not a problem, for he was no stranger to boredom and tedium. He also knew of the dangers, and would not willingly have risked his employment or freedom.

Yes, John Collins was aware of all this, but could the same be said for his friend Franz, who now lived in Russia? No, it could not, Franz Müller was becoming a real problem for John, or was it perhaps the other way round?

John was pleased, of course, that his friend had made the effort to search him out, to make contact. Well, he had known all along that he must have settled here in Russia. As he had suspected, Franz had made a home for himself near Leningrad. It had been good of Franz to telephone him like that. If only he had left his address or 'phone number though, if only he had been able to speak with him personally. But at least he'd left a message.

"Should a Mr. Müller telephone again," John said to the lady assigned as his secretary-cum-housekeeper, "please be sure to get his address, for I'd like to arrange to go to Leningrad to meet him."

Well, there were no more 'phone calls, and for just a while Franz began to feel dejected. It was bad enough to be forgotten for all those years when the Iron Curtain had prevented any form of communication, but now he worked for the British Embassy in Moscow, that should not have been a problem. Had he only imagined that his foolhardy Englishman from all those years ago, in that tiny little island, liberated from democracy by the valiant German forces, was to visit Russia? Where had he got that idea from? Surely John Collins must have assumed he was dead? It was too silly for words to think that he'd have kept Franz in his thoughts all these years!

Anyway, everyone knew what Russian telephones were like. No, it would have to be a visit in person.

Strange how the British, when they go abroad, like to take a little piece of their home country with them, be it the caravan with things familiar, or the fish and chip shops sought out on the Spanish Riviera. For diplomats it is the same; still the before lunch sherry, the gin and tonic prior to dinner, complete with full evening dress. Even the after-dinner port still flows as though they were still in London. Roast beef with Yorkshire pudding is as common fare as bacon and eggs or porridge. Similarly Sundays, even in this haven of atheism remain so very British. Nobody works within the compound on a Sunday.

Usually, John Collins, so steeped in hard work during the week, was able to remain himself, plain, conscientious, hardworking, successful negotiator that he was. In the little non-working time that he had to spare on those days, it did not really matter who he was, for he (that is, he and Franz) remained within the Embassy and, even then, in his private quarters. They had such a lot of catching up to do, such tales and adventures to recount.

Sundays were the problem. Sundays provided spare time for

160

John. On this particular day, he had not intended to go out, especially on his own, for he was well aware of the advice he had received against such actions. However, it was such a beautiful day, and there was absolutely nothing to do at the Embassy. Besides, if he went out just for a while, he would not be entirely alone, would he?

Well, here he was, out in the suburban streets of Moscow in Mother Russia itself. John could not really see what was monstrous about the place. True, it did not have as much colour as England. In that respect it was more like Guernsey towards the end of the Occupation. There were no bright and cheerful hoardings telling people what to buy. Well, that was quite understandable really, for the people had no choices, so why advertise?

The streets reminded him of his time in Germany, with the ancient cobbles tangled with tram lines here and overhead cables there.

It was true the buildings were all rather drab, mostly not knowing what fresh paint was, and squeezed in between the older grimy structures, heavy-jowled with dated neo-classical influences. There were also the recently built State's flats, bland and regular to the point of ugliness, their plain uniformity only broken by large identification numbers or the hanging and fluttering party slogans in the obligatory large red lettering.

From time to time as John walked, he would suddenly come across relics from the past, small islands of religion, little churches resplendent with their onion-shaped domes, isolated amid the drabness. There were even to be seen, too, the occasional comings and goings of scarf-shrouded old ladies, in and out of these anomalous buildings.

And what a bustle of people there was. It might be Sunday for John Collins, but here it was just an ordinary day. Bicycles jostled for position with the noisy jerking and clanking trams, whilst the occasional car or lorry wove in and out, passing by the horses and carts and hand-pushed trollies. Yes, everyone was busy about their work, with smoke and steam issuing from the factory blocks which existed alongside the residential quarters, and everywhere people rushing to or from their employment.

John came across a State shop, where curiosity rather than

161

necessity took him inside. Again he was transported to the
Guernsey of his youth, where all shops had been counter-
service for the precious little which was for sale or barter. Not
for the people of Russia, the aisles of well stocked shelves for
choice and self-selection, but instead, the distant brown bags
of commodities where words, not pictures, told of the
contents. Not for them to choose an item against how much
it cost. No, the question was, did they have enough ration
coupons to buy a particular thing if, in fact, it were available?

Franz should remember those days and those shops. Had
they not spent evenings, while walking through Town,
looking in at the empty shop windows? Had not Franz
recounted how the Guernsey people always asked him to pay
in cigarettes rather than money. Oh yes, Franz would recall
all this as clearly as he.

Franz? But why should John suddenly be thinking of his
friend from so long ago? Thinking of him? Should it not be,
talking to him? Was it not the case that Franz Müller was here
with John in Russia? Was Franz really here, or had John been
dreaming again? He felt confused.

'Yes, of course I'm here,' thought Franz, 'I'm here, but
where is my friend John?'

Chapter Twenty-four

As old Frances slips into her nightie, as she pulls back the cool white sheets of their 'put-u-up' double bed, she feels excited. She feels she has been here before. What fun it is to visit Granny's like this, how exciting to be away from home. Granny always spoils the two sisters. She and Rita will have a lovely time.

Where is that girl? Oh yes, she must be preparing their midnight feast. What fun!

"Come on Mum, wake up dear," urges Gerda. "You're dozing off before you have this lovely cup of tea I've made for you."

Gerda wishes that she could be as relaxed as the dear old lady. How she longs to sink into that bed beside her second 'Mum', but no, she must stay awake, she must remain alert in case they call. Well, at least Little Franz has come. He won't forget his Mama if the time comes. Perhaps she will indulge herself, perhaps this anguished and distraught lady who carries all the cares and woes for both herself and Frances will trust Little Franz to do the right thing when the time comes?

* * *

Well, they were ready to move now. Any moment now John and Franz would be taken aboard the 'plane. It was good of Franz to stand by his friend so, especially after all the trouble and embarrassment John had caused everyone, not least the British Ambassador. What a way to end a promising career!

At least it was to be a 'plane bound for London. It could have been worse. John Collins had been told he was lucky he was not facing a term in Siberia. No, John could not have expected Franz to have accompanied him there. The poor German had suffered enough bitter cold at Leningrad all those decades ago!

The diplomat at John's side shifted uncomfortably from foot to foot, the two plain-clothed Russians looked uneasy. John felt sure he must be the reason for all their awkwardness.

"Well, Mr. Collins," at last spoke the Englishman, "Give my best wishes to London for me . . ."

He paused, as though he could think of no more small talk to fill the hiatus.

The loudspeaker droned out a message, and the two Russians looked one to the other. This was it.

The diplomat hesitantly extended his hand towards John.

Franz, always the formal one, inclined his head slightly as he took the gesture of well-meaning, which hid a distaste and abhorrence for the troubles his friend John had caused.

"Cheerio, old boy."

The two Russians closed on either side of Franz, so tightly and so aggressively that John was pushed aside.

"Up Englander lover!" yelled the Corporal to the wretch who lay exhausted and bruised before him. "Now we take you to learn what the Führer thinks of traitors and spies!"

Franz heard the voice, it was in his, the master tongue, but it was not part of him. It was for Franz Müller, but Franz Müller was now no more.

The prison rumbled down the bumpy track runway. It turned and first one engine revved and then the other until they seemed they would disintegrate, to crush Franz's mind. As it gathered speed, accelerating towards doom, ever faster, faster, faster, all the bumps and jolts fused into one mighty upheaval, so that all the floor-bound males were forced into an involuntary silent laugh, as jaws forced back and heads struggled for support. All that time Franz held just one thought, just as when Morten had abused his innocence. He held in his vision the picture of his friend, never again to be seen.

Suddenly the great jostle ceased and a leaden force pulled his stomach down on to the steel floor, while he lurched sideways. The craft was airborne. It had happened, he had died.

No, the Russian authorities had not taken kindly to John Collins with his activities. That Englishman had pushed himself too far. He knew his travel documents did not permit travel out of Moscow. The comrade at the station had been quite right to report the man's attempted flouting of security.

It was indeed fortunate for John Collins that Franz had decided to stay with him throughout his interrogation. Franz had certainly matured. John recalled what a baby of a coward that German had once been at the prospect of a little bit of questioning by the Gestapo.

"I think they'll interrogate you."

"Interrogate me! Why?" shouted John. "Why should they interrogate me, eh? What have I done?"

"Don't shout at me! It's not my fault!"

"Well, it's not mine either! Why would they interrogate me? What have I done, eh?"

"I don't know. You keep ask these questions," replied Franz. "Why don't you think about me? You might get interrogated, but what will to me happen?"

"What do you mean, what will happen to you? You've done nothing wrong, have you?"

"I don't know John. Maybe there'll be a lot of trouble for me."

"Why?"

"Well, for a start, we were fighting in the road. You could be sent to prison for hitting a German, John."

"I know," breathed John dejectedly, "but we weren't fighting."

"We were, it started as a fight."

So, John Collins was expelled from Russia? So what? John could not feel ashamed, his conscience was clear. Besides, they were only Reds, just Bolsheviks. Had not Franz been fighting to rid the world of their like?

Well, at least before his arrest he had had a fruitful final day of freedom in Moscow. His visit to Russia had not been altogether futile. At least he now knew Franz was still alive. He had always believed this, of course, but now he had proof that his brother was alive. Well, certainly no evidence that he was dead.

Before his arrest at Moscow Central Station, John had been very industrious, very industrious indeed. It had all happened when Franz had decided to leave him for a while. Yes, Franz had said he was only going for a minute and John had believed him, but he had not returned. Well, that was Franz! Was it surprising that his friend, who had been missing for years and had suddenly arrived, should just as quickly have disappeared? To John, it seemed perfectly acceptable. Oh yes, Franz would come back when he was ready.

Perhaps it had been Franz's way of telling his friend that he should really concentrate on important matters while he had the chance. Maybe Franz realised that the longer he stayed with John, the more he would put him off the task in hand? That was it, of course! Why had John Collins come to Russia in the first place? Why, to find definite evidence that Franz Müller still existed. He needed to research his private thoughts.

This was all a bit ridiculous, however, for why did he need to search for Franz when he knew that he had just been with him? Had he not been looking for the German in Germany itself, and had not he and Gerda made enquiries in Guernsey? Gerda? Oh yes, Gerda, that was it, Gerda Collins, his wife — well, former wife. Yes, that explained it, Gerda must be here in Russia too! So it was Gerda, not Franz who had persuaded him to come out and look for his friend. How he held the two so confused! Yes, it was all so confusing, and yet, what else could be expected, for this was Russia?

Yes, John Collins, member of the British Delegation, accredited member to the British Embassy in Moscow, used his time well. When he was arrested, he was found to be in possession of much information.

Did he really have with him lists and numbers, or was he thinking of that court case in far off Guernsey? Had the Russians really interrogated him continuously, hour after hour? Had they kept on and on about his lists, so carefully researched in all those museums, or had that all been when he had truly known that he was young John Collins, when he had been but a boy?

They had certainly not been rough with him. On yes, they

had raised their voices from time to time and had stood up angrily, as though in prelude to some violence, but they had not, in fact, touched John physically. Well, that had confirmed it was in modern Russia. If John had been confusing all this with Guernsey, he knew they would have smacked his face and caused him pain. The Gestapo would not have been so gentle.

Well, it did seem very clear to John, just as when Franz had come along to point him in the right direction. Yes, of course that was it. Franz now lived in Russia, so he knew his way around. It had been thanks to his friend that he had found the right museums, and the libraries, where such records were kept.

John had seen the recorded evidence of war. He saw the photographs of the terrible havoc created by the Germans, in their unprecedented attack on the innocent peace-loving Russians. He saw too, how great Mother Russia had fought back to protect and avenge her innocent children. He was witness to the records; great long lists there were, with names too numerous to be counted, lists of the dead, lists of prisoners taken who had subsequently died of their wounds, shorter lists of those who had survived their capture, to be honoured with hard labour to help make amends for the misdeeds they had perpetrated.

John had even seen a very much shorter list; it was strange, that. Why had Franz directed him to that particular list, a list of repatriation? It did not make sense to John that his missing friend seemed to be telling him he had been repatriated to the Fatherland after the war, as that German's own mother believed. Most contradictory, when they both now knew he had decided to settle here in Russia. It was as illogical as the scribbled information they had found in John's pockets.

Well, someone had been lying, but who? One moment, John had been aware of mass graves with countless Germans unidentified and unidentifiable, the next, he had seen lists showing names, ranks and numbers. What a contradiction!

Yes, John Collins was sure he had seen many 'Müller F.' entries in the lists of death, but none of them could have been Franz. No, Franz had to be on one of those shorter repatriation lists, the lists with personal numbers which could now be cross-referenced. At last, John Collins had known he was close to a definite conclusion to his search.

There had been a conundrum however, for despite Franz's guidance to these appropriate places where John was to discover the truth, once and for all, Mr. Collins, of the British Delegation had felt it to be all too easy, too simple, almost as if it had been some sort of ironical trick to delude him into believing what could not possibly be proven. Why had he, then, after all the years of fruitless search, learned numbers and ranks, as well as names and initials, to lead him to speedy conclusions, when previously his researches and enquiries had told him no such detailed records had been kept? Why also, had his Russian captors been unable to make sense of his notes? Why had they kept them, returning in their stead such nonsensical scribblings?

Chapter Twenty-five

Gerda cannot relax. She should be mourning, nothing less. But how with decency, can she mourn the still living? The ultimate has to be quick. But that is wrong! What a thought! Then John must linger on and must she put her misery into abeyance for his sake, for that of Frances? But that too is hard. Neither course can be easy; both are destined to hurt her. Already the seeds are sown and one day she will reap their harvest no matter what. At least it is all outside her control so the choice is not hers. That impossible choice! And yet for as long as she is waking she has the impossible conjecture there, invading while she has no other occupation.

How can she go to bed? How can she get in with Frances, the sweet old lady who, no matter how dear, how helpless, has usurped her darling's place? How can she sleep in this tiny room so strange, no windows open, the excessive heat of the hospital pipes contrasting with the cold of the floor? She cannot rest in this strange place, she has to be ready at any call.

Will they call her? Of course they will! What if they forget? No, that is silly! How could they set up such a place as this and then disregard the very purpose for which it existed? Gerda keeps posing herself these questions as she drinks her second and then her third cup of tea, all the time answering herself and reassuring herself.

It is late now, but still she is not drowsy. What a quiet place this large building is at night! How can it be so full and yet so quiet? Where are all the patients, all the wards full of the sleeping, the ailing, the dozing and all the recuperating? Where are the nurses and the sisters, the Matron in her office, the doctors and the auxiliaries? Why was no one here? Don't they know she cannot sleep, cannot live alone with this time which does not move?

169

They must be there below. She should join them, talk to them, drink tea with them, make tea for them, just watch and listen. Anything, but she has to escape.

* * *

And so, John returned to his quiet comfortable home in Hampshire, weathered out the storm of annoyance with his superiors and settled once more into the mundane routines of work and private life. He had his thoughts for company.

As the years moved him onward from the inconclusive evidence he had discovered in Russia, he found that he had two ideas which would fit the fate of Franz, ideas which could be taken on to fit his mood. At times he would acknowledge the stark lists of death and would accept that Franz was one of the F. Müllers indicated, that he had in fact been dead since 1942 and had tricked and deceived his friend in so being. At these times John felt let down that his erstwhile brother had haunted him so and had allowed him to ruin his life in searching for the unattainable. At other times John knew that Franz had been on that list of repatriated Germans and was now somewhere in Germany.

Of course, that was why Gerda had come all that way to Moscow to tell him. Gerda knew, she had known all along.

"Don't worry about Franz," she had said, "He's quite safe. He got sent back to Germany after the war. I should know. His mother told me."

Why though, had Franz's own people classified him as missing without trace? Why had he not bothered himself to look for John? Could it be that Franz no longer cared, perhaps had never cared? Was it as that evil man, that Patrol Leader, had suggested, that he had associated his whole misfortune with his illicit friendship with the enemy youth John, and so had grown to despise him?

Perhaps it was John Collins who had cause to forget his friend? Maybe he should have detested his friend for the evil plans into which he had been entrapped? Possibly, Franz felt so guilty at the very memory, that he had deliberately deserted John and repressed all recollection as too unbearable to sustain?

"And what a pity you won't be able to warn your friend," sneered

Morten. *"If only you could let him know, so he could avoid the danger!"*

"Also, dear Franz, when it has happened, and your friend is full of hate, who do you think he will hate most? Will it be David Hüffmeier? Well you might think so," he effected gleefully, *"but no, it will be you!"*

He prodded Franz to make his point.

"You are the one he will loathe, for it will be you who brought him into contact with our nation, you who taught him to become friends with Germans. He will hate you for ever!"

There was only one way Franz could save his friend . . .

Had John really been prepared to make that awful sacrifice for the sake of friendship all those years ago? And had Franz too really been willing to place himself in such peril for the sake of their continued comradeship?

There was no choice. John could neither stay nor go.

"You have one minute to decide," was Hüffmeier's ultimatum. *"You go now to put off for a few days more what will be anyway, and you leave your dear one to us, or you stay and share his experiences with him, and keep him for a while longer. We go now to bring back drinks, four drinks to celebrate your decision."*

"Go John, please," insisted Franz in his misery. *"You must go. You are good, you are decent. Please go for me, John, for your mother, please!"*

As if oblivious to the pleadings, John could only waste the rationed time, permitted for deliberation.

"What did he mean, 'show your buttocks'?"

"It doesn't matter, John. You just go please!"

"I can't leave you to them, not two of them, not like that!" replied John.

"You must, John, you heard them. Can you take the things they want to do?"

John would not, could not, answer such a question.

"But they'll prevent us from meeting ever again," intervened John.

"No, they won't," urged Franz trying to sound more convincing

than he felt. "There's our plan, remember? Tuesday and Thursday. Please go, my friend!"

Hüffmeier and Morten were returning, confidently.

"But you, Franz. How can you take it?" whispered John pathetically.

"Just go. I'm all right. I know what it is now. You get used to it," insisted Franz in his urgency.

The two stood, smirking grimly as they proffered drinks to the perturbed youths.

"That's true," mimicked Hüffmeier, "you get used to it. You certainly will, Müller, before this war has killed you off!"

"Get used to it?" questioned John in a daze. "If you get used to it, Franz, then so must I."

"Quite so!" concluded Hüffmeier. Morten clicked his heels and smiled. "Now we will all drink, yes?"

No, John could not reproach his lost friend for what might have been, but which had never happened. They had both been rescued from the unimaginable, well, certainly so John, thanks to the timely intervention of his father and his parish priest. In his own mind, John had been able to forgive his German friend for the potential moral danger into which he had placed them. He had never despised Franz for all the trauma their friendship had caused his life and the fortunes of his whole family.

No, Franz had gone away, he had deserted his Guernsey friend. As John Collins, with the onset of years, lonely, independent and work-driven, he too had to forget his erstwhile friend, be he alive somewhere but oblivious to times past or no longer caring, or even no longer existing at all, but gone by deceit, and dead all these years.

Chapter Twenty-six

As she ventures out she looks back at the old lady, so peaceful. Gerda is about to join the living, and yet she cannot. She cannot even allow the door to take the vision of her darling's mother from her, to venture into the lonely silent light.

The lights out now, the curtains drawn back, it is Gerda who sits in bed next to her frail old in-law, slumping down into the surprisingly soft and cool sheets with pillow so luxurious. Gerda is resigned to an eternal night of wakefulness, chased by thoughts revolving and returning, as if for reassurance that their concepts have not changed. Gerda falls asleep with the deep sleep of the exhausted.

* * *

In some ways John was surprised to get a letter from Gerda after all those years, and yet, in another way it seemed quite to be expected, for had she not fleetingly visited him in Moscow? Not that she mentioned their recent meeting. It was almost as though she had forgotten it, as if for her it had not happened. Well, that was a surprise in itself.

John found himself not only surprised but, to his amazement, invigorated by the communication. So not all his past was completely dead.

The letter was quite brief and formal as if to gauge the temperature to see if there would be a reply before bearing her soul of all its thoughts.

Gerda told him in quite a business-like way that she was now staying with her mother-in-law, John's own dear mother, who was now quite frail from old age and years of over-work. She said she would probably remain in Guernsey, at least while the Guest House business affairs were wound up, and possibly after that. She was prepared to absent herself at any time if John could spare the time to visit his mother who, in her eighth decade, did not have much more of a life expectancy. She told him also that his son (she used 'son' deliberately, perhaps sensitively avoiding the name Little Franz), now a young adult, had completed his time in university and was intending to get married. The young man particularly wished to meet his father and to introduce his wife-to-be.

John quickly replied. The letter from Gerda had bridged the gap of all those lonely years to the period when they had both been so happy.

The letters began to flow in a triangle, Guernsey, England, Germany, and it seemed no time at all from there that he was speaking on the telephone first to old Frances and then to his second mother and wife, Gerda. He even received a 'phone call with the very formal and cautious enquiry;

"Father? . . ."

Frances came to England for an extended holiday while Gerda remained in Guernsey. Frances had come, ostensibly to look after John, but in the event she was the one who needed the care and attention.

It was for this reason, out of a sense of duty to his mother, that John invited Gerda to stay also. Out of courtesy, John reciprocated Gerda's earlier offer, saying he would absent himself from the household if his presence was thought to be an impediment. Secretly however, the good man was relieved that his former wife and friend disregarded his selfless offer to remove himself and arrived one evening, soon after, unannounced.

And so a reconciliation was effected. John now had both mothers to look after him.

It was not long after this happy and natural reunion that their temporary setting back of time to happier days, was made complete.

Gerda knew that John was ready to accept his only son once more, for she had prepared him. He had not enthused at the idea of meeting his offspring and his daughter-in-law to be, but neither had he resisted, acceptance indeed! Both mothers waited expectantly for the couple, the one as proud Grandmother to meet yet again her own dear boy incarnate, the other as justifiably proud mother. Meanwhile John forgot, or appeared unconcerned, at the coming event.

As last he came, Little Franz, yet little no more. Tall he stood there at the front door, tall and robust, blond and blue-eyed, a true Aryan like his father. His wife-to-be, as nervous as the fiancé who held her hand, was at his side.

So John greeted his son, and both slipped back the many years since they had last met, the one with anxiety, fearing an extension of his former hurt and rejection, the other with guilt at how he had torn up his own image in the little boy's eyes and transformed himself from doting parent to despicable deserter.

"Father . . ." hesitated Little Franz, for that was how he had started life, and that was forever to remain his title, the incongruity of it long since forgotten and accepted, ". . . Father, it is so good to see you . . ."

"My boy," almost shouted John, experiencing real joy at this reunion, joy that he had not thought himself capable of since a youth, "You have come! You have come home at last to Papa!"

All formality was gone now, there was no more stiffness or insecurity. For a few seconds, seeming to last forever in its completeness, the two were reconciled, as father hugged his son and Little Franz felt at peace once more.

"Franz!"

"Yes, it is I," announced Franz, beaming. "What do you think, John? I have a bicycle for the day. Now I can ride with you, yes?"

"This is super," John replied. "Yes, let's get going quickly, away from this place. I've a lot of deliveries so we can ride together and talk as we go."

Papa was back and they could play their games once more. He didn't even mind if Papa wanted to call him Patrick like he used to. It didn't matter so long as Papa stayed.

And all the while, as father and son stood locked in joy, so did Frances and Gerda and Little Franz's fiancée witness, and all with absolute well-being.

Little Franz accepted that his father would never call him by his given name but got round the impasse by employing the familiarity of 'son', while occasionally lapsing into Patrick. Little Franz was puzzled by it, just a little hurt but then hurt was the strongest memory he carried of his father. Gerda helped him to shrug it off and his fiancée just put it down to one of those extraordinary English eccentricities.

John and Gerda did not re-marry. It did not seem proper or necessary, but they gradually grew from friendship to love again, while old Frances looked on and waited for the day she would be great grandmother.

John continued working long hours but the two women became the good home-makers, the one instructing and the other implementing, or not, as the mood took her. All three were happy and each had sufficient to fill their days.

John had the occasional dreams, but Gerda was always there to soothe. The difference being that these days he shared his thoughts with her. He would confide his discoveries in Russia and they would discuss. She agreed that there was no conclusive end to the conjecture and she helped him to see that perhaps putting the thoughts into abeyance was the best course.

There were regressions of course, when at times, the most simple incidents could trigger his memories and fill John with an intensity as though he were actually re-living past events, just as the drug misuser is reputed to have flashbacks to his moments of trauma.

On one such occasion, despite his personal wishes on the matter, John was inveigled into attending a neighbourhood party, which seemed to be a frequent habit of those nearby. John had not been keen but had reluctantly, for appearances sake, agreed to join Gerda later, once the party was in full swing. He reasoned that by that time all the party-goers would be well into things and he would not have to make too much intense conversation.

He also decided that once he had made an appearance he could creep away without causing offence to anyone, for he would have been registered by the collective memory.

176

The party had been going for some while and the host and hostess, of a genuinely hospitable nature, were anxious at John's absence, but Gerda reassured them he would be along. The hostess persuaded her man to nip along to speed John's arrival, but this idea was discarded at Gerda's insistance. She settled down to relax on the sofa, enjoying the luxury of being waited on, and so was slightly heady, what with the general good atmosphere of the place. She could relax, relieved that John was not to be rushed and that she had skilfully put off his collection.

Unbeknown to Gerda, one of the men had, in fact, gone to collect John. John had just completed seeing old Frances safely in bed and was slightly annoyed at this intrusion on his timetable but decided that, as he was going anyway, it was better to put a bold face on it and go.

It must have begun as they left the front door of his house, John remembered he had left the television on. He could hear it clearly but it did not matter, it would not come to any harm. The sounds of martial music tantalized his ears as he closed the door.

John had enjoyed the Mickey Mouse film. The whole cinema was in uproar, both Germans and civilians forgetting their differences and indulging in amusement. It was so much appreciated that it was shown for a second time.

The Berlin newsreel film was completely in German. It showed the full glory and might of Herr Hitler's victorious forces. At every scene showing the devastation of British cities, and the advances made against the Bolsheviks, there would be sporadic clapping from the German side of the cinema.

One shot showed a British warship. At this there was a jubilant shout from the civilian side of the rail, followed by some half-hearted cheering and clapping. The locals were damned seconds later when the same warship was shown in all its devastation.

He was quite pleased then to leave behind the devastation of the British navy. He was pleased to step his way upwards through the dark narrow streets and alleys to arrive at the party where he would meet . . . Meet? Whom would he meet?

His companion was a little on edge, for he did not know John too well and he would not have undertaken this mission with such a sullen uncommunicative man if it had not been to placate his wife. He therefore must have seemed a little brusque in his anxiety to get back to the good time he had just left.

He thought how wilful this boy was, how stubborn. What a challenge! He had not come across his like before. In Germany one look, one word, and the young boys obeyed him, for he was the S.S. He was Hitler's chosen man, was he not? He had never felt his power to be ineffective. This was a new experience, coming across one so young who had such a mind and will of his own.

He wondered how to handle this predicament. He knew he could use force, for such action would be thought quite legitimate owing to his uniform. He did not want to alienate this beautiful John though.

It would have been different if he had been a mere Jew. David had a particularly good reputation where Jews were concerned. He had to have with a name like his. He had to prove, contrary to his Hebrew label, he hated them as much as the next man or even more. He felt he had established his point with his comrades and was no longer teased by them in that regard.

"Your friend wishes with you to speak."

The man gave a nervous grin. John kept well back. Although he was keen now to arrive at the party, he did not wish to have to walk with, or get into conversation with this man dressed in black.

As they entered the hallway, many sounds and smells assaulted John's senses. He followed the uniformed one into the reverberating cacophony. Involuntarily he tried to take steps down into that room, steps down on a flight which did not exist. Momentarily he stumbled but, as he regained himself, he knew that the assembly had all frozen. They were all petrified for just long enough for him to take in the whole scene, the food laid out on the table, the glasses held, the chatter, the cigars, the gramophone, the orderlies assisted by officers as they decanted yet more drink to the empty glasses. And there, yes sure, there he sat, sprawled between the Patrol Leader and that strange effeminate creature, there sat the friend of almost four decades previously, Franz Müller, glass in hand disgustingly drunk and careless of what was being perpetrated on him as he allowed those caresses and let the excesses of food and drink soil his uniform. How could he, after all these years, return in such a way? How could he insult John like this, showing that all he cared for the years of search, and night time trauma of hopelessness, was to indulge himself so and be so careless of his friend's effort?

Why was he behaving so? Why was he so dirty, so drunken and debauched? Who were those men? Why was that sickly-looking Patrol Leader fussing over him so? Why was he so familiar with Franz. Franz was nothing to him, just one of his soldiers. He was too young to be the Patrol Leader's friend and too subordinate for him to be so familiar. Why then did he allow this person to be touching his leg? What was the reason for such behaviour? And why was Franz lying sprawled across that other person, that fellow dressed like a young girl, with his silky blouse and tight slacks? What was going on? Why was the creature kissing him?

With all these angry, unanswered questions racing in his mind he turned upon his heel and, before S.S. David Hüffmeier realised what was happening, had left the party.

John, in his disgust and turmoil, rushed from the house pursued by S.S. Hüffmeier whilst Gerda, hardly aware of this rapid course of events, was persuaded to stay and finish her relaxation for the host would see John was all right.

He rushed from the room and was outside the house before he heard David's voice as insignificant background to his crude nightmare. As he rushed up past the police station, neither sure whether he was walking or running, awake or asleep, he heard the plaintive voice of the S.S. as background only.

"Wait John! Wait I tell you. . . . Wait!. . . . please!"

The cry was not part of him, it was all unreal. He was in a dream or nightmare. He knew he had only to will himself awake to find it was not true, that his innermost fears and realisations were only figments of his troubled imagination. He could not wake however.

The journey home, although several minutes, was insignificant to the trauma in his mind.

He crashed through the front door and up the stairs.

Chapter Twenty-seven

John's night was quiet. All night he dreamed he was asleep. Well that was how it seemed. He was not really aware of anything except his dream, for nothing was real. All was from his imagination and only there with his permission. He imagined at times, in his timeless cushion of well-being, that he saw intrusions in his dream but of course they were not real. If they were they only were if it was his wish for them to be so. Like the bright light, which he could exclude at will, so the various people he imagined looking at him, the nurse adjusting tubes and clips, the Sister watching the nurse's efforts while helping her to alter his position in his cushion, while they did things below, which he could not see or feel, like the doctor with his hyperdermic syringe.

All these people are no more real to him than his recent dream, or was it nightmare? Yes, that too had to be unreal, just a figment of his imagination. And yet, was it? Had he really only dreamed that he had been somewhere alone, surrounded by that terrible cacophony, while his small enclosed world had tumbled and crashed around him? Had it just been one dreadful nightmare? If that was so, then why had he let the illusion go on for so long, why could he not dispel the fleeting glimpses of contorted memory?

Well, it is all too much effort to reason, especially while he floats, the one ingredient of his recent entanglement missing, even from his recall. No, John feels no pain, he experiences no fear, thanks to the doctor.

* * *

So finally, John Collins had reached the stage in his confusion where he could not be sure what was happening to him, whether his fantasy was his reality or the routines of his life were just figments of his imagination. He became as the man, long since blinded, not sure if he were awake or still dreaming, with both states being so similar in their reality.

As John progressed into the second half of his century, as he faced the run down of his life, knowing for sure that the years remaining could not be expected to equal those which had passed, either in quantity or what they had to offer, so he realised his own insignificant place in time and in the universe.

He had his two mothers, of course, and he knew that he had a son, and soon the line was to be extended into his first grandchild, but even so, he knew he was incomplete, for he had taken of the world but had not repaid, and he had outstayed his welcome in this life.

What did he have to show for his time of stewardship on this earth? True, he had kept a good job going, he had enjoyed steeping himself in his work, and he was respected for it. In consequence of his toil, he had a comfortable, modern and material home, and the two women in his life wanted for nothing, and both were uncomplaining.

But what else did John Collins have to show for his five decades? What did he have which was of true worth? Had he friends? Were there memories which were good, which could fire his thoughts and colour his moods with the same pleasures as when they had once been real? Did John have the satisfaction of knowing that he had used his time well, and that the world was perhaps a little the richer for his having existed?

For one so insignificant in the great scheme of the creation, had he not had far greater influence for ill in the world than his mere insignificant status should have been capable of? Was, in fact, the world a worse place for his having existed? Had he not replaced trust with treachery, joy with despair and love with disgust?

No, John Collins, a man with a past best forgotten, but which would not go away, and no future except this bland remorseless run down until he once more returned to the utter insignificance of eternity, had no hope, no joy in his life.

Work and routine, interspersed with a repetitive ritual of home life, were John's only high points, and any time in between, any spare moments, where conjectures and memories would creep in, were his low points.

Logically, John knew he had to steep himself in the peaks of his existence so that he would not descend to the depths, and at most times he maintained his course. When, however, he slipped and lost his way in those misty dark valleys, he knew he was trapped in timelessness and that his unease, which would drain him mentally, while taking away any resolve to be rescued, would remain with him permanently.

To those who worked with John and respected him, and to the two women in his life who loved him, these periods of observed melancholy became ever more frequent and a cause for anxious concern. For John, they were clamped on to his every moment with a sense of depressed resignation.

If only his friend would come and talk to him, but no, Franz did not talk to John any more. Even his only friend had deserted.

Since John's return from Russia, when he had been sure that Franz still lived and had forgiven him for causing him such troubles, his friend had not made contact. That had been so strange, for why was it that, once they had become reconciled, the fraternization should cease? To find and then to lose was worse than to have gone on searching without reward.

It was all so confusing too, and John Collins was not always sure what was tangible and what was in his mind. Often he would explore these ideas and re-trace events in his thoughts, but always his journey would terminate and he would travel back in one great leap to the Guernsey of his youth, when he and Franz had been such friends together.

Yes, all that part of his life had been real and true. John remembered as clearly, as if it were yesterday, how they had spent their happy hours together, their laughs, their explorations, the fun of playing together like children, as each had regressed through sheer joy at finding a friend, how even the bleak aspects of their short time together had been gilded by the passage of time. In memory, even their very real worries, anxieties, fears and deceits took on a lighter aspect. Yes, he remembered the hunger and the shortages, the doubts and mistrust, even the hurt and rejection, but all those could almost be considered blessings for, like some unpalatable meal transformed by a tasty sauce, they had been accompanied by friendship.

But now, what did John have? He used to be able to talk with his friend and meet with him at will, until quite recently. Now it seemed, though, that Franz no longer wished to go along with this game. Could it be that he felt let down that Gerda had returned? No, it couldn't be that, surely? Besides, Frances was here now, and John knew that his friend looked on her as a mother. Why, then, did he keep away?

It could only be that Franz had not truly forgiven his friend. Oh yes, he had said all was well and that there was nothing to forgive, but had he meant it? Was it true what poor old Dad had said about the Germans, that they would say one thing to your face while meaning another? Hadn't Franz himself almost admitted such a duality of standards? Yes, John recalled so clearly how he and Franz had argued about the 'two truths,' the one for mighty Germany and the other for the nations the Nazis regarded they had liberated from democracy.

Even his own dear Gerda, long-suffering and forgiving Gerda, had implied that Franz was no more. Was that true for her, yet untrue for John? Could the two truths co-exist?

Hadn't she come all the way to Russia to tell him this, or was it Franz who had visited John there, to say that it was Gerda who was really just imagined?

Why couldn't both answers be true? Why did it have to be 'either, or'? It had always been possible before. John had only had to think of a possibility for it to have become real. So why not now? Why could he not get back to reality and be with his friend once more? Why did this present dream, this strange place, a wife, an old lady of a Mum, monotonous never-ending employment, have to dog him so and exclude him from reality?

Poor confused John, the youth John Collins now enclosed in his ghastly hallucination that he was an ageing grown-up, so needed his friend to tell him that all was all right, that the Germans were still good and were the saviours of mankind!

At the same time John wanted Franz to be with him. He needed him to

184

look after him, to tell him it was all right, that he, Franz, was not like that. He needed Franz to explain that the German people were basically good, that it was just a few who did these evil things and that the rest were all right really. The German people were still the friends of the British and still needed them as cousins to help build that better world. Better world? With bombs and broken bodies? With punching and kicking?

John had to know Franz was still his friend, unchanged. He wanted to talk with him. He needed to walk with him. He wanted to be with him. Franz seemed to be the only real German left at this moment. Franz had taken him home and looked after him last night. Franz had not punched him. Franz had not taken his father to the police station, or just now beaten that poor man who had shouted in anger, at the destruction of his children.

John's confusion grew. It took over from Franz and became his companion at home. At work, as he tried to lose himself in his routines and tasks, that same confusion crept in. It kept him company, but was not satisfied with that, for its familiarity led to its posessiveness, and John's confusion resented sharing him with any person or any thing. Mr. Collins became so confused by the presence of his new companion, confused and slowly but surely dominated.

Mr. Collins had always been held in high regard where his business acumen was concerned. Even his trouble in Russia had been relegated to just a temporary aberration, such was the value of this good negotiator to his Company. All transactions touched by John were sure of success, as the graphs of sales flickered and accelerated upwards whenever his involvement was evident.

It was such a day, when good negotiations were drawing to a conclusion and John, to any casual observer, seemed his usual efficient self, as he clinched a deal with a lucrative new client. John's Company was about to become further indebted to its most efficient servant. But then the ever-present confusion finally broke out and intruded at a crucial stage.

"Thank you," said John, holding out his hand to the client who stood before him.

Both were satisfied. The client, who had just signed a deal

worth many hundreds of thousands of pounds to John's Company, knew that he too was a beneficiary.

"Thank you," he replied with enthusiasm. "My business is well pleased with this arrangement, and we will look forward with pleasure to receiving your first consignment."

This was all small talk now, but all part of the etiquette associated with the conclusion of long and fruitful discussions. Nothing could go wrong at this stage, both could feel satisfied.

"Eh?" Mr. Collins' query was little more than a whisper, the intervention hardly noticed by the man taking his leave.

"What you say. . .?" continued John. His diction was coarse, not within the experience of the other.

"Sorry?" asked the man, confused, anxious to leave now. His chauffeur must already be waiting.

"Is it that you're pleased then, eh?" John chuckled, as he let out this stream of Guernsey accent, not indulged in for oh so many years. "So it's pleased then that you are, eh? Cor demme, that's good then, eh?"

The last words were shouted as John, eyes glassy, watering with an angry stare, stood to glower at the man who stood before him.

"We will win this war!" his words lisped with the authoritative lilt of the master tongue, as he thumped the good Aryan table in front of him.

John knew not who he was or what he was doing, his only consciousness being that he felt angry, that he, expatriate Guernseyman and son of the Fatherland, had become anger itself. His confusion had finally engulfed him and taken him over.

Chapter Twenty-eight

Frances is first to wake. She lies there trying to clear her mind of dreams, to face the reality of day. She often dreams, now she is old, often remembering her nocturnal excursions well into the day so that, if they have been enjoyable, she keeps them a little longer to colour her reality. If not pleasant, then she lets them fade. That is one of the blessings of her advancing years. She has many memories upon which to draw, to select for her subconscious journeys.

What a strange night she has spent. Still part of her knows she is in Granny's attic and there is Rita still asleep! Always lazy that girl! But of course, it is not Rita.

During the night Rita had been Larry. Frances had woken, (or had she dreamed that she had woken?), and there he had been. Well it had been a good meeting. Why not pretend Larry is still there beside her?

No, she has other things to do. Yes, she has been up half the night. It has not all been a dream or peaceful rest. Her little boy is sick. Yes, of course, hadn't they fetched the Doctor in the middle of the night? Hadn't her poor John been in such a fever? And who else had come? The Chief of Police, that was it!

As the Chief moved towards the door he said, almost apologetically, almost as if it were anathema to him;

"He'll have to speak to me soon, Mr. Collins. You know that, don't you? If he doesn't speak to me they'll do the interrogation. You do understand that, don't you? They won't worry about injections or the health of the patient."

187

Or is she dreaming again? Surely that was real though? Surely her little boy is ill and needs her now? That is why she is here.

This is not Granny's; she is not a little girl anymore. She is John's old Mum. He is in hospital and she must be with him now!

"Wake up Rita!"

Gerda wakes with a start. She feels very cold. She has slept deeply and still she feels quite chill.

*   *   *

John Collins' time in hospital was a relief to all. It gave respite to his family, who were relieved immediately of the pressure of his irreconcilable contradictions and his deathly contagious, stifling depressions. Also, they had the positive blessing of observing his slow but sure return to normality, to a former self which had so gradually diminished over the recent years that they had not noticed the individual steps down into degradation, but just the loved one already at the foot of the cliffs of his despair.

At John's workplace too, his removal to hospital had seemed a fitting outcome, the very burgeoning of his illness explaining and excusing the enigmas of late.

John left behind no enemies at work or home, but was followed by the thoughts and well wishes of those who loved him and those who wished him well. No, his only enemies were within him, as part of him, and this was why he and they had come for treatment.

The time was pleasant enough. At first, disturbed John slept a lot. Yes, the poor man slept and dreamed, for he and those enemies which he carried within his poor mind, were so old and so terribly tired.

There were consultations, of course. Yes, confused John, despite his exhaustion, knew it was required that he should talk with these white-coated men. He had experience of life; he knew doctors were for his own good. They seemed to understand him too, and it was good to talk with them, for they knew he held others trapped inside his mind, and they understood and let John know that it was all right, that they would repair him.

The old Sarnian was not stupid. Despite his fatigue, he

knew he had to talk and reason with these doctors as surely as he had to tell the unseen companions what was going on, for how else would they know which medicines to try out on him? Yes, this ancient and care-worn man was a willing patient. He wanted to be made better.

As the drugs and tablets were absorbed, while always he was carefully monitored, so did John gradually shake off his years, and his fatigue and lethargy with them, so that slowly but surely he became part of his surroundings. Each day, Mr. Collins became more and more aware of things around him, and the inner voices lessened their efforts to isolate him.

John was in no rush. He was as relaxed as the staff who cheerfully, if a little patronising, jollied him along and made him feel one of the family. Yes, John had always enjoyed being fussed over, and now the younger he became, the more he enjoyed it.

The building was old, its high ceilings and lengthy windows giving it a certain sense of splendour. One might have expected it to be cold and draughty through its very pretensions of spaciousness, but on the contrary, the administration kept it over-warm as though to compensate.

The wards were good, old-fashioned places, where there was constant companionship for those who needed it. There was a certain lack of privacy, as would be expected with the great number of beds mustered militarily on either side of this corridor of a room, but this to John was a bonus. He had always wished for that companionship of sharing a room at night, perhaps the unspoken need of an only child. It made going to bed exciting somehow, childlike even. Besides, what need had he for privacy? Anyway, he could always retreat under the bed-covers or just immerse himself in his reading or drawing or even his private thoughts if he chose to.

Not that the patients were allowed to linger in bed all day, either. What fun it was to be cajoled in the early morning, to be nagged into getting up and to have breakfast and take a daily interest in such vital hospital routines as washing and grooming. How John began to enjoy joining in with some of the other patients, to moan and groan about these impositions.

No, once it had been established which medications worked best for John, he also was released from his bed.

Released at first, but actively encouraged soon after.

"Come on, Mr. Collins," jollied the sister with arm muscles bulging, suggesting she would make a better friend than a formidable enemy. "Can't have you lazing in bed all day, can we? Doctor says you've got to get up for meals now."

"What was that?"

John smiled, he would not risk repeating what he had just muttered.

"Nurse!" bellowed sister, "I think Mr. Collins here wants another blanket bath! Cold water this time!" Her smile belied the contrived aggressiveness of her quip.

There were all sorts in this place, from people who had almost destroyed themselves through various abuses, or quicker attempts, to the ultra-shy and withdrawn, still awaiting to be released from their private incarcerations, to old and feeble people who could not express themselves other than through anti-social habits.

But here in this place, no-one minded. What in the outside world might have seemed unusual or abnormal was accepted here as part of the rich pattern of life. No, John Collins, as he got ever younger through the application of treatment and therapy, was no more bothered by the shuffling old gentleman who struggled in vain attempts to expose himself to the completely disinterested nurses, than by having to share the day-room with women, some of whom were still in dressing-gowns. Everything was accepted here, and he was beginning to feel so good.

"How are you today, my dear?" asked Gerda, pleased indeed to see her man looking so much better and taking noticeable interest in his surroundings.

"Me? Oh, I'm all right me, eh?" he joked, exaggerating his Guernsey diction for old Frances' sake.

"Oh, that's for sure, eh?" echoed the old lady, while John fussed to fetch his Mum a chair.

"And is it that you're all right you, cor demme me?" continued John, as both Donkeys indulged in some long past, but not forgotten humour.

Gerda did not understand the private Island fun, but she

did know her dear husband was laughing, and that was all she needed.

As companionship-filled day followed worthwhile day, as medication followed psycho-therapy sessions, so did John more and more recover. Not only was he working out his own fears and anxieties so that they could no longer intrude, except by his specific invitation, but he was involved with the help of others in this happy family.

John became involved with group therapy where he, almost recovered, would help those who still had far to go. Yes, John was now giving. The former taker was now the willing donor, and he enjoyed it. John Collins was aware that others too were capable of suffering, as once he had been tormented. John was never more to feel that he was the only person in this world capable of feeling pain.

Even Gerda had become involved at this stage, and as a sign of John's recovery, her presence was not resented by him. No, she was actively welcomed, for she was now his real and tangible friend. She would help him to accept that Franz had to be relegated to memory.

When John had reached the point to acknowledge the wrongs he had brought to his wife and son, she had been there by his side to help him to forgive himself, to remove the pain as the guilt had been recognised.

"So, John," started the psychiatrist, who insisted on being referred to as psycho-therapist or just plain therapist, for his informality was the gift of his art, "You tell me you're ready to fly the nest."

Yes, it was true, as much as John loved it here, and would miss the routine and the companionship, he was well enough to recognise his own reinstatement to the normal human race. Not that he thought of what he was going to as any more normal than his friends and helpers in here, such was the good repair that had been effected on him.

"Yes, Doctor, I'm ready to go home now, to my family."

191

"Good. And what about your other things?" The therapist's words were well-meaning, his questions always open-ended.

"You mean my friend?" asked John.

The therapist just shrugged, but his lack of spoken response was kind. It was his trade after all–his patients had to do the speaking, not he.

"Franz?"

The therapist just raised his eyebrows, as his eyes smiled at his patient, willing him to proceed.

Many hours had they spent discussing the inconclusiveness of John's quest, hours of outpourings, begging, pleading, beseeching. There had been times when John had viewed this doctor as the foe, the one who was keeping Franz from him, telling him that Franz had deserted him, that he hated him, that he wished no more to do with his disgusting and traitorous erstwhile friend. And yet, the man had never said these things, never suggested nor refuted, he had simply let his patient bring them out of his own mind to explore and examine his own thoughts.

There had been times when John had tried to convince this man that Franz lived, for had he not met him in Russia? Other moments there were when he wondered if it had all been a delusion and if, even then, he had been displaying warning signs of his recent illness.

"I'm really not sure, doctor. You see, at times I know, yes I really know, Franz is alive somewhere, and then again at other times I just know he has to be dead. Why else has he not contacted me . . .?

"Go on, I'm listening, John. Then what?"

"Well, I sort of believe both in a way." John felt as a young lad trying to explain to his teacher what he had newly discovered and as yet hardly understood. He did not feel awkward about saying it, however, not to this man anyway, for this man always listened and never condemned. He knew everything there was to know about his patient, and yet he still liked him and was never impatient or rushed him.

"I know it doesn't make sense, but I sort of think Franz is alive some of the time and dead at others." John smiled at the therapist, he smiled, embarrassed at the irrationality of his own thesis, but still that good man just kept him fixed with his gaze, willing him to go on.

"I don't really care now though, because when he is dead I can keep him alive by remembering our good times together. When I think about him, about us, then it is all real, for it all happened, so is still there. Do you see what I mean?"

The therapist nodded.

"So what will I do now, doctor? Should I keep on looking, or what?"

"Well, John," replied the patient man, "You must choose, really. I can only remind you what you decided the other day . . ."

"What? You mean, Gerda and all that?"

"Tell me then, tell me again," suggested the therapist. He needed to hear it once more, he wanted to feel that John Collins, now in receipt of a generous pension from an appreciative Company whom he had served well, a man with the prospect of time on his hands, would be able to cope, and use this blessing to build himself up.

"Well, I really love Gerda, and I know I've been a bad husband to her in the past, but now I'm going to make it up to her.' He paused.

"And?" The question was kind, more of a cue than inquisitorial.

"And I'm going to share Franz with her, even if he is dead."

Chapter Twenty-nine

The final day lasted an eternity, or so it seemed. Yet, unlike many traumas, which extend for ever while they are executed, then fade like the sun-chased morning mist once their time has gone, this one would live with the two women until their own extremity, whereas with John it had to die with him.

* * *

John's Company had been extremely generous in their recognition of a good and faithful servant and they made it possible for him to retire early on the grounds of impaired health, while removing from him all possible financial anxieties which might otherwise have been an impediment to his enforced leisure.

John Collins had certainly been a model patient in hospital. He had been declared cured, well, at least equal to any of his peers, for who can claim to be wholly sane for all of the time?

With the pressure of work removed and with the absence of guilt and anxiety from his bygone years, John was able to find himself once more.

Perhaps for the first time in his life, he began to appreciate fully the efforts of others. Where previously he had taken for granted that the role of the two women in his life was to attend to his every need, now he was grateful and full of humility that anyone should so concern themselves with his well-being.

Now, the days were John's to fill. He was not an old man any more. He had his health back and his mind was completely his. Had he not successfully come through his alcoholism of years gone by, then his depressive illness which had been equally banished, leaving him fit and well? Yes, John was truly thankful that he had been saved from himself on both these occasions, thanks to the love and concern of those around him. He now knew that despite his years, he was still a young man, and would enjoy his early retirement to the full.

It is not always easy, when a person has been driven by hard work all his life, suddenly to take on the luxury of leisure. It is a blessing which has to be used wisely and not over-indulged.

Having given himself completely to his work and search, all those years, John Collins had developed no other interests. Try as he might, he could not interest himself in gardening, and he had never been one for working on home improvements. Nor could John read for long, for his concentration would go, or he would find himself identifying too strongly with this character or that, which would lead to confusion.

Gerda tried to involve her man in aesthetics as much as she could, so that often they would indulge in visits to live theatre, ballets and concerts, for they were well-placed by car to attend many venues. When visits to London were required, the train put them within seventy minutes of the capital.

John even got himself talked into galleries, and exploring gardens and stately homes at every opportunity. If there was anything of interest in their surroundings, the Collins family would be there.

Then there was their son, his wife and their newly-born little child. Oh yes, the time was filled adequately. It seemed they were frequently visiting their little grand daughter in Germany, or else she and her mum, and sometimes Little Franz as well, were staying at their house.

Life was full, life was varied and it was good. Even so, there were times when though feeling younger by the day, John needed to get away, to be completely by himself. Well, not completely perhaps, maybe he just needed to get away from other people to have only his thoughts for company.

John's wish for solitude was not a cause for worry, it was rather a refreshment for him, and he began to indulge in it frequently, knowing that Gerda did not mind, that she accepted this need in him, just as she had accepted long ago that there had been a little part of her man which she was not permitted to know or share.

It could be said that Gerda actively encouraged her dearest to go off on his own as he did, for perhaps she too needed her space, the better to appreciate their togetherness when it did happen. John always returned happy and refreshed after his excursions into solitude. Everyone had to acknowledge that, so it could only be good.

Some days, as though he were still at work, John Collins would rise early, go through the hurried ritualistic routines of one with little spare time before the onset of another working day, wash and groom himself, put on his formal clothes and take his leave.

"Goodbye, Gerda love. I'm off now. See you later, my dear." Gerda would rush to his side.

"Goodbye, darling, have a lovely day. Drive carefully."

They would kiss goodbye, and Gerda would wave her man off as he reversed the car from its garage. The whole community of neighbours would accept John as one of the club setting off to earn an honest shilling, just as they were.

Gerda and Frances never quizzed John as to where he had been. Occasionally he would drop snippets their way, describing some incident he had observed, or telling of a lovely view and how he planned to take them to it next time they were out for a Sunday afternoon drive together. Mostly, it was as though they were playing some sort of game, a pretence even, that John was employed. Well, it was true, he was employed but not with the work or chores imposed by others. No, John was employed with his own activities, his own pleasures.

"Where does Papa go?" asked Little Franz of his mother. He was at home on one of his frequent visits with wife and child.

"Oh, you know your father," laughed Gerda. "He's really happy on his own sometimes."

"But Mama," started Little Franz, more puzzled by this new habit than confused, "Are you sure Papa is all right to go off on his own like this? You know with . . ." This idea trailed for too many painful memories, recalls which he thought

196

forgotten and buried, were beginning to ghost themselves upon him.

"No, he's fine, Franz. Your father is just lovely," reassured Gerda, cutting short any misgivings her son might have had. "You'll see how happy and relaxed he is when he comes home this evening. Papa is a changed man."

Little Franz certainly hoped so. He did not really relish the idea of his Papa going off on his endless search for his namesake once more, not if it meant he had to abandon his name to that figment and adopt the title Patrick once more. But no, these were silly thoughts. Everything must be as Mama said, or she and Grandmama would not be so happy about it all.

When he was out on his own, be it driving slowly in the car or walking on solitary paths, John Collins was at peace. He enjoyed indulging his thoughts. This was not a conscious pursuit, nor was it in any way compulsive. John was not really aware that he was thinking. He certainly was not searching into his memory, it was more that his memories were seeking him out and introducing themselves one by one.

It was strange how one thought would lead to another without any conscious effort or ordering. Consequently, his train of recall was haphazard, well, to any form of logic, but for John it was quite natural and unforced. It was a therapy.

He did not embark on a journey thinking, 'What shall I consider today?' No, he would set off as a writer with a blank page, just waiting for inspiration. Just as when the writer has penned his first line, then the ideas flow as though from some unknown source, the instrument not knowing what comes next, but having just some vague goal or ending, so it was with John's thoughts.

Perhaps he would remember a dream he had recently experienced. Quickly, as his mind relaxed, that dream would trigger the memory of another dream and another and yet another. Scenes and memories of dreams long since forgotten would flood into his mind so fast that not all could be grasped, but they would have only sufficient time to colour his mood. It seemed to John that he had so many sleep time memories, that they all formed some part of a parallel life. He had a parallel Guernsey, a replica England, Germany also was duplicated, even Russia had its twin. The one thing these thoughts had in common was that they were all good, all soothing. None of John's free-wheeling thoughts disturbed him, but all confirmed him in his relaxation and the new found contentment in his life.

Not only dreams did John have, but memories, memories of his distant past, right back to childhood, the days of his youth, early manhood, adulthood, maturity and recent old age, before he had reverted to find himself back in his young middle-age.

Yes, these memories also flowed, flitting from one to the other with almost the speed of light, for was he not able, through this power, to move instantly in the merest fraction of a second from one place to another, hundreds of miles or thousands of days apart? What power, what freedom, what absolute control!

In order to achieve this state, it was imperative for John Collins to have solitude. Solitude yes, but John was never alone or lonely. Previously, when he had been a youth in turmoil, his thoughts had made demands of him. As he had aged, his guilt and conscience had manipulated his ideas and his confusion had grown, so that his thoughts had become unwelcome intrusions. Now, since hospital treatment had brought him back to health, it was different. Now, John was in charge of his conjectures, and they would come or go to keep him company, or respect his privacy, as he pleased.

Now, if it was the good man's choice, he could conjure up his friend from all those years ago. He no longer had to have his friend intruding, uninvited, to reproach him for his shortcomings. If Franz came to mind, it was because he had been invited. After all, John was not sure if Franz Müller were still alive or if he had perished long ago. He did not have to know, for when he chose to, his friend of all those decades previously, could be conjured up, whether in fact he were alive or dead. The present did not matter, for it could not undo the past.

So John could conjure his friend Franz at will, and could sublimate his logical thoughts, just as the reader of a story can identify with a character. As the atheist can temporarily believe the tenets of the religion held by a written character, as the reader can accept magic and mythology while held in the attention of a novel, so it was with John; when in a relaxed state, he knew it was often easier to believe than to disbelieve.

And if belief is faith, then the believer is in charge of his own imaginings, and what is right for that person must be so, for it is real to him, therefore it exists.

So with John and Franz; it took little effort to believe and therefore to feel sure that he was alive, less effort than to accept that he had died. At other times, when in energetic and vital frame of mind, John had the mental energy to acknowledge the logic of his friend's demise. Both possibilities could co-exist, both contradictions need not conflict, for was not John Collins in charge of his own thoughts? There were, after all, two truths, and who was to say which had more force than the other?

John no longer held conversations with Franz. No, even though he could hold the memory of their comradeship as clearly as if it had been only yesterday, he was not deluded by the image. The hospital time had done well for John. Nor was he ever confused as to who he was. No, he was quite clearly John Collins, and the memory of his friend was without doubt Franz Müller, but it was good to hold the memory alive when he chose to do so.

Not all John's thoughts were about his absent friend. At times his free-wheeling took him to other places, other times. He would examine himself as he had been, he would examine and judge himself as though he were considering an entirely different person.

Yes, the John Collins he observed in the dealings he had had with his parents and with his dear Gerda and Little Franz left a lot to be desired. If he had not accepted that he was looking at his past self as an entirely different person, he would have felt consumed by shame. As it was, he had learned to accept his former short comings as being now outside his control. He knew now how to forgive himself and to make a fresh start. Though it sometimes might have seemed almost too late, it was never quite so, at least to try to make amends.

So it was then, that he would set off early in the mornings, taking leave of his wife and mother, to the whole world as if he were setting off for work.

How he filled the time until he returned home was often unknown to the two ladies, but all they knew was that after such an absence he would return to them unharmed and relaxed, and oh, such a welcome and lovely man.

After one such excursion into his recent past John was driving home tired but exhilarated. He had enjoyed his day of fantasy and only he would know where his thoughts had led his body.

Almost home now, he was relaxed. At times like these he always considered his car an extension of his own limbs. No more thought was needed to guide the vehicle than a walker gives to his walking. He and his car were at one.

John, the driver, would soon be leaving his faithful servant. Just eight miles more. He absent-mindedly fiddled to tune the radio.

The appliance, unlike his car, was not subjugated to his will and resented the intrusion into its peace.

It was a September evening, just dark now, the air was cool and still, autumn not far off. The sky ahead, which had lit his journey with a brilliant red, and was now the deepest purple, indulged a whim and permitted itself to wear its first evening star, as John absently toyed his receiver, while the cool air allowed the first mists to rise and set above the ground.

The stations were myriad on a night like this, the words of the many foreign commentators, and sounds of international music, galumping into each other jerkily as the tired hand grew impatient with his set's disobedience.

What was that? That voice, what was it? Whose was it? That voice picked up then so quickly missed and lost, that voice come back through the dark, through almost a lifetime.

Who was that, who had spoken? Who was he?

The fumbling, now involuntary, persevered. The car continued to drive itself – as the legs walk – independent of the master it carried.

There it was again. That gentle, clear, smooth, youthful sound, its timbre laden with laughter and enquiry. The words were German, the voice was that of an old friend, his lost friend.

The car drove on. John would talk to the long lost enemy returned from yesteryear. At last he had found his friend.

The car sped on, oblivious of the green light which had turned amber then red, as it had been oblivious of the sky changing from red to purple, whilst its master had been its decision maker. The master was listening to his brother long since lost who had once been his enemy, but also his friend.

Neither the car, nor John, nor the German friend saw or heard the other traveller at the cross roads, until they felt the impact which turned them all, in an instant, from immortal dreams to vulnerable metals, glass, and flesh, and bone.

Chapter Thirty

The priest came, at the request of Gerda, at the suggestion of the Sister. It was a new Sister on duty now and the nurse was a man.

The priest, a local vicar of High Church persuasion, befitting her little boy's upbringing, was with Frances and Gerda quickly. Gerda wondered if he had already been prepared in the night and had just needed Frances' permission this morning. Perhaps permission was the wrong word anyway? Why did Gerda feel so touchy about it? She loved old Frances so why should she, who focussed her love of equal yet differing intensity on that same dying John, resent that the old lady had been asked and the old lady had assented to the final rites? Was it because it emphasised that the old dear was his mother and that she had known her son for ever? Yet it had been Gerda's permission that had been sought for the kidneys when the point of expiry should come. If it were a case of point scoring then surely she had been given the more valued task? Was it that her's was just temporal and only associated with living and dying, with mortality, whereas Frances' part was spiritual, eternal? They were silly thoughts anyway. She was just on edge.

Frances had not queried the Extreme Unction yet she was aware of this seventh sacrament. Had not she invoked it on dear departed Larry? Strange that she had witnessed these last rites impassively, yet with understanding, and had then reverted to the belief that John was on the mend.

John had been unconscious or asleep during his final service, and the medical staff had discreetly left the family with God's servant. At least he was still alive as witnessed by the incessant motion of his dials and graphs. It did not matter, so the rotund and draped little man, rich in the plainness of his regalia, had informed them; the Holy Spirit would work regardless of the state of the one receiving. Gerda had felt almost cynical, except she had not had enough understanding to fight against anything so foreign. Besides, she had then no fight left in her, except to hold back her mourning until her John could be released.

* * *

The man pauses. He feels chill. He looks up from his task and rejoins reality. Yes, he has been sitting a long time, his joints feel stiff and he is suddenly aware of aches and pains which have been there for a long time but of which he has been oblivious. Better to get back to the job in hand, to join once more the unreality which will render the reality unreal for a little while longer. The man is beginning to feel his age, the first cold winds of approaching winter in his life.

Before he sinks back to his task, which has been his joy for many years, he surveys his surroundings. He sits in a place steeped with childhood memories.

The sun has gone now, it goes early in late summer. Probably this is why the visitors do not invade this place or, if they do, they go early to leave it as a haven for the locals. But where are the locals now? Where the brave bundles of bravado and self-boasting noise jumping from the top, reacting to, and leading their audiences?

The breeze ripples across the almost calm expanse of sea between the Castle and this pool, this tidal pool, the first along the coast from St. Peter Port, known to the locals as the Gents' Pool. The fast escaping sun in this chill September, portending the winter to come, the winters gone and the winter of life ahead, still lights the Castle which throws its angular reflections on to the water, reflections every so often shattered by that sudden assault of the east wind.

The pool is no longer a pool, as the first ripples flood over the ancient smooth granite wall, sweeping the grass-like, sun baked, wind-dried, hardened sea-weed and transforming it back into the soft hair of mermaids, to cascade faster and faster into six inch waterfalls, replenishing the loss of leakage and evaporation since the last high tide.

Soon it will be deep enough to jump off the top. Who is going to be first this time? Who dares not to be? Look, it's right over the wall now, it must be six inches deep already. What about the slab, eh? You mate, stand there and show me if it's up to your belly button yet! They're stalling for time. They always do. Each painstaking step of the little boy or little girl down the brass ladder, each furtive step onto crackled dry seaweed, some splashed now and soapy, the horror of sudden cold between toes and the self-imposed torture of slipping first a foot and then a leg into the first foamy ripples of high tide, is derided and hurried by the impatient performer, but inwardly welcomed as a respite as perhaps a further six inches was needed on that frighteningly shallow mattress of water above the slab. Was it really true the Germans built that slab? Maybe? Didn't they build the south slope too, for sunbathing?

'O.K., stand clear, I'm off, me! Is it all clear below?' Back to the top wall now for a run up. 'Yes, it's all clear!'

'Go on. You scared or something?'

'No, I'm not mate. You watch this, eh?'

'Go on, then!'

'Still all clear?'

'Yes. Course it is.'

'Right!'

That fast acceleration. Has he enough speed to get airborne, to get far enough out in space for that twenty foot descent, to land properly in two feet of water?

'Hurry up and get it over with. If you're going to injure yourself do it quickly, I hate to watch.'

Almost at the edge. He loses his nerve. Are they sure the tide's coming up this fast?

'Move out the way, you bloody little fool! I nearly landed on you then! Good job I stopped myself.'

The little depth gauge mite shivers closer into the wall where she was. She can't understand why that big boy shouts at her so. She was nowhere near the slab, but she won't argue as he's a big boy.

All the others think it, but they can't talk. If they do, then they have to be first. Come on, tide. Come on mate, jump please, then we can all bundle in after you, if you're not hurt!

That yell! Was it fear? Was it exhilaration? Arms waving, legs still running through the air. Falling like a stone now. Yes, targeting right on the slab, well away from the steps. This is it! Is he going in too steep?

Pull out a bit! Bend your legs up, let your bum slow you down and take the speed out of your impact! No, not that tight! It's not deep enough for a bombshell! Hell, he's gone in badly!

The great splash, the frozen silence. Will he rebound from the bottom, thrown out of the water? Will he take the force on his bent legs and rebound like a released coil? Will he just lie there? Who will go in for him?

The craters of foam wave outwards and ripple their way to join the rising tide. He slips under, straightens out his sprung legs. His heels hit the furred concrete obliquely and his legs slide along unobstructed. Instinctively his hands go to his side, the spread palms jacking his descent as the wedge of water is forced aside to allow his bottom a safe landing.

Fear over now. He springs to attention.

'Easy. Look at that, everyone. I did it! I was the first and the water's only up to my arse!'

Everyone jumps in from the side. Soon it will be deep enough for them to go off the top too.

But where are they all? Where are the brave children now? Is it that even the children of Guernsey, the children of the man's youth have been seduced from their fun-loving inexpensive course, by the modern attractions of mindless games and pastimes? Is it that they're all gone soft now and prefer the heated, chemical water of the indoor pool at Beau Sejour? Is there no-one to stand the chill of the cold east wind?

Chapter Thirty-one

From time to time John heard their voices as they took turns to speak to him. He quite liked it when he felt their voices too, as their lips had touched the bristles on his ear. Yes, he had enjoyed that. He had wanted to tell them so but that would have meant speaking. No, he could not go to all those lengths. Besides, he did not know how to express his feelings. He had forgotten what feelings were. As for words? Well he didn't feel the need for such communication, he didn't think he could remember how to speak. Anyway, they kept doing it so they must have realized what pleasure it gave.

Perhaps they had seen his smile? He couldn't tell really, not that he was sure he had given one. Maybe he had just dreamed he had? Perhaps he was dreaming these voices too? He could check. He could always lift up the shutters and find them there as part of his day, reality in his dream. No, that was too much effort too. Why exert himself? He was quite content like this.

"John, hello darling. This is Mum here. Are you awake, my love?" Frances spoke quite casually. Her boy was fine really, just a mum trying to reassure him.

"Gerda dear, you have a turn, I think I saw his mouth move then. I think our little John was smiling."

Didn't he laugh last night! How Frances remembered. He had laughed, and laughed, at the Chief of Police! She had felt quite embarrassed, almost as much as when he had screamed out in fear at the Doctor, such a good man too, to have come out like that after curfew and all.

"Hello, John darling." Gerda was speaking now. Her voice was stilted as she fought back the tears. She could not break yet, she had to hold on. "It's me, Gerda. Can you hear me, John?" She was on his good side, on his left today. She took his hand and held it with a gentle squeeze.

It was cold, his hand was cold! He was dead! She gasped. She looked round. Frances was still there, the nurse was there, the tubes and bags of transparent and red were still there in their varying stages of emptying. The panels were still lit. All was the same except they were all attending a corpse.

"You all right, Mrs. Collins?" asked the nurse as he rushed forward. Gerda saw him coming. He swayed towards her, first to the right then to the left, a bizarre half melted snowman! Everything was so cold! She was cold, the ward was cold, the nurse was made of cold and the corpse was cold.

* * *

She is ready for bed now. Soon it will be dark. She could put on the light. Ah yes, these modern times, she has electricity now, but why bother? Why not follow a life time's habit and go to bed with the night and rise with the sun?

Her old companion, her dog, whines at her feet. She looks down at her old friend, her only family. He looks away pretending not to appear to want but letting out just a slight whimper in case she really does believe he is unconcerned.

"Yes, I know," she whispers. "It's our walk time. I know, you old thing."

His old threadbare tail rustles the cool air. Strange to have such a worthless creature in the home, but then she is a strange woman.

The old woman moves slowly. She has worked hard all her life. There will be no rest for her, she has no-one to support her closing years, only memories, all harrowing. Yet she has love in her heart, she always had and she always will have. She has no-one to support her dark end but her old dog needs her. It is good to be needed.

She takes her thick winter coat from behind the door. September is quickly beckoning the winter.

She feels the old cold of mother Russia as the cold winds from Siberia strike through her open door.

An old priest smiles as he sits alone. He is a priest, for tonight he is wearing his clerical collar set smooth against the wrinkled indentations of the past years. It is not yet dark outside his tiny bungalow but he has the light on, for his eyes are not what they were.

Tomorrow he will be preaching again in his old, loved church. He has been invited to preach. He loves the challenge. He will see the rapt attention of the flock, no longer his flock but someone else's. But he will be happy for, just for a little while, they will be his. He will see familiar old faces and there will be gaps where the many have passed on. But he will see them. They will be there with him.

He turns himself to his task once more. He is amused. 'Turn the other cheek', indeed! That old theme! It was as familiar now as it had been half a life time away. Things have changed now, for then he was young and now he is almost at the end, but life is still full of fun as he indulges in the present, revels in the past and allows his hand to stay, while the two concepts intermingle. There is no need to rush. Time is his for this evening.

She reaches home at last. How she hates the thought of winter, but how this cold east wind forces it into her consciousness. Another cold winter without the warmth of her darling in bed, like those cold winters when she was young and he was stolen from her.

She sniffs and, with the back of her hand, wipes a tear from her cheek. Was she really crying or was it just the penetration of the breeze?

How could she manage yet another cold and lonely winter? How would she survive without him? Perhaps it would be better if he had died and then she could have mourned away his parting. But to face old age alone and yet to know he was still an entity, and to have her lonely burden added to by guilt that she had felt compelled to allow her dear Keith to be taken from her, to be looked after with professional care, was more than she could contemplate. She had to live one day at a time, never planning ahead, for there was no future for them, not even a past to devour for comfort.

She has her daughter though, Anne de la Haye has her daughter and she will lean on her. It is good that her daughter is warm and comforting and wind-proof. She and Keith have at least created some goodness out of their misery.

The wizened old chap chuckles inwardly to himself and his old eyes twinkle. Despite his years the aged bundle of wrinkles and sinew has never lost its deceptive piercing light blue smile.

He has been put into the television room and will be permitted to enjoy the whole of the football match before the staff take him along to his bed. He spends a lot of his time in bed these days and more and more of that asleep. He does not resent or regret though and is stoical, accepting the signs of his ancient years. He has had a good life.

He is amazed and amused, his enthusiasm transmitting into a dry cackle as he realizes the irony of one of the first matches of the new winter season. The other inmates do not respond, except that one turns towards the twinkling visage and then gives himself back to the screen.

Germany playing against England! What a travesty! What a complete about turn from all those years before, years which now seemed like only yesterday. Playing each other like brothers too! The bitterest of enemies turned to become brothers! Was there not treachery somewhere in this? No, those were old ideas, Sebastian had had to unlearn such ideas after the surrender. Well they couldn't see into his mind so he could still hold such thoughts and they would never know. What fun!

He thinks back. There always had been those who had propounded the concept of brotherhood. But had they really meant it? Would they really have allowed it to have proceeded to this, or was it just propaganda gone wild?

Sebastian remembers now the two boys who had taken the ideal literally. Hadn't they been ahead of their time? The one a gullible defeated Britisher and the other a traitorous failure. What had become of those two, he wonders. Had they ever got together after the war?

"I think I'll close the curtains now, Herr Tropp," fusses the nurse. "It's almost dark outside and the autumn winds are coming early."

Herr Tropp just smiles, he keeps all his thoughts to himself.

Anne is pleased to sit down and to know that soon her only child will lovingly bring in a cup of tea for her Mum. She is a good girl.

She never really gets used to visiting her Keith at the Duchess of Kent Home, perhaps she never will. She always longs to go but she always comes away in pain. It's not just the knowledge that her poor strong man of yesteryear is now a broken wreck of his former self, completely dependent on others in his wheelchair and with his incontinence. No, it's not just that, and the knowledge that his mind is still whole, that he is in fact still the young Keith that he always was, strong, fearless fisherman, trapped in an old and useless body. It is not altogether the bitterness of the four years of separation and longing, three of which had undermined the foundations of his good health, for their separation and great longing had carried them over the hiatus of reunion after the Occupation, with its trauma of the lost first son. Wasn't their sweet daughter the enduring proof of this?

No, the visits, as comfortable and welcoming as the staff were — and no-one could do more than them — always remind her and take her back to times better erased; to the States Emergency Hospital to visit little Patrick, poor fatherless little child who was not permitted to survive to see his Daddy.

How is that other poor lamb, she wonders. Whatever became of John? How he had been a support to her in her loneliness! How little Patrick had always smiled when he saw the Collins boy! How they had loved each other like a father and son!

"Come on Mum, perk up a bit, there's a love. Here's your cup of tea." It is her daughter. She had never met Patrick either, or his proxy father.

Strange to have met Bert Bisson today too. Maybe that is why she is now thinking so of John. It all seems to be focusing somehow on those dark cold and lonely years of all that history ago. Bert was not a happy man either. He'd lost his new young wife. Tragic early death it had been. They said he'd lost all his fight and will to go on after that. He had really gone to pieces. The Duchess of Kent is obviously the best place for him.

Chapter Thirty-two

"That's all right now, love." Gerda came round to the kind ministrations of old Frances. She had been seated in the corridor, near a hastily-opened window.

"I'll be back in a moment, Mrs. Collins," the Sister addressed Frances. "I'm sure she's all right now. Don't leave that window open for long, mind. We don't want her taking cold. There's a bitterly cold wind outside today."

Today? That was it. It was a new day! Gerda revived, with a jerk of panic. It is today that John is going to die and then I'll be free! That is a terrible thought though. I have killed him! That is why he is so cold. I have killed John by my wishes and nobody knows yet, except me!

"Come on now, Gerda, drink this water, you'll feel better," coaxed Frances kindly. "I don't think you slept much last night, that's the trouble. Come on now, perk up please, we must look our best."

"Our best?" she quavered.

"Yes sweetheart, for John's sake." Frances was putting on a cheerful front but ill hiding her own deep-felt misery.

"John?"

"Yes dear, John . . . you know?" Frances choked as she tried to say more.

"But he's . . .," Gerda could not quite bring herself to facing up to her liberation.

"No, dear. He's not dead yet, but it's just a matter of hours now."

She knew, Frances knew all along! Or did she? Did she think he was living, that he had a future? Or did she realize he was dead already but was pretending just for Gerda that this was not so?

"But he was so cold. He must be . . .," Gerda persisted.

"No, darling," was Frances' gentle and knowledgeable

212

reply. "No, my love, he is not dead yet. He's just gone very cold because his poor body has almost given up."

* * *

The youth lets the door click quietly behind him. He does not feel too bad at leaving the old man like this but he did not really want to wake him. Not that the old man could have stopped him really. No, the youth tells himself he wants the old fellow to stay asleep as long as possible before discovering he has gone.

He could have left the tenement door open, thus avoiding the chance of the old man hearing the lock. He had thought of it as he had made his way towards the fast life and the living, leaving behind the mundane and the dying, but he had stopped himself. It is true he has stolen the old man's pension so any thief would not find anything of worth in that pensioner's home, but the youth cannot bear to think that another might come and rob the old chap, assisted by his own carelessness. It is in order for him to rob the old man, but not for a perfect stranger to. It is permissible to rob someone you have loved but not to let them be violated in that way by someone unknown.

Not that he has loved the old man really. How could he have loved someone so old, who had just picked him up like that? But even so he wishes the poor veteran no harm. The old man has loved him, that is certain. He had shared all of his meagre existence with him. The youth knows that half of what is the old man's is his for the asking, or the sharing. The old man loves him, he has told him so. He had not really loved the old man and yet no one has ever treated him so kindly as he has. He had stayed there a long time too, of his own free will.

If the police catch him he knows he can get off, for he only has to say how the old man had kept him and loved him. Yet he could not say he had been kept prisoner there. He had wanted to stay.

Does a part of him love the old man? He prefers rather to feed his anger than to subdue his love. No, the old man deserves to lose his pension. He has had other boys, he will find more. He deserves what he had got! Yet the lad hopes, as

213

he sets off for his new life, that the next boy will treat the old man kindly.

The old chap would probably have given his pension to the youngster and gladly have gone hungry and without heat for days, if he had asked for it. No, the boy could not ask, but he knows, even though he did not exactly reciprocate old Morten's love. Deep down he cares and will probably return some day to see if he is all right.

"Mr. Bisson, you'd better wheel Mr. de la Haye in now," orders the Duty Sister, "there's a cold east wind coming up now. We don't want him to catch cold do we?"

Old Keith smiles. He can still command his facial muscles. His old body might be ready for the scrap heap but he still has that smile, which can at will belie the blackest gloom of innermost feelings.

"D'yer hear that?" chuckles Bert. "Ruddy nagging women, eh? Can't get rid of them, anyway."

Keith coughs out a weak laugh. It is true, now he suddenly feels cold but he doesn't see why he should give in. He's weathered far worse out in his little fishing boat.

Strange how Bert puts Keith's very own thoughts into words.

"You know, Keith, these first cold east winds like this always remind me of that time we got sent to France back in 1941. D'you remember?"

What a stupid question! Keith nods.

"D'you remember we thought it was cold as they took us across? But that was nothing to that first prison, eh? One blanket each, as I remember, and those hard plank beds too." He grins at his own musing.

"Yeah. Those were the days, Bert. Those were the days, mate! Take me in now, please. I'm not the man I was. I feel the chill of death right through to my old bones."

It is a silent Bert as he wheels Keith into the warmth, accompanied by death. Larry is dead. Where is Frances, Frances and that boy of her's, the one who set all this trouble in motion? He's no boy now and that's for sure! What's happened to everyone?

Can he really stand up tomorrow in that same pulpit and pour out those same sentiments as he did all those years ago? Can he really expect people, these days, to understand what it is to forgive his enemy? Has he managed it?

Old Father Peters indulges in his memories. 'Did I really give Adolph Hitler and his ilk such a great build up, only to dash it so vitriolically right at the end? I must have done a good job though, for they certainly had their revenge.'

'Was that turning the other cheek though? Shouldn't I have been asking them to forgive the Occupiers and not have been seeking to gain unfair advantage from my rhetoric?'

'It seems hardly possible that we can have been such bitter enemies then. Now look at us. We are two friendly nations as if we had never hated and sought the downfall of the other.'

Father Peters contemplates his life since the coming of peace. Yes, he really has tried to forgive and forget. It is true he was separated from his wife and sons but that has all passed long ago now and his blessings far outweigh his tribulations. He is a great-grandfather even. That is wonderful. His great-grandson is almost ready to leave school. He is almost a fully grown young man.

Yes, the thought of his youngest seed now in mid-teens reminds him of the two lads who, ahead of their time, forgave the enemy. They were both brave in their way; well, ahead of their time.

It is quite cold now, exceptionally so for September. Father Peters draws the curtains early to exclude the draught from the cold east wind, as he wonders whatever happened to the two; the one of his flock, the other the enemy. He shudders involuntarily as he turns back to his task.

The man, with his ghosts real and ghosts imagined, turns back to his writing. He wishes to lose himself in it once more before the light, too, matches the premature chill of the air. Better to imagine life and activity than to be forced to acknowledge none, as an omen to his thoughts.

The waters lap up higher now. No danger to even the most inexperienced jumper. Little waves flip their spray into the air.

Voices; are they real or are they of his imagination? No, they are real, there are still youngsters in Guernsey who will visit and appreciate the simple pleasures of the pools at high tide, even on a prematurely cold evening such as this.

The group of youngsters change and jump around to keep warm, and to expedite their resolve to take their quick dip. How the man would like to join them, in their cold flagellation, but he has work to do as he turns his now not-so-lonely-hand to his pen. He is not in control; his pen controls.

Chapter Thirty-three

John clearly heard the man's voice, it was a young man. Had he been looking for this man, for some reason? Was he the one he was searching for? Who was he searching for, anyway? Who was he, come to that?

The injections came regularly now so that no more was he permitted the luxury of pain to clear his muddled mind. With each injection came too a slowing of all his functions as witness his battery of friendly dials. This was slowing of life while a hastening of death towards its natural conclusion. And all the time he grew colder. What a feeling! What luxury, the cold and comfort of death stealing over his broken body.

Whose was that voice? Was he cold too? Yes that was it, the man had a cold voice. No, his voice was cold. No, the man with the voice was cold. Or was it, the voice with the man which was cold? It didn't matter.

More chill, cold sleep.

* * *

The old man sprawls out in his chair as the flickering flames of the first autumn fire reflect from the pallor of his skin. His chair is placed so that he will feel the warmth of this early fire, and that his still, almost inactive body will lose its potential hyperthermia. There is much activity in the room around him with excited giggles and whispers of the gathered generations, all thrilled to see the first fire spitting and crackling from the logs, to help dispel Grandpapa's cold German air. The stationary old man seems impervious to the noise and ecstatic concern around him, as though unaware of any sense except the warmth.

The old dog ambles ahead, every now and then pausing to look back, just to make sure his good mistress is still there. She struggles on behind, uncomplaining, on their well-trodden evening route. She is glad that her old dog is happy, his happiness is hers.

The wind comes in occasional strong buffets now as the sky darkens rapidly. She does not mind, for she has on her winter coat and they both know this path so well, the dog his pilgrimage all his life and her's the mission of almost four decades.

Does she imagine it or was that a flake of the first snow on her cheek? Well, so what if it was? It does not matter. She is old, she has her fire, she has her dog, she has her coat. She will not want for food, she has her neighbours and the State will provide her against starvation.

Times have changed! As she has aged and turned from young woman to old crone, so has the world about her. Not her world but the world of others, those who have had power over her to direct and control her. They have all changed, but she has kept her course.

She reflects that through her unchanging role she has experienced much, but it has not all been bad. Now in her closing years, she can better accept the colds, as sampled today, for her cruel time in Siberia has weathered her. Nothing of the cold of mother Russia will ever match the naked cruelty of frozen Siberia. This she has suffered and survived and now the very State which had condemned her to such privations has itself changed and is the Mother Russia which will sustain this independent and odd old woman to her grave.

Pieter is too old to feel the indignity of being tended and fussed over by his sister and niece. He is too unwell to be concerned that his place, as head of the household, is being usurped by the younger women. It is less stressful, so his doctor tells him, just to go along with people's plans rather than to try to fight them for the sake of it. He is less likely to get another stroke that way.

Besides, it is good at times to be well cared for. He has

218

done enough of the caring and looking after and organizing for the family in the past. It is he who has held this family together, what remains of it. No Müllers to bear the family name, but at least Ilsa has married well and has off-spring.

His sister-in-law still has that photograph on the piano. This annoys Pieter at times, for he has demanded its removal but she has just refused. Strange, in this one thing, his sister-in-law has been steadfastly disobedient. Not that it matters now anyway, for whether Franz be dead or alive in some part of Russia, he is far too old to have any Müller off-spring. If he has fathered some Russian peasant brat then Pieter prefers not to know.

Strange, Ilsa is visiting today. She must have known her old uncle is feeling cold. She has lit a real log fire. Not that he would have asked her to, he'd not wish to be indebted to anyone so young. But it feels good, it is good to be warm. Pieter thinks they must be lighting the first fires all over Germany today.

Ilsa comes in to tend to the fire. She is glad to think the old man looks warm now. To think she used to fear this old wretch. Yet there is in her a sense of duty. Did he not, in his way, try to look after her little brother in the war?

He suffered for it too; dishonour and demotion, not that he had ever talked of it, but she knows. She had found out lots of things in her searches in Guernsey and back home in Germany.

She steals a glance at the picture of young Franz. Well at least he will never grow old. His memory will be forever young. Perhaps it had all been for the best that she had never located Franz's whereabouts or discovered the circumstances of his disappearance.

She remembers now how her mother took the confirmatory news of her father's death. They had all known he was dead but actually to have had it confirmed boldly and cruelly as it was, had finished her mother. She had become a bundle of nerves.

It had been then that Uncle Pieter had stepped in and ordered their lives more and more.

She now supposes she has a lot to thank him for, although she cannot think that she ever appreciated it at the time. Well, at least her mother is still alive and well. Perhaps it is thanks to Uncle Pieter? Perhaps Mother really needed a domineering man?

Whatever became of that Gerda woman? She never did meet the husband, Franz's enemy friend. Strange that! Almost as if Gerda did not want a meeting to take place.

But why is she thinking like this? Why bring up all the past again? She feels cold as she shudders and draws up a chair also, next to the fire.

"Do not bother Grandpapa, Franz," Bern chides his youngest infant, as the little child crawls on to Grandpapa's knee. "He does not want a bundle of energy like you crawling all over him."

The words are not hard and the harshness is not meant, for all the family present knows that Grandpapa dearly loves his little Franz.

"Hey, Mister! What you doing?" The writer is drawn back from his other world as one of the erstwhile aquatic performers drips cold brine all over his characters.

"Eh?" He slips into the language of his youth.

"Who, me?"

The gang gathers, potential curiosity.

"Of course," injects the curly-haired one, leaving unsaid the collective response, 'Who else?'

"I'm writing."

"Oh he's writing," says the dark haired one of whom the description 'hair brush' seems most apt.

The writer looks up and grins. This group has real Guernsey spirit. Couldn't he use some of this repartée in his work?

"What you writing then?" enquires the tall one with genuine curiosity, edged with a trace of lively impertinence.

"I'm writing a book," replies the man, "a story." He carefully avoids the pretention of referring to it as a novel.

"Let's have a look then?" asks the chirpy one.

"Hold on a minute," orders the man, in mock severity, "you get dry first, I don't want my efforts turned to pulp."

They all laugh.

"What's your name?" asks the man, of the hair brush, feeling it must be his turn to ask the questions.

"Mark — Why?" answers hair brush.

"Mark-Why. That's a good name, eh? Hello Mark-why, mine's Mick." He proffers his hand and they all laugh with him.

"Mine's Chris." volunteers the little chirpy one, who is obviously the leader, "and this one here is Nigel . . .," indicating the tall one, "and this here is Steve."

He holds out his hand and the writer takes it, not quite sure if the friendship is genuine or humorously derisory.

"Glad to meet you," he says.

"And we're pleased to meet you Mickey," concludes Chris.

"Come on then Mickey, what's this book about?" asks Steve.

"Well you might not believe this but it's about Guernsey."

"Yeah?" gasps Nigel. "That's good, eh?" He is serious. The others laugh at his enthusiasm.

"What about Guernsey?" asks Chris adding, not waiting for the writer's reply, "Hey lads, what if Mickey puts us in his book, eh?"

What the writer at first understood as a humorous quip, he realizes is loaded with seriousness.

"O.K.," he says, "I'll write you in, you'll see."

The infant, the last of Bern's large family, named Franz to please Grandpapa, also loves his Grandpapa.

As he crawls on to the old man and is clutched and held safely by the sinewy gnarled old hands, and as all look on, Grandmama with tears of thankfulness, tears of regret, in her eyes, her son and daughters by her side and an uncountable number of grandchildren, little Franz's actions say it all. They put into action the feelings they all have.

Little Franz is unaware of his old Grandpapa's appearance. Little Franz, the youngest blessing in the Schmidt family, does not see the unseeing eye-sockets in his faceless grandsire, he is not cognizant of the bald and scarred protuberance which was once a delightful head, or of the stump, with skilfully moulded nostrils, which was once a human nose, or of the tattered flaps which must once have been the Corporal's ears. None of this he sees, or if he does, like all the family, he does not consider it worth a second thought, for he loves his Grandpapa.

"You a visitor?" asks Chris.

"Me? No, I'm Guernsey me, eh?" replies the writer.

"Is it?" adds Nigel.

"That's for sure, cor demme!" laughs Chris, "He's from yer him, eh? Eh?"

They all indulge in the language of the writer's youth, and of John's youth. It still lives on.

"That's for sure," he concludes, "Cheerie, mes vieux."

They all go on their way. It is a little darker now.

The children have all gone now. All that remains to the writer is the memory of presence. Perhaps they have not been real at all? Perhaps the writing is the only real thing?

The Castle reflections have faded now, the first lights are coming on in Town. The writer is all alone. He shudders as he sees the smoothing and shattering, as a blast of cold wind races across the sea towards him. He is chilled right through before the buffet hits him.

Yet still he writes, feeling the discomfort, yet oblivious to it. He pulls the ideas out of the cold air. He is a receiver for a story which is there in the ether. He is just the tool, directing the pen to create the story which is all around him.

He will stay until it is too dark to write any more.

Chapter Thirty-four

"It is not long now," said the nurse. The ladies and Little Franz did not answer. He was glad of that.

Gerda nodded as she slipped her hand from John's for Frances to have her turn.

The nurse had experienced the cold theft of death many times. He knew death was more beautiful, more natural than anyone could imagine. Death was a release. Death comes to all; it is the ultimate goal of all our lives. He was going to leave the family now to share alone the death of their dear man.

He had first a duty to do. It did not concern the recording machines for the pulse now was fast and slow by fits and starts, while the blood pressure was as low as it could be. The heart was quite weak and irregular now and breathing almost without evidence.

No, he had to prepare them for the pleasure of death. He did not find it hard, for his experience had always vindicated his advice.

"I'll leave you now," he said. "You can be alone with John." He was familiar, Gerda appreciated this.

"It is good that you can all be here for the end," he added. "So many people miss it." Frances clutched at John's cold fingers.

"You will be glad you were here right at the end," he continued. "You see death is so natural, so easy. There is nothing to be afraid of. It will seem like the most natural happening in the world when it arrives."

Frances knew. She had been with Larry. Death held no sting for her. She accepted it, as this kind nurse said.

"He will stop breathing once or twice you know," he addressed Gerda, "and then he will start again. You might think he has expired but then there will be a big intake of air and he will take a few final breaths. Please don't be alarmed. This is the way it is."

Gerda nodded.

"When he's finally stopped, call me please. And I want to see you crying out all those tears you're holding back at the moment, right?"

She nodded again.

"Talk to him. You never know, he might still hear you."

*　　　*　　　*

She stands there now. Her dog sits still by her side, whining slightly. She stays longer tonight, it is darker than when they usually come and colder now than it has been since last March.

She wipes the tears from her eyes. There are more tonight than usual. There are always tears, but tonight she is taken from the present and her short sojourn, at this point of pilgrimage, is expanded to allow her nostalgia to complete itself.

She surveys the great pile of stones, the cold wind whistling through them, rusticated and mellowed as they are since their laboured construction by her bare hands almost forty winters ago.

Her husband did not return and no news was heard of him once he had gone off to fight the Fascists, but she had not expected more and she still had her son to comfort her and work their peasant plot.

Then the States had taken her only child. He had been requisitioned and taken by the government to help with the siege of Leningrad. Her little thirteen year old man had been stolen from her, hastily trained and used to save his nation. He had not been permitted to write to his mother, nor she to him, for it was their duty to be parted and to suffer. And he had been killed. She did not know how he had died, or where he had died, or what his last words had been, or his last thoughts and hopes. But she had expected this, for they were Russians and Russians expect to have things imposed upon them without their consultation. She had known her son was dead, before she had been given the blessing of confirmation, but she had not cried. She had never cried for her son's death, nor had she built the stones for him. She had been unable to cry for him these last thirty-eight years, for she had loved him too much and been devastated too much.

The tears she allows now are not from the cold of the wind, they are not for her husband, or for the son who had been destined to die for his country, from the moment he was born, or for her wasted years of correction in the camp in Siberia. She cries now freely, more than she usually permits her self-hardened being, not for her two men but for her other son, the one for whom she had been martyred to Siberia after the war, and gladly so.

It had been on a bitter winter's day in 1942. She had not eaten for three days. There had been precious little food in the house, for no supplies had got through to the nearby community, not that Mother Russia had much to feed her children at this time anyway, but she had trained them well in hardship and those worth anything to her would survive. The useless would perish.

The peasant woman had been recently bereaved, that is, it had been confirmed about her little boy, what she, as his mother, had known in her heart. She had sat hungry for three days, the official horse rider dispatch on the table in front of her. For three days she had neither eaten nor slept. She had been hungry but unable to stir even to fetch roots from her shed. Her primitive fire had gone out from lack of love as she had felt the cold devour her, but she had not cared. She had suffered the pain of the winter's frosts, which had seeped right into her tiny home, but she had done nothing to alleviate its scourge, for to act for herself was of no consequence. She had no purpose to life.

At the end of the three days, still conscious, almost revelling in the misery, as some necessary purging of her circumstances, she moved her frost-stiffened joints, awoke the pains of hunger in her belly and permitted herself to feel the misery and discomfort of the cold dry thirst which had dehydrated her suffering frame. She had to drink. She was alive, the thirst had vanquished the self-imposed death wish of mourning.

She had stumbled her way weakly to the door, dizzy with hunger, head aching and throbbing with pain, half frozen joints aged like those of an old woman.

There was no water in the house. There was snow in abundance outside, but no fuel with which to melt it.

Painstakingly she had faced the outside rawness so that her gasp had all but frozen her lungs. She had staggered her way to her outhouse to find kindling to make water to drink, in order to continue this suffering.

It had been there in the outhouse that she had found him. There, flesh as pallid as the very snow, had lain that pathetic little green bundle, huddled in the manner of the Pompeians, petrified against the searing cold.

Gone immediately were her pains. No longer did her head ache or her stomach twinge, or her throat rasp, or her joints rack her. No longer did her dry eyes, tearless through abject devastation, feel the guilt of not crying.

Here was God's angel come to comfort her, to give her a reason to eat, to drink, to keep warm, to stay alive.

She was oblivious that her helpless little guest wore some foreign uniform, that, even though she was not well versed in current affairs, only which was fed to her by the matron State, it must not be right for him to be here.

The little man was still alive but very ill. She took him in, cared for him, mothered him, nursed him in her own son's bed. She lit the fire, cooked up roots, fed him, bathed him, comforted him. She ministered to his every need. He passed from pallor to high fever. She did not sleep, except to steal a few minutes by his unconscious and writhing side.

When he was too hot she cooled him and when too cold she fed his shivers with more fire.

Gone was the bottle green uniform with its metal insignia of eagle clutching the square web of swastika. With its dispatch gone too to the far reaches of her mind was the uneasiness. She knew that what she did was for the memory of her husband and the love of her son. She did it for God, the God who, in this devastating winter of war, could still send His angel to give her a reason for life.

She nursed the child and at times he came to consciousness. He had been confused and frightened but he had trusted her. At first he had been unable to speak and

226

when he had, it had been in an unintelligible tongue. Their communication had got little further than for him to say that his name was Franz and that he was a German on the run from the Bolsheviks, the Reds from Leningrad who were taking no prisoners.

She had been clutched with fear to have her secret but repressed suspicions confirmed in this way and she had known that one day she would suffer for this act of love and mercy to the enemy, in memory of the very husband and child that same enemy had slaughtered. But she had been unable to sustain the fear or the warning pangs, for the love of the angel was far stronger than the hate of warring men.

Young Franz had known only a temporary reprieve from his terminal fever. She had been unable to fetch a doctor for him, for the doctors were all members of the Party and would only have speeded both their fates. Besides, all doctors had gone to war to fight the invaders. Those left were not in need of doctors for it was better for the weak to die, better that the nation should be purged of such incumbrances in order to rebuild itself afterwards.

He had died in fever, bathed by his third mother and loved by her equally to his other two. Her angel had left her in that cold scourge but he had parted in love, as her memory still enshrined him till this day.

She had carried his vision with her at the inquisitions, after victory. He had been there in the court rooms as she had been condemned and reviled. He had held her hand as they had tried to heap shame on her.

She was a traitor to Mother Russia, she had sheltered and fed one of the invading Fascists, almost as if she had thought him to display human attributes.

They who condemned her, all knew that she had been misguided and reckless, evil and corrupt, as with delight they had confirmed her punishment. She had taken their open shame but had travelled, with secret pride, on her journey to Siberia. Five years she had spent in the punishment camp, five long, hard, cruel years, but her angel had not left her side.

Franz had stayed with her also, in her ten years of exile following the camp.

And when she had returned after those long dark cold years which had been warmed only from within, she had found her little home. No-one had touched it. They had neither harmed it nor preserved it for, to the community, she had not existed and what was hers had had to stay so, for they would have none of her.

Her tiny home was little more than a ruin, but it was still there. Still there too, amazingly, untouched, perhaps through ignorance of its existence or fear of its presence, stood the mound of stones marking the spot where the angel rested. This mound of stones, now moss and lichen, embroidered with a permanence of the rocks themselves, was her inspiration. She had been still a young woman and she had owed it to the memory of her husband and son, and the visiting angel, to build it up.

And so, with time and versatility on her side, she had repaired her little home and had cleared the land and taken up the peasant way of life once more. She had received no human for company but she had expected none would see her grow old.

She had known only dogs, for they are faithful. They do not bend with the breeze of man's decrees.

She is cold now. Too many cold memories to chill her soul. Even her friend whines, ready to slink his way back to the warmth of their little home.

The wind picks up suddenly. It is a cold cruel wind. She shudders. It is getting dark early now. She is getting old. The cold wind makes her think of the winter to come and that winter of so long ago.

"Come," she orders, as she wipes the tears with her gloved hand. "We must go now."

Chapter Thirty-five

And so they sat there, all three chill, sharing gladly the death of their loved one. First one holding his hand and then the other, each clasping the other's hands to share the cold chain of nature.

"John? You listening?" asked Frances, almost the trace of a girlish laugh in her old voice. "Can you hear me, dear?" She thought he could.

"You're going to join Dad, John. You're going to see my poor sweet Larry." She allowed herself just one sob. She thought she felt his hand tighten in hers.

Gerda's turn;

"Sweetest, I love you, we all love you. Wait for me. Oh my darling, wait for me!"

Frances hugged her daughter-in-law. They both cried freely, their hot tears tingling their chilled skin.

"I think his eyes flickered," gasped Frances.

He stopped breathing. They stopped breathing too and waited.

Then again the slight heaving, accompanying the gasp of intake, as he fought and searched. Not long now.

"John love . . ." It was Frances, "Be a good boy."

Gerda's turn, "Give my love to Franz."

Little Franz hugged his Mama to him. He could only choke out one word, almost a cry, "Papa."

John took his final breath. He was released from them.

They thought he smiled. To their memories of that moment he did. Perhaps he did?

* * *

A cold gust sweeps across the sea. It is almost dark. The writer had forgotten the changing scene, so lost was he, so intent to complete his task.

229

The cold rippling warning across the lonely stretch of chill water has reached him now. He shudders. He is cold but he is glad. He has completed his creation.

It is now complete. He has drawn from the air, drawn from the soul of the earth, his creation, the story that was there for his taking. He is cold from the wind and cold inside with a deep sadness that it is complete. He had accomplished his aim and now his mind is alone once more. His task is complete.